Praise for Natasha Preston's

THE CELLAR

A *New York Times* Bestseller

"[A] ripped-from-the-headlines novel."

—*School Library Journal*

"A well-written, completely absorbing nail-biter of a book…[with] a powerful, suffocating atmosphere of dread and uncertainty."

—*Bookish*

"A real treat for avid mystery and thriller fans… Never a dull moment."

—*Teen Reads*

"A gut-wrenching, suspenseful novel."

—*Teen Ink*

"Constantly has you guessing what will happen next."

—BookReporter

Also by Natasha Preston

The Cellar

Awake

The Cabin

You Will Be Mine

THE
LOST

NATASHA PRESTON

sourcebooks
fire

Published by Sourcebooks Fire, an imprint of Sourcebooks, Inc.
P.O. Box 4410, Naperville, Illinois 60567-4410
(630) 961-3900
Fax: (630) 961-2168
sourcebooks.com

Library of Congress Cataloging-in-Publication Data

Names: Preston, Natasha, author.
Title: The lost / Natasha Preston.
Description: Naperville, Illinois : Sourcebooks Fire, [2019] | Summary: While investigating the disappearance of one of their classmates, Piper and Hazel are kidnapped and taken to a building designed to keep them locked away, where every room is a method of torture and a test of survival.
Identifiers: LCCN 2018052409 | (trade pbk. : alk. paper)
Subjects: | CYAC: Kidnapping--Fiction. | Survival--Fiction.
Classification: LCC PZ7.P9234 Lo 2019 | DDC [Fic]--dc23
LC record available at https://lccn.loc.gov/2018052409

Printed and bound in the United States of America.
VP 10 9 8 7 6 5 4

For Elizabeth

I was blown away when you told me you'd driven for fifteen hours from Florida to Texas to come and meet me at a signing. I will never forget getting to hang out with you for a while, and I'm so incredibly proud of where you are now.

1

Ten *runaways*. That's what the police are calling them.

Ten teenagers have disappeared from our town this year, and it's only June.

I gaze out the window of the aging café, the chipped, pale, magnolia paint making it look borderline derelict, but the food is good. It's summer, but the weather hasn't gotten the memo. Dark gray clouds swirl in the sky, threatening rain again. It's been like that all day, short smatterings of drizzle. Rain that fizzles out as quickly as it appears. We have a long, school-free summer stretching out in front of us before our senior year. But we won't be able to have any fun if the weather doesn't get with the program.

"Piper, another one bites the dust," Hazel says, waving a news article on her phone at me from across the table. She pushes her shoulder-length, dark curly hair behind her ear. "Look."

ELEVENTH TEEN RUNAWAY.

Eleven gone.

"Who is it this time?"

"Lucie Bean, sixteen years old. Same age as us again. She lives about thirty minutes away. Last seen two days ago outside Huck's Café with friends. It says she left on her own but never made it home."

We live in Mauveton, population 5,839. It's a densely populated but small town with nothing to do, and the biggest city near us is more than an hour away, which makes it one of the most boring places on earth.

But still, eleven *runaways* in seven months seems high.

They've all completely vanished without a trace.

"Where did Lucie go to school, Hazel?"

"St. Drake's."

"Wow. Isn't that, like, the third person from that school?" I chew on my lip as I reach for her phone, so I can read the whole article.

"What are you thinking?" she asks, her eyes narrowing in suspicion.

"I'm thinking it's only a matter of time before someone we've shared a classroom with disappears." There's always been a high percentage of people taking off from this dead-end town, but over the last year or so, it has gotten worse. Much worse.

Hazel puts her phone down and drops her hands to the table on either side of her plate of fries—fries that she ordered for *breakfast*. Gross. "You seriously think they're missing, like someone has taken them, and they haven't just run away?"

"If people are going to take off from here, they tend to do it when they're eighteen. The number of younger runaways is multiplying. Don't you think something is very wrong with that?"

She chews another fry and swallows. "Maybe. The cops don't seem to share your concerns."

I shrug at her comment. "Well, they probably know better than me."

"I don't know… What if you're right? What if they don't think anything strange is going on?" She's playing devil's advocate here.

But what are we supposed to do about it? Just because I love watching mystery movies and TV shows doesn't mean I'm qualified to find actual, real-life missing people.

Potentially missing people.

"What do you recommend we do, Hazel?"

"Duh. We can try to find them."

Oh, simple as that. "How?"

"By acting like average teenagers." Lifting her eyebrows, she looks at me in triumph. "We're going to go to parties and hang out with them…wherever they hang out."

"I'm not following you here."

She rolls her dark brown eyes. "To find teens, we need to live like teens. Stereotypical ones, I mean. I don't think we count."

Hazel has a good point. Neither of us are extroverts. We spend most of our time hanging out at my house or hers, watching rom-coms after creepy mystery and thriller movies.

"We definitely don't count," I confirm.

"We're going to change that."

"Why? I mean, why are you deciding to try and figure this thing out, Haze?"

Tilting her head to the side, she replies, "What else are we going to do all summer?"

Well, nothing. Maybe we won't find anything, or maybe we'll discover where these people have run away to.

But either way, it seems like a maybe we'll end up having a decent summer instead of spending the whole time indoors.

The call of even a smidge of social life is too loud to ignore. It might actually be nice to get out. We might be missing something by staying inside and by ourselves all the time. "All right, I'm in."

"Yes," Hazel cheers. "Ooh, do you think we'll uncover some sick serial killer's lair?"

"No, I think we'll find nothing, but we'll end the summer with the knowledge that we have soaked in some vital vitamin D and aren't total losers. So that's a plus, right?"

Hazel's shoulders sag. "Is your glass half empty today, Pipes?"

"No. I do believe something more is going on than teens skipping town, but I don't think we're going to find ourselves in the middle of some crime drama. We don't know what we're doing, and if the police can't find anything, there's nothing to suggest we'll be able to."

"I'm going to need full commitment from you here. We go into this with nothing but positivity."

"Fine. Whatever. Let's go catch a killer," I say to appease her.

"Yay!" She picks up another fry. I have two pastries and a coffee. Hazel has fries and a cup of tea. "Where do we start?"

"The lake?" I offer.

Her eyes widen like she's suddenly realized what this whole social life thing will entail. "Can we go there?"

"It's not private property. Why couldn't we go?"

"We've never been there. We've never been asked to go there."

"It's a public lake, Hazel. You don't need an invitation."

But I know what she means. Lake-related conversations echo down the halls at school. Everyone who is anyone goes there most weekends. Most weeknights, too, in the summer.

But no one has ever suggested Hazel and I should go. *We* haven't even suggested it to each other. We really do need a life.

"Okay," I say, taking a hair elastic out of my pocket and tying my long, dark hair on top of my head. "Let's do it! Let's meet at the lake tonight. And please act normal."

She scrunches up her face. "I don't know what you mean."

"That's what I'm afraid of. You know you can't hold back from telling people *exactly* what you think, and not everyone appreciates that. I'm not always going to be there to back you up."

"Ah, but you will be there tonight."

"Best. Behavior." I raise my eyebrows in warning.

The last thing we need on our very first outing is to be ostracized. I'm not really sure what kind of reception we're going to get anyway.

The café bell dings obnoxiously from the force of the door being shoved open.

Hazel and I look over at the same time to see two handsome college guys walk into the café, dressed in clothes that probably cost more than my parents' car.

I think their names are Caleb and Owen. I know of them because their superrich parents are part of an organization that donates a lot to local charities.

They live a few miles out in a development with the other wealthy people, and only come to this part of town when they're dropping off donations.

But are they donating to the café? Not that it couldn't use an injection of cash, but it's hardly a charity.

Hazel cranes her neck to get a better look at them. In fact, everyone in here is doing the same thing. I glance over my shoulder as they head to the counter. I can't figure out what they're saying, even though the room is so dead quiet, you could hear a mouse sneeze.

After a minute, they're handed two takeout cups of coffee. As they turn to leave, I swing my head back, biting my lips together.

Oh crap. I hope they didn't catch me staring.

My face heats up like an inferno, and Hazel's eyes widen at me. I don't know if she's trying to tell me that I'm busted? Or is she marveling at their chiseled beauty and matching, sleek haircuts?

What products do they even use to get their hair that shiny?

They pass by us, and out of the corner of my eye, I see one of them turn his head to look at me. What do I do?

Against my better judgment, I look. Crystal-blue eyes peer at me, unashamed and unapologetic. I'm very sure my eyes do not convey the same thing. I think the guy looking at me is Caleb. Both have blond hair, short and styled in a swept-to-the-side fashion. Both wear crisp, navy pants and button-up shirts with the sleeves rolled to the elbows. It's like the rich-guy uniform.

Caleb dips his head in my direction, his blond hair falling just a fraction out of place. And then he's gone.

The bell dings again as the door opens and closes.

I let out a breath I didn't know I was holding, my head spinning from the lack of oxygen.

"Did you see that? He looked at you!" Hazel gushes. "Like, he looked at you! And you know I love you, babe, but your hair is a total mess right now."

"Thank you," I mutter sarcastically. I push the rest of my pastry away. After that, I suddenly don't feel much like eating. Caleb couldn't have been looking at me really, though, could he? Not that it matters. I'm too young for him. "Let's get our bikes. I need to go home and figure out my makeup before tonight."

Hazel stands. "Don't forget to do something with your hair, too."

2

I lock my bike to the rack outside the library.

It's eight at night, but the sun hasn't yet set yet behind a sea of gray clouds. Shame it's still drizzling, too. I walk down the long path to the lake and pull my hood up.

I straightened my hair, and it now hangs to my waist. It took forever, but it does look much better. I didn't bother with much makeup since I'd probably come out looking like a clown. But I have on mascara and some lip gloss, which is more than I usually bother with.

I reach the path leading to the dirt trail down to the lake when a guy, an impossibly good-looking guy, runs across the road from the other side. He doesn't even look where he's going…because his eyes are on me. Wait. It's Caleb. Again?

He stops in front of me and smiles. Wow, he has a nice pearly white smile. "Hey," he says.

"Hi," I reply, trying not to frown. "Are you okay?"

Why is he here?

"Yes. Sorry, I saw you from back there." He scratches the back of his neck as if he's nervous talking to me. "And this morning. Are you going to the lake?"

He remembers me from this morning!

"That was the plan. Can I help you with something?" I say, keeping my voice ice cool like a total champ. Inside, I'm somersaulting.

"Kind of," he replies with an amused grin. "You could talk to me."

Sort of an odd request from a virtual stranger.

"Talk to you?" I ask.

Shrugging a shoulder, he replies, "Why not?"

Oh, he smells nice, too, like he's fresh out of the shower. I want to step close.

"I don't know you."

"I know. Do you see my problem now?"

I shake my head. "No, not really."

Laughing, he steps closer. "I'm Caleb," he says.

I know who he is, but I don't know him.

"Piper," I reply.

"Nice name."

"Thanks." What is he doing talking to me?

"Are you at the university here or…?"

I shake my head, feeling like a child. "High school."

"Ah, I thought you might be."

"I look like I'm in high school then," I mutter. Maybe I should have tried a little more makeup. *Nah, I would've looked like a clown.*

"No. The opposite actually. It's just my luck that you're not yet eighteen, so I can't ask you out."

Lifting my eyebrow, I feel some of the initial shock of him coming up to me beginning to wear off and the snarky girl returning. "What makes you think I would want to go out with you anyway?"

His blue eyes shine in amusement. "I think I could convince you."

I think he could, too.

"Well, Caleb, I guess we'll never know. I'm not quite eighteen yet."

And by *not quite*, I mean my eighteenth birthday is ten months away.

Chewing on his lip, he watches me for a second, his mind seeming to work overtime. God, I would love to get inside his head right now. I wait to see whether I'm going to be privileged enough to hear what he's thinking. "I'm twenty-one."

Four years isn't that much of an age gap. Okay, who am I kidding, and why am I even thinking about this?

Dusting off the stupid thoughts running through my mind, I take one step back as if the slightly larger distance will somehow make me think straight. "I should find my friend. She's waiting for me at the lake."

He looks down the trail, his eyes scanning for something or someone, then his attention is back on me. "You're going alone?"

"Yeah. I left my bike at the bike rack outside the library."

He looks back at the trail to the lake. "Let me walk you."

"Thanks, Caleb, but I've done this tons of times before."

So, maybe not *tons*, because Hazel and I haven't been here before, but I don't want to sound like a loser in front of him. For some dumb reason, and this is the first time this has happened, I care what someone thinks of me—what a *boy* thinks of me.

Oh, how things can change in a heartbeat.

"You're sure?" His prominent frown deepens. "I don't like the idea of you walking alone."

"Totally. Thanks anyway." I turn to leave, but Caleb captures my wrist.

"Wait a sec. Are you on Facebook?"

"There are still people who aren't?"

He chuckles. "I'll find you, Piper…?"

"Willis."

With a sharp nod, he lets go of my wrist and walks away.

He's going to find me on Facebook. What is my life right now?

I head down the trail to look for Hazel, and the rain finally stops. There are people from all three high schools in the area. The size of the crowd is easily over a hundred, so finding Hazel isn't going to be easy. She left before me and lives closer, so she has to be here already.

It's really warm tonight, so why anyone felt the need to light a damn bonfire, I'll never know. Though I'm impressed they got the fire going with the drizzle. Hazel hates heat, so she won't be near that. I'm the opposite; I'd rather be too hot than even a little bit cold.

By some miracle, I spot her right away. She's talking to three girls I don't recognize. Her arms are folded, and one of her eyebrows is arched. She looks as if she's giving them attitude.

This will be fun.

I power walk over to her, and it's only when I get close that I realize what this is about: Lucie. Missing girl number eleven.

"How do you not know? She was your friend!" Hazel says.

The three girls look at each other.

"What's going on?" I ask Hazel, stopping beside her and smiling at the girls who look a little scared of my socially awkward friend.

Hazel's head tilts in my direction. "Lucie's friends don't know why she left or where she's gone."

"Everyone wants to get out of this hellish town," the one in the middle shoots back, firing one impressive death glare at us.

Hazel might be a little blunt, but she's my friend. "Still weird, though. I mean, she was your friend and you had no idea that she was going to take off?" I say.

They turn their attention to me, and the girl in the middle, the spokesperson for the group apparently, huffs. "Get out of our business. You don't know Lucie, so save your opinions."

"I'm not judging you, but who runs away without telling a single person where they're going? Or at least leaving a hint?"

"Well, obviously people who don't want to be found, like Lucie."

I raise my palms. "Okay. We were just curious."

"Well, don't be. This has nothing to do with you," the girl snaps. She walks off first, and the other two follow like good little puppets.

I turn to Hazel. "What was that about?"

Shrugging, she raises her eyes to me. "I overheard them talking about Lucie, saying she hadn't replied to their texts."

"And you couldn't help yourself?"

She turns her nose up. "I think it's a disease."

Laughing at her, I nudge her toward the cooler. "Come on, let's at least act like we belong here."

"You don't think it's weird? Lucie's best friends know nothing about her wanting to leave town. I mean *specifically*. Where does Lucie want to go? What does she want to do? Surely those are things that her friends would know?" Hazel asks as we head to get a can of…something.

"Sure, but I don't think they're going to tell us anything since you didn't exactly make friends back there."

She scoffs. "Whatever."

"Do you think anyone here knows anything about the runaways?"

"I bet they do."

I stop walking. "Ooh, maybe some of them are involved in human trafficking? Or doing some creepy, cultish sacrificing?"

"Calm down with the horror movies, Piper."

"You never know," I grumble.

Hazel reaches down and grabs us two Cokes from the cooler. "I'm bored of this now. It was a mistake, it's not fun. When can we leave?"

"I *just* got here!"

She turns her nose up, her curly hair bouncing in the breeze. "That's your problem. I've already been here for ten minutes. The only people I've spoken to are those girls, who are super-hostile, and this guy who thought it was appropriate to kiss me."

"Someone kissed you?"

"He *tried*."

Yeah, we're definitely not going to make friends here.

"This is a bust," she says.

"I did mention we wouldn't be solving crimes by being stereotypical teenagers, if you recall." Not a total bust, though, because I did get to meet the cutest guy on the way here. Why haven't I told Hazel? She would relish the thought of me talking to a guy, even if I never see him again. Because I'm too young to go out with Caleb, but Hazel would try to convince me to do it anyway. I haven't had a boyfriend in a year, and I can't really call him a *boyfriend* since we were together five days and I only got a peck on the cheek. Apparently, I was too boring for him. I could have saved him five days if he'd just asked me if I was an exciting person at the start.

"We should Facebook stalk Lucie's friends," I suggest. And also maybe check to see if Caleb has found me on there yet. If he even bothers to look me up at all. He wouldn't be the first guy to say something and not follow through.

"You know Lucie?"

I turn to the owner of the voice. A guy, probably our age, glares at us. From the dark look in his eyes, I think it's safe to assume he heard every word I just said.

So now, not only are we accusing people of being terrible friends, but we're also advertising the fact that we're indulging in a little online stalking.

Fantastic.

Hazel takes a small step back. "Not exactly. We heard about her taking off, but we didn't know her."

He watches me for, like, an hour. Well, it certainly feels like an hour.

"Why are you questioning Lucie's friends?"

I shrug. "We just bumped into them."

"You here to gossip? She's not just another runaway, a number. She's my friend."

This is going swimmingly. "We don't think she's just another runaway. It's weird that people keep disappearing. No one else seems to be all that concerned."

He folds his arms and looks at me the way Hazel was looking at those girls.

He can bring it. I'm not intimidated.

Straightening my spine, I gain an inch and stand almost as tall as him. "Do you think Lucie ran away?"

His left eye twitches. "No, I don't. But she obviously wanted out of here more than she wanted me."

Oh, she was more than a friend to him. He's hurting. Of all the people who could have overheard us talking about Lucie, it had to be him. My traitor of a friend seems to have lost her voice. How convenient.

"I'm sorry your friend isn't here," I say. My words are sincere. I am sorry.

Shaking his head, he turns on his heel and walks off like he doesn't want to waste another second on us.

"Well," I say, turning to Hazel. "Is there anyone else here you feel like insulting, or can we leave?"

"We can so leave."

In unison, we turn and head up the path.

"Thanks for the backup there," I say sarcastically, tossing my Coke can into a recycling bin.

Hazel laughs. "You seemed to have things under control. I didn't feel like you needed backup."

I glance over my shoulder to take one last look at the group at the lake. Around the back of it is the river that runs through town. Lucie's boyfriend stares at us with folded arms and a deep frown. Whatever.

"What do you think is going to happen if we find her? And the others?" Hazel asks. "They might not want to be found."

"I don't know. But I can't imagine it's easy for the people who love them not to know where they are and if they're okay. Besides, what are the chances of us actually finding them? Because I'm thinking it's an absolute zero."

"We're not trying to solve crimes; we're looking into the weirdness of all the runaways, and it still beats sitting home all summer, remember?"

As we walk, I twirl the cotton friendship bracelet on my wrist. Hazel and I made each other one when we were ten. Mine is black and purple, and it's a basic braid with black beads at each end where the knot is. Hazel's is black and pink.

Neither of us like purple or pink anymore, but we both keep them on.

We reach the end of the path, and a car pulls up beside us.

The dark window slides down.

"Caleb," I say, my heart doing a little flip. Beside him is his friend Owen, who lifts his hand in a lazy greeting.

"Get in, Piper. I'll give you a lift."

"Err," I say, turning to Hazel…whose mouth is practically sitting on the road.

Maybe I should have mentioned meeting Caleb to her, after all. She's going to have a lot to say when we get back to my house.

Caleb laughs. "Both of you."

"We have our bikes," I start to explain, looking back.

"I know, but more rain is forecast anytime now. You can get your bikes tomorrow."

Hazel's mouth snaps shut. She nudges me. "Yeah, we can just get them tomorrow, Piper."

"Okay," I concede. I don't really want to get soaked anyway.

Hazel walks around to the other side of the car.

I open the back door and get in. "Thanks, Caleb."

He looks at me in the rearview mirror and smiles. "Anytime."

Hazel shuts the door.

Caleb drops his eyes and pulls out onto the road. I watch him in the mirror, though he's now focused on the road. His eyes turn hollow, and his smile falls. He presses something on his door, and the car doors lock.

3

Don't. Panic.

How humiliating would it be if I freak out and he's just locked the doors for safety? My mom does that. No one is going to carjack us because our car is old and there is never anything valuable inside, but she insists on having locked doors at all times.

He's not your mom.

Hazel either hasn't noticed or she's not worried. Her eyes flit between Caleb and Owen like she's not sure which one of them to crush on more.

I swallow. He hasn't asked either of us where we live.

"So, my house is on Park Lane," I say, tugging at the sleeve of my top.

Owen looks over his shoulder. "We're going somewhere else first."

"Yeah? Where?" Hazel asks. She sounds unconcerned and intrigued. Why isn't she concerned?

"Don't worry, you're going to love it." He grins. "Where are my manners? I'm Owen. Caleb told me about meeting you, Piper, but he didn't mention your friend."

He told Owen about meeting me? Is that good or bad?

"I'm Hazel. Nice to meet you, Owen." She's all smiles and long, lingering looks. So, I guess Owen is the one she likes. I should be relieved, but I'm not sure how I feel about Caleb at the moment. I don't know where he's taking us, and he's not exactly forthcoming with information.

"You look alarmed," Caleb says. I glance up, and my heart jumps. He's watching me in the mirror again. Gone is the dark expression from before. Was I reading too much into it?

Maybe I have watched too many horror movies.

I shake my head, but inside I'm screaming *yes*.

"Don't be, Piper. I'd like to get to know you better, and I can't do that if we never hang out. Was it the lock? It's a habit I picked up from my mom." He presses the button again, and the car unlocks.

My stomach settles, and I breathe. Also, I feel a bit stupid now, too.

"Sorry," I mutter. "My mom does the same."

"No need to apologize. I didn't think how it would look to you."

Owen watches our exchange with curiosity. Does Caleb not talk to girls much? That seems incredibly unlikely. With his movie-star good looks, charm, and charisma, I would have thought he had girls falling over themselves, eager to spend time with him.

I'm too young for him, and my ex will attest to the fact that I'm not very exciting.

Caleb could have his pick of girls, so why choose me, who he shouldn't actually date? Unless that's it. He likes that nothing can happen. Some people want something they can't have purely because they can't have it.

Okay, there's a chance I'm overthinking the crap outta this.

Holding my hands up, I say, "I'm done being an idiot."

Hazel arches her eyebrow, and I want to whack her. We both know I'll never be done being an idiot. My mouth engages before my brain too often for that.

Caleb chuckles and shakes his head, but he watches the road. "You're not an idiot, Piper."

Hazel snorts, and this time I do whack her arm. "Violent much, Pipes!" She turns her attention back to Owen, who is still craning his neck to see into the back of the car. "Where is this place we're going?"

Owen's toothy grin widens. "A place that isn't full of high schoolers."

"We're high schoolers," I say, folding my arms.

"Yes, well, Caleb seems to have made an exception for you, so I will, too."

All right, then.

We turn off the main road and head down a dirt road. I've never been this way before. It's private property, according to the passive-aggressive signs pinned to a post at the entrance, and as far as I can tell, it's just open fields and overgrown woods.

"Are we allowed down here?" I ask, adrenaline starting to tell me this is going to be exciting. I've gone from barely leaving my or Hazel's house to trespassing in the space of twenty-four hours.

Owen laughs. "Caleb's family owns it, so I would think so."

Hazel's wide eyes meet mine, and her expression is screaming *marry him*. She's buzzing over this. I knew he had money; he drives around in expensive cars and wears nice clothes, but I didn't realize he owned a lot of land.

Sure, Caleb is good-looking, duh, and knowing that he might like me back is making my heart leap with excitement and nerves. But I'm certainly not thinking about marrying him just because he's rich.

Relaxing into the seat, I look out the window. We're surrounded by acres and acres of cornfields. The light splattering of trees around start to get thicker just outside of town until it turns into forest.

I watch the clock on the dashboard. There's plenty of time until I need to be home; my parents are just happy I'm getting out. But I don't know how far we're going and how long Caleb intends to stay there.

"Where do you hang out, then? You know, to avoid high schoolers?" I ask Owen, earning a chuckle from Caleb.

"There's a place here that we've kind of fixed up a little." He turns to Caleb. "I feel like we're committing some sort of sin bringing them here."

I roll my eyes.

"You'll get over it, buddy," Caleb replies flatly.

He turns around. "No offense. We just have rules."

This should be good. "And what rules are they?"

"No outsiders."

"Hazel and I are outsiders."

"Caleb's breaking the rules, not me."

Caleb keeps his eyes on the bumpy road and shrugs.

Owen chuckles. "Right. You actually like her."

"Can you shut up now, Owen?" Caleb growls.

I press my lips together because I can feel the strength of a smile fighting to come through.

We drive for a few more minutes in silence before pulling up at a decent-sized, single-story building made of brick and metal siding. It's one level but easily bigger than my house.

"You built this?" I ask.

Caleb cuts the engine. "No, it's been here for years. We renovated the inside a while ago, so we'd have somewhere to go. In case you haven't noticed, there isn't a lot to do around here."

Oh, I've noticed.

Owen is out first, so I follow. Caleb smiles at me as he gets out and locks the door. Hazel is looking around, her eyes flicking back to Owen every few seconds.

"You brought me to the place you renovated so you wouldn't get bored?" I ask.

Caleb takes a step closer to me but keeps a respectful distance. "It was this or turn to petty crime."

"Good choice."

"Do you want to come inside?"

Laughing, I reply, "You didn't give me the option to come here, but you're asking if I want to go in?"

Resting his arm on the car casually, he reaches for my hand. "You could have told me to take you straight home at any point, and I would have."

"I'm kidding. And yes, I want to go inside."

His Hollywood smile makes my stomach flutter. "You're going to love it here."

4

glance up at the building. It's not much to look at from the outside, it's been neglected. There are dents in the metal siding, and it looks like something has cut into it. An axe maybe? I don't know.

The sun dips below the roof and the sky darkens around us.

My arms prickle with the chill from the breeze.

Caleb doesn't drop my hand, so I don't bother pulling away. Owen and Hazel are a little ahead of us, just going through the door.

"When do you have to be home?" he asks as we slowly walk toward the door.

"Ten." I suddenly feel very childish having a curfew. I wonder if I can talk to my parents about staying out later since school is over for the summer. Though, if I do, they'll start asking questions. And if they find out that I'm talking to a boy and getting into a car with him to go hang out somewhere, they will never let me leave the house again.

He stops walking and nods, his blue eyes dancing in amusement. "I'll be sure to have you home every night by ten."

Every night?

"You look lost for words," he says, turning his body so we're face-to-face.

"That pretty much sums it up."

"Why do you think I can't care about you?"

"Because you don't know me. Because I'm too young for you."

He tilts his head. "You can't control a feeling, Piper. All around the world people try to hide who they really are and what they really want. I'll never understand it. Sure, I'm not going to try anything with you, but that doesn't mean I don't want to."

So, he's honest. It's refreshing.

"I agree with that. So many people around here hide how they really feel until all they can do is run away."

"Exactly." He blows out a breath of relief, as if he's glad he's finally found someone who agrees with him. "If people were a little more honest with themselves…"

"You don't seem to struggle there."

"I used to. Then I gave into it and…wow."

I bite my lip to stop from asking what he gave into and started doing, but that feels a little intrusive. Also, if it's gross, I'm going to regret asking. Some things are better left unsaid.

"Shall we follow the others?" he asks, tugging my hand so I step closer to him.

Dipping my chin, I reply, "Let's do it."

We walk through the door, and my mouth falls open. It's *huge*. It's one large room with sofas, a massive TV, arcade games, a pool table, and bar.

"This is amazing. No wonder you don't hang out at the lake."

"I don't really like large groups of people."

Smirking at him, I add, "Or outsiders."

"Very funny. Okay, phones on the side table," he instructs, taking his phone out of his pocket and setting it down, indicating for us to do the same.

"Why?" Hazel asks.

Owen puts his on the table, too. "Everyone is glued to social media. In here, we talk to each other. It's more fun that way. House rules."

She shrugs and puts her phone beside theirs. I hesitate; my phone doesn't often leave my hand or my pocket.

"This isn't school, Piper," Caleb chuckles. "It hasn't been confiscated. You don't have to turn it off and leave it here until the end of class. If you get a call, you can come and pick it up."

Hazel widens her eyes at me, as if to say, *Don't embarrass me again.* "Come on, Pipes, then we can challenge the guys to a game of pool."

Neither of us can play pool. But I'm being silly. "Okay." I slide my phone from my pocket and place it on the table.

Caleb smiles. "Now, do you want to see the rest before we kick their asses at pool?"

"The rest?" I ask.

"You didn't notice the building is significantly bigger than this room?"

"Well, I did, but I figured you'd just renovated this part." Against the back wall are two doors with keypad security locks. "What do you have back there?"

"Which door do you want to go through?"

"Where does the one on the right lead?"

"To more rooms."

"Where does the one on the left lead?"

Squeezing my hand, he replies, "If I told you that, I would have to kill you."

I roll my eyes. "Really?"

"You have to choose one. Kind of like *The Matrix*. Do you want the red door or the blue door, Piper?"

"They're both white."

He laughs and takes a dangerous step closer. We're almost chest to chest, definitely not a position we should be in considering we can only be friends. Besides, I don't know him well enough to have him invading my personal space.

His smile dies as he looks into my eyes. *Is he going to kiss me?* I can't have my first proper kiss with a virtual stranger.

He takes a deep breath. "I shouldn't do this."

Hazel shouts, "Come on, Pipes!"

I take a step back, and he lets my hand drop. Caleb shakes his head slowly. "Which door, Piper?"

"Well, I have no interest in being dead, so I'm going for the door on the right."

With a breathtaking smile, he nods. "Good. Come on." His posture changes; he's taller, more animated.

"You really are proud of this place, aren't you?" I tease.

He looks at me over his shoulder. "You have no idea. Owen, you two in?"

Owen looks up from where he and Hazel are playing pinball. "Sure." I follow Caleb, intrigued by what else they've done here. He punches in a code and opens the door.

Caleb lets Owen and Hazel go in first and then turns back to me. "Okay?"

I nod, and he holds out his hand again. We probably shouldn't, but I take it anyway and let him lead me into…a really long hallway. Huh?

Gazing up at him, I arch my eyebrow. "What is this?"

On each side of the hall are more doors, at least three on each side and another one at the far end. It's dimly lit, the metal light shades casting circular shadows on the floor.

He laughs and lets go of my hand. "The building used to be offices when my dad ran his business from here. There's that big room we came in and another one up ahead, then lots of smaller rooms."

I turn back to the hallway as Hazel take a few steps down it. "Have you done anything with those rooms yet?" I ask.

He presses his chest against my back. I freeze as his breath blows against my neck. "Why don't you find out?"

Yeah, I don't think that's going to be happening.

"I think I'm ready to go back to the other room now," I say as his body moves away from mine. "Hazel, come back."

I take a step closer to my friend, who is padding toward the first door on the left.

Behind me, I feel the atmosphere change. It chills me, causing my skin to pebble. Hazel looks past me and her face pales.

My back is still to the door, but I hear a loud clang and know the boys have gone.

"This isn't funny!" Hazel shouts as she spins around.

Seeing her panic, I turn and sprint the few steps to the door.

There's a handle on this side, but the door's lock is attached to the keypad, and I didn't look when he punched in the code.

"Caleb!" I shout. "Let us out!"

Hazel slams into the door and hammers on it with tightly clenched fists. "Open the door now!"

"Caleb!" I shout louder. "You've had your fun, now open up."

Pressing my ear to the door, I wait. They must be right out there, so why do I feel like I'm shouting to an empty room?

I stumble back a step and grab Hazel's wrist. "What's going on?" I mutter.

"What's going on is that they're dead as soon as I get out of this corridor."

Oh God, this is not good.

"Caleb, please!" I shout.

Hazel and I jump as bright overhead lights blink on.

Caleb's voice rips through a speaker: "Piper, Hazel, welcome to the game."

5

elcome to the game.

"Caleb!" I scream, panic searing through my veins.

"Go through the door at the end of the hall," he instructs, his voice cold and tinny through the speakers at the very top of the wall.

I shake my head vehemently. "Not happening. Open this door *now!*"

"Orientation is in the room at the end of the hall," he says. His voice sounds like a recording. But if it is, where is he?

"Caleb, you've had your fun, now let us out!"

"How do they find this fun?" Hazel snaps.

My head is dizzy. I slam my hands into the wall to steady myself. I don't like this; I need to leave.

"Orientation is in the room at the end of the hall."

"Shut up!" I scream. "Just shut up and open the door!"

Hazel slaps her hand over her mouth and sobs. "What's going on, Piper?"

"They'll let us out in a minute," I reply. My voice sounds monotone even to my own ears. They have to let us out. They can't hold us indefinitely. How long could they keep us? What would they want to keep us here for?

The speaker crackles with static. "Orientation is in the room at the end of the hall."

My heart races, pounding in my chest as if it's trying to escape.

"Hazel, maybe we just have to play their stupid game."

"What? I'm not going through there."

"Well, they're not coming in here, and that might be a way out," I say, pointing toward the door at the end of the hall.

She shakes her head. "I want to go home right now."

I grip her hand, my fingertips tingling. "So, let's do that. I don't care if we have to walk home when we get out of here."

"Orientation is in the room at the end of the hall."

If I hear that one more time...

"Let's get this over with," she says through gritted teeth, her eyes narrowing at the speaker on the wall.

If I could reach it, I would rip it down.

"Okay," I reply, very unsure if this is the right thing to do.

I don't know why they are doing this or what they're getting out of it. But if they think they can laugh it off when we get out of here, they're mistaken.

Hazel and I hold hands as we slowly shuffle toward the door. Her breathing is heavy...or mine is. At this point I don't know. I'm just glad I'm still breathing. The tie of her friendship bracelet brushes against my skin.

Neither of us speak as we approach the door.

There is no lock on this door.

Hazel shakes her head. "I can't open it."

Her eyes are wet with unshed tears.

"It's okay, Haze. I will," I whisper.

Reaching out, my hand shakes so hard I almost miss as I grip the handle and push down.

"I changed my mind," Hazel says, gripping hold of my wrist to stop me from opening it.

"What other option do we have?"

"Orientation is in the room at the end of the hall."

We both jump as the recording of Caleb's voice plays again.

"I'm scared, Piper."

"I am, too, but we're in this together, and when we get home, we're never going out again."

Nodding, she presses her lips together like she's trying to prevent herself from falling apart.

"Okay, I'll go first, and we'll be out of here soon."

Her grip on my wrist loosens, and I push open the door. We take a step back, afraid that one of them might jump out at us.

They don't.

The room is dark, the lighting from the corridor offering a glimpse of what's inside. The only thing we can see is the herring-bone wood floor.

"Caleb?" I tentatively call out. How could I be so wrong about him?

"Orientation is in the room at the end of the hall."

"Oh my God, okay, we're going in!" I shout. Fire ignites in my stomach. We need to get out of here right now.

I walk ahead, my desire to get this over with outweighing my fear. Hazel, still holding my hand in a death grip, stumbles inside behind me.

"Close the door, Piper," Caleb says through the speaker. This time his voice is soft and human.

Turning on my heel, I grab the edge of the door and slam it shut.

Almost instantly, the door makes a clang.

My body overheats. It's locked, and we're cloaked in darkness.

I take a step closer to Hazel, pressing my side against hers. She's trembling, her body causing mine to shake. The loss of my sight makes my other senses run wild. I can smell paint so strong it almost chokes me; I can taste it. Hazel's heavy breathing rattles in my ears.

"Where are they?" she whispers.

"Shh."

Even though I can't see, I close my eyes and listen. The space around us is dead, like there has never been any sign of life in here, like we're the only ones.

Before I can take a full breath, light floods the room. My eyes blink open, and I whip my head around. Hazel whimpers as I spin us so our backs are to the wall. We can see more from this angle, and no one can sneak up behind us.

My gaze tries to take in everything at once. A relatively small room with two armchairs and a TV screen. In the corner is a water cooler. There is another door opposite the one we came in.

Caleb's voice rings through the room: "Piper, turn the TV on and press play on the remote."

"Don't," Hazel warns.

"They're not here; we have to."

"Get comfortable, Hazel. You're going to want to be sitting for this next part," Caleb says. Laughter feeds through the speakers.

My breath catches. "Did you hear that?"

"Them laughing at us? Yeah, I heard."

I nod because I know they can hear us. But I definitely heard three voices laughing. Who is the third person?

"Just do what they say, Hazel."

She sits, and I turn on the TV and press play. Retreating back, I forgo the spare seat meant for me and huddle next to my friend.

The screen flashes to life. Caleb, Owen, and another guy I've never seen before are grinning at the camera. They're sitting behind a long table with their hands placed palms down on the wood.

"Welcome, player...or players," Caleb says. His eyes darken the way they did after he locked the car doors. He almost looks like a different person.

"What the hell?" Hazel whispers.

"We know you must be wondering what you're doing here," Owen says and chuckles. He sits forward, his fingers spread wide like he's excited. "You're here to play."

The third guy runs his hands over his face and says, "We don't want to give too much away, the games will become crystal clear in due course, but I just want to take the opportunity to wish you luck."

Owen's head tilts. "Luck? How odd."

Caleb nudges him with his elbow. "Through the door in the far corner, you will find another room. Grab one bag each from the hooks, choose the bag marked with your clothing size. Then go through the next door. You'll know the one."

"I'm not going anywhere," I mutter.

Caleb sits back in his chair. On either side of him, Owen and the guy with no name stare into the camera and smile.

The video ends and cuts to black.

Hazel and I look at each other. "What do we do?" she asks.

Shaking my head, I shrug. I don't know what to do or where to go. I have no idea how to get us out of this or even what Caleb really wants. The idea is to scare us, right? Well, he's already done that. How much further will he take it?

And what's on the other side of this door?

Hazel sobs. "We can't stay in here. You said this is a test, right?"

"Yeah, I *think* that."

"Do you think they're going to let us go back the way we've been if we refuse?"

"Why are you asking me? Do you think I'm the one with all the answers?" I snap, surging to my feet.

Hazel flinches and drops her chin.

"Damn it. I'm sorry, okay? I didn't mean to shout at you, but I don't know what to do, either."

"Please proceed through the door on the far wall," Caleb's robotic voice booms through the speakers.

I take a breath, close my eyes, and open them again, more composed than before. Clenching my trembling hands, I look at Hazel. Her eyes are wide, confused and fearful. Out of the two of us, I'm probably the stronger one, the one who will jump right in and take action, but just barely. Here, though, she's leaving it all up to me.

This is my fault. If I hadn't started talking to Caleb, we would be at my house right now.

Oh God, what are my parents going to do when they find out I'm missing? And Hazel's parents?

"Please proceed through the door on the far wall."

The speaker is above the door we're supposed to walk through. I glare at it, knowing Caleb and his friends are watching. They're probably loving this. Our fear is what they want.

If I had any control, I wouldn't show them fear.

"We have to go," Hazel says, standing. She holds onto the arm of the chair to steady herself. "Like you said, let's get this over with so we can go home."

"Right," I reply. I nod, but underneath I'm petrified.

Hazel walks ahead and wraps her hand around the handle. Her knuckles turn white the harder she grips. With a deep breath that whistles past her teeth, she shoves the door open.

This next room is small, more of a hallway. It's painted mint green and brightly lit. Along one side is a row of hooks holding cloth bags with *S*, *M*, *L*, and *XL* embroidered on the front.

At the opposite end of the room from us is the door.

Instead of white like all of the others, it's red. But there is a white lily lying on the floor.

6

A white lily. The flower that symbolizes death. My grand-mother is super traditional and only wanted white lilies at my grandpa's funeral.

They are just trying to freak me out.

I gasp, my heart beating so wildly I have to press my chest to relieve some of the pressure. Is this another test? Part of the game they're playing? How is this even a game?

"Grab a damn bag, Hazel. Let's go."

I reach out and swipe a bag marked *S* off the peg.

"Piper, no."

"Take a bag and come on! I want to get this over with."

Without any thought, because I'd probably only get a headache if I think too much about what is going on, I stomp to the red door.

Hazel sobs. I hear the cord of a bag rub against the metal peg as she hurries after me. Slinging my own bag over my shoulder, I reach for the door handle.

"Shouldn't we look in these first?" she asks.

Grabbing the door handle, I twist and push. "What's the point?" The bag is light and soft, likely holding some sort of clothing. I don't care what its contents are right now, I just want to keep going. I don't know how many rooms are in this building, but the sooner we start, the sooner we'll finish. And we both want to go home.

As my eyes adjust to the darkness of the next room, I grab Hazel's hand. It's not pitch-black like before, but the only lighting is a dim band of LEDs on the floor. It frames the large room but gives no clues to what is actually in here.

"What now, huh?" I shout. They'll be listening. This whole thing is one big game to these bored, rich college students.

They're sick.

"Would you like the light on, Piper?" Caleb asks through the speaker. His voice is soft and musical.

His voice startles me. It's not a recording. Sweat beads out on my forehead.

"Don't talk to them!" Hazel whisper-shouts.

"Piper?" he sings my voice. "Would you like the light on, sweetheart?"

I swallow hard. His amusement at our situation turns my stomach. But we don't have an option. I have to converse with him.

"Yes!" I snap, glaring at the corners of the room. It's too dark to see where the speakers are, so my eyes follow the faintly illuminated perimeter of the room. The intercoms and cameras must be up there somewhere.

Caleb laughs. "Ask nicely."

Ask nicely? Is he serious?

Gritting my teeth, I seethe, "*Please* turn on the lights."

Light floods the room.

It's…empty. Aside from another white door in the corner, there's nothing here. There's a keypad on that door, though. Why that one and not the others we've been through?

"What's this?" Hazel mutters, turning to look at the space. We haven't missed anything. We're standing in an empty, sterile-looking, pale gray room.

"I don't know," I reply, glancing up at the camera by the speaker. "They're trying to scare us, make us think something is going to jump out at us—or someone, maybe?"

She shakes her head. "Why?"

Isn't that the million-dollar question?

"They're pathetic," I say, loud enough for the intercoms to pick up. "Playing with people to satisfy their own creepy needs." I harrumph. "This isn't funny to anyone but you."

"Shh," Hazel hushes. "Don't aggravate them."

"Or what? They'll lock us up in their labyrinth? It's a bit late for that, Haze."

"Oh my God, Piper, let's just focus on getting through this. *Please.*"

She's right. I sigh. "What now, Caleb?"

"I see you're beginning to enjoy our game, Piper," he replies.

"You think this is fun? This is sick. How did you even get into college?"

Hazel nudges me, her bony elbow digging into my side. "Piper!"

My fingers curl into my palms with anger. Damn, I hate him, and I hate that I can't stay calm. I hate being trapped. I don't want to do this. I just want to go home.

I shuffle forward.

"Do you think they've done this before?" Hazel whispers.

I focus on what is in front of me, blocking out her question. Blocking everything that my reeling mind wants to tell me.

"We need to get through this door," I tell her.

We'll be on the outside when we're through this door, I convince myself.

The room is so long, it must span the length of the building. But it's narrow so we only have a few feet to reach the next door. We both take small, cautious steps.

"Nine. Four. Nine. Six," Caleb announces.

The code to the door.

Though it doesn't seem like there is anything in this oppressively empty space, that doesn't mean there isn't anything waiting for us behind that door.

Caleb and Owen could be lurking, waiting to jump out at us. They'll laugh and pretend it's a joke. They'll probably tell us to lighten up when we don't think all of this has been funny.

I lick my lips, my tongue sticking to my dry skin.

"Open it," Hazel whispers.

I draw in a breath. With trembling hands, I punch in the code and the tiny red light on the keypad turns green.

My fingertips graze the door handle as if it might burn me. But it's not hot; it doesn't electrocute me like some prank out of a *Home*

Alone movie. It's cold. Pushing down, I shove the door and Hazel huddles into my side.

Sitting in the next room on old leather sofas are four people, all around our age.

A girl I recognize stands, her tear-filled eyes staring back at us.

Oh God. It's her. Lucie Bean. The girl from the newspaper article.

This is where the missing people go.

7

Lucie's red hair is still in a side braid like in the photo she posted the day she went missing. That was days ago. She's been here, a few miles from home, the whole time.

I lock eyes with her and hers widen, as if she knows I recognize her. As if she's hoped people were looking for her.

Before she went missing, I'd never seen her in my life. But now I would recognize her bright green eyes and dark red hair anywhere.

"You know me," she whispers.

I want to answer, but my mind is spinning. Lucie isn't the only one here. There is another girl and two boys. All look around sixteen. All high schoolers. All, I bet, so-called runaways.

No one is even looking for them because there are always missing clothes and bags from their rooms, so the cops assume their disappearance was a choice.

Hazel and I didn't choose this. I don't think they did, either.

The two boys move closer to Lucie. One is tall and skinny with dark skin, black hair, and brown eyes. The other is much shorter and muscular with light blond hair and pale green eyes.

I don't recognize them, but I do recognize the other girl from the newspaper. She ran away—she's been missing—for a few weeks. Her hair is raven black and her eyes, which seem haunted, are the darkest brown I have ever seen.

"What's happening?" I ask, fear trickling down my spine. Hazel and I aren't getting out.

The tall guy takes a step forward, still keeping his distance, though clearly we are all in this together. "I'm Theo. This is Kevin and Priya. Looks like you know Lucie."

I shake my head. "We heard about her. We met some of her friends earlier tonight."

Lucie whimpers, leaning against Kevin's shoulder.

"What…? How…?" I don't know what to ask first. I have so many questions, so many thoughts whizzing around my mind that it's impossible to pick one.

"What is this?" Hazel whispers.

Theo tilts his head. "They keep us here. It's their idea of fun," he spits. "There are rooms." His eyes darken, as does his voice. "Challenges."

"Challenges?" Hazel asks.

"They like to see how far they can push us…how much we can take," Kevin explains.

I don't want to know what he means by that. I don't ask, though, because in this moment, ignorance is bliss.

"How long have you been here?" I ask, trying to concentrate on when Hazel and I might get out…not how long we'll have to stay.

What could they challenge us to do? How bad could it be? Why do they all appear defeated?

Theo looks into the distance like he needs a minute to think about it. "It's not easy to keep track of time. There are no calendars, but I've been here the longest, about two months. Kevin's one month. Priya, three weeks, and Lucie is new. It's sometimes hard to keep track of the date if no one new has arrived in a while."

"What date is it?" Priya asks, her voice soft and timid.

"July twenty-fifth," I tell her.

"I thought so. I've been trying to keep up with the days."

"How?"

She looks up. Above us is a small window, way too small for someone to crawl through. It barely even lets in light. "I've been tracking the days, making a note of them. I was only a day off when Lucie arrived."

Wow.

"No!" Hazel snaps. "No way. I'm not watching for the sun to rise to tell me the date, and I'm not staying here for weeks or months!" She pulls her hand out of mine and spins, pounding her fists on the door behind us. "Let us out right now, you sick bastards! Let us out!"

"Shut her up!" Kevin snaps.

I ignore him. Hazel is only doing what I want to do. I'm worried she'll hurt herself if she keeps slamming the door. I grab her wrist and tug her backward. "Haze, shh. It's okay. It's going to be okay."

Her legs give way, and we both slide to the ground. Her shoulders slump, and she sobs against my side, gripping my arm like I can somehow protect her.

I hope I can. I wish my confidence, my strength, my stubbornness were enough to break down all the doors in this building.

Why so many doors? And so many locks?

"Are we going to die? There's no getting out, is there?" she cries.

"Hey." I grip her upper arms and turn her so she's facing me. "Hold it together. There is always a way. *Always*. That's what you told me when I lost my sister and thought things would never be good again."

There's a hard determination to my voice that surprises me.

"You can't know that."

"And you can't know it's hopeless. There's a way in, so there's got to be a way out. Okay?"

She nods, but she looks as defeated as the rest of them here.

Kevin and Theo have been here for so long, and they haven't found a way out.

But that doesn't mean there isn't one.

Maybe someone could play dead, and when Owen, Caleb, and their other friend come to investigate, we could jump them.

Theo kneels on the floor beside us. "Come and sit. We'll get you some water. Then you can change, and we'll answer all those questions I can see in your eyes."

"Change?" I ask. Ah, the bag on my back.

He smiles weakly, almost in apology. "They require it."

That's when I notice they're all wearing the same plain, dark-gray sweatshirt and sweatpants.

I close my eyes. Caleb and his friends are trying to strip us of our identity. Like in prison.

They've chosen the wrong girl. I've never been into fashion. I always wear jeans and T-shirts. I don't care what I'm wearing, so they can do their worst. They are not going to break me by making me wear some uniform.

I look at the camera square on as I stand and drop the bag from my shoulder. Bring it on.

Hazel rises to her feet as well, her body visibly trembling. She's scared. I am, too. But I won't be used as some sick form of entertainment. My life...our lives are worth more than that. She doesn't want me to anger them, but I'm not about to give in.

"Let's get changed, Hazel." I turn to Theo. "Is there somewhere private we can do that?"

He shakes his head. "There's a bathroom through there, but it has a camera, too."

Closing my eyes, I nod because my voice isn't working. There is nowhere we won't be seen. Caleb and his friends will see me in the bathroom. I know in the grand scheme of things, with us being trapped here, someone seeing me pee isn't the biggest issue. But it's still twisted.

"Come on, Haze." I tug her toward the door Theo pointed to, and she reluctantly follows. I literally have to drag her. She's not helping this situation at all. "Hazel, snap out of it. I need you," I whisper in her ear, hoping that no one else can hear. I don't know how sensitive the intercoms are, if they can pick up our voices when we whisper.

Which makes me wonder if anyone has checked to see if there are intercoms we can reach and rip down. We could stand on something or boost each other, but I would have thought there are more than what we can see mounted to the ceiling, for that exact reason.

Theo, Kevin, Lucie, and Priya watch us as we go into the bathroom. Their gazes burn into the back of my head.

I close the door behind us and drop my bag to the floor.

"They can see us in here," she whispers. Her eyes fill with tears.

"Forget about that. They want us to feel uncomfortable, so pretend you don't care." I keep my voice low, but there is a good chance *they* can still hear what I'm saying. I suppose it doesn't really matter. Of course, we're not going to be okay with being kidnapped and watched.

Would it even be considered kidnapping since we got in the car willingly? False imprisonment, maybe.

I tug on the hem of my top with my heart racing and pull it over my head. Hazel and I have changed in front of each other hundreds of times before at school and home, so I focus on that, pretending we're back in her room getting into sweats before a movie marathon.

"It's just us," I say. Though it's a total lie. We might be the only people in this room, but there are at least three sets of eyes watching us.

Hazel slowly lowers her bag to the floor. She pulls the drawstring open.

I take out my own clothes and tug on the sweatshirt. It's lined with fleece and super-comfortable, I'll give the psychos that. The sweatpants are the same. It's something I would wear for lounging around. I stand tall.

Hazel is the polar opposite. When she's dressed, her shoulders hunch.

"Hey." I grip her shoulders and push them back, forcing her back straight. "We have each other. You are not giving up. Promise me, Hazel."

She takes a breath, emotion passing across her face. It looks like determination. She's trying at least. "Okay, Piper."

"Let's get back out there. I really want to hear what Theo and the others have to say."

And I also really don't. Then it will be real, all of this will be real. I won't be able to pretend that Caleb will let us out when we've been scared enough.

Do they plan to keep us here forever? What happened to the other missing teenagers from before Theo's time?

I have so many questions, though I'm not sure I am ready for the answers.

"Piper," Hazel says, slamming her hand on the bathroom door as I go to open it. "We're getting out of here, aren't we?"

"Damn straight, we are."

One way or another, we're getting out.

She lowers her hand slowly. My heart doubles in weight with the responsibility. Hazel is counting on me. We've always had one another's back, but the dynamic between us has shifted tonight, and I'm the one bearing the responsibility. It's not her fault that she's terrified and probably in shock. But I do hope my Hazel comes back to me soon, because I'm not sure I can do this on my own. I need my partner in crime.

We exit the bathroom. Theo, Kevin, and Priya sit on the sofas arranged in a square, facing inward. Lucie is pacing in the middle, chewing on her fingernail. She stops and looks up as we walk toward them.

Hazel and I sit opposite the three and wait to see what Lucie does.

She sits next to Priya, staring at me with a fiery expression. I can tell she wants to ask about what's happening outside, if people are looking for her, if her family is frantic with worry.

I don't want to tell her the truth: They all think she took off. Other than her mom's initial Facebook plea and a few posts from her friends wishing her well and asking her to keep in contact, no one seems to be looking for her because it seems as if Caleb and his friends packed some of her things to cover their tracks.

Our dead-end town is perfect for people like Caleb.

Ignoring Lucie as best I can, I ask Theo, "What do they want with us?"

"Control. Fear. We're pawns in a sick game to them."

"Pawns? How?"

He licks his lips. "Who will mentally survive rooms one to five." He takes a ragged breath. "And who will *physically* survive room zero."

8

P hysically?" I repeat.

I don't get it. My mind rejects his words and their meaning every time I try to put them together.

They want to see who will physically survive room zero.

They kill people in that room?

"I don't..." Hazel is trying to make sense of it, too, but like me, she's coming up blank.

Theo shifts in his seat. "We knew someone was coming."

"What?"

Kevin claps him on the shoulder. "Last week, Sophie...died. They always find a replacement. It's a surprise that two of you turned up. I don't think there has ever been a double abduction."

He's calling it an abduction. Oh God. He's right. Even though we got into the car willingly, we were abducted.

I close my eyes and rub my forehead. Hazel and I were abducted.

"What happened to her?" I ask, nausea washing over me in big tidal waves.

"She didn't have a choice," Kevin says defensively.

I'm certain I don't want the answer, but I have to ask: "Sophie didn't?"

"Priya didn't."

Hazel grips my wrist, squeezing hard.

My gaze flicks to Priya. Her head is hung low, black hair falling in her face like a cloak. "I didn't want... We had to f-fight. I didn't want to."

"It's okay," Theo soothes. "Sophie's blood is on their hands, not yours."

I can't believe what I'm hearing. They make kids fight to the death?

"This isn't real," Hazel mumbles.

The thought of ending someone's life is abhorrent. "I can't do that. I can't," I protest.

"You will," Priya replies. "When someone is coming at you to kill you... Trust me, you'll do whatever you have to survive."

"Have you three ever been in room zero?" I ask Theo, Kevin, and Lucie.

Lucie and Kevin shake their heads. Theo takes a breath. "Once."

He's been in here two months and been in room zero once. Less time for Priya.

I want to ask Theo who else was in room zero with him. Would I recognize the name from the long list of missing kids? It's definitely gotten worse in the last eighteen months. Is that when Caleb and his friends decided to *play* this game?

"Are you okay?" I ask Theo. Taking someone's life, even if it is in self-defense, has to make an impact on who you are, your psyche. I can't imagine what it's like to have to do that. My only experience with death is my sister, but I had no hand in that. I know what it's like for death to strip everything good from your life and leave you hollow and broken on the floor.

He tenses, muscles bunching along his forearms as if he's in shock. Like no one has asked him that before. "I'm fine," he says, but his ashen skin tells me otherwise.

I'd never be the same again if I committed murder. I know that.

"What happens in the other rooms?" Hazel asks. "I need to know what we're up against."

It's the first spark I've seen in Hazel since we got here. Is she finally ready to fight alongside me?

Theo threads his fingers together, leaning his arms on his knees. "There are six rooms off the hallway to hell, like I said. We just explained what happens in the final one, room zero. The other five are…difficult, too."

Get to the point, Theo. "What happens in them?"

"Room one is sound. Room two is temperature. Room three is light. Room four is sleep deprivation. Room five is water."

I slump back in my seat, his words sucking the life from my body. Those all sound like methods of torture. I've watched enough crime shows to know that. Hazel and I went through a medieval torture phase. We binge-watched documentaries about people discussing all sorts of horror-filled torture devices. Some of the engineering was pure brilliance, even if it was evil to the core.

The realization makes me dizzy. "What happens in those rooms *specifically?*"

"Room one," Theo says, "is loud. *So* loud. Then there are quiet moments so devoid of sound that every breath you take and every beat of your heart hurts your ears."

"Room two?" I ask.

"Temperature. One minute, so blistering hot you almost pass out, and the next, so cold you feel your life ebbing away."

Priya and Lucie curl into each other, hunching their backs and pressing their arms together. Kevin's jaw clenches so hard I'm surprised his teeth don't snap. And Hazel, well, her eyes are round like saucers and staring off into the distance as if she's been possessed.

"Three?"

"Light. It starts dark, so dark that you can't see your own hand right in front of your face. Then it's like you're staring at the sun." He closes his eyes. "It gives you the worst headache."

My hand clutches my throat. How am I going to survive that?

"Four is sleep deprivation."

"That one doesn't sound as bad," I muse. Sleep isn't something that I've needed much of, never has been, and it's something my parents told me tested their patience when I was younger. I usually fall asleep around one in the morning and wake up at five.

He shakes his head. "It's killer, Piper. They put you in for days. The lighting is dull; it's warm and comfortable. But they use methods from the other rooms to keep you awake."

My body temperature dips dramatically, and I shiver.

"Five?" I ask quickly, needing to move on. "You mentioned something about water?"

His head dips, and he grips his neck. "You're strapped to a bed, and they place a cloth over your face…"

I know where this is going so I hold up my hand. "Enough."

His eyes raise. "It's the only room where they're present, too. Caleb, mostly. He loves that room."

"Piper, we can't," Hazel says. "This can't be real. I can't go into those rooms. I can't make it through those things! They can't do that to us!"

Except there's no one here to stop them. They're in control.

I clear my throat, threading my fingers together. "So, what else can we expect?"

Theo raises an eyebrow. "That isn't enough?"

"More than enough, but I don't want to be caught off guard. Theo, please."

"This room is where we spend most of the time. Through the archway behind you is a kitchen. The two doors next to that lead to a bedroom and bathroom."

I turn up my nose. "One bedroom?"

He smirks. "Everything I've just told you, and you most react to sharing a bedroom?"

I used to share a room with my sister. Her empty bed is still there. There's a new cover on it, for guests apparently, but only Hazel sleeps over, and although neither of us have had a conversation about the bed, she sleeps in mine with me.

I swallow the stab of pain my sister's memory brings. "I'm trying not to think of all the other stuff."

"Bunk beds. Kevin snores, but if you throw something at him, he'll stop."

Kevin gives Theo the finger.

"I want to go home," Hazel says. "I don't want to share a bedroom.

I don't want to share a bathroom. I don't want to go into those stupid rooms or cook in—"

"Haze, stop," I say, wrapping my arm around her back. "We'll get through this together." I want to tell her that my parents won't believe I've run away—and neither will hers. Yes, we have told them we want to move to the city someday. But we'd never just pick up and leave, cutting all ties with our parents.

They will look for us. The police will look for us, and someone will make a connection. Maybe someone saw me talking to Caleb earlier today or maybe someone saw me and Hazel getting into his car. There's not a lot of traffic by the lake, but someone could have driven past. Someone could have left the bonfire early and seen us.

Did I see another car or a motorcycle? I don't remember, but Hazel and I were very focused on Caleb and Owen. How stupid.

She looks up at me and her brown eyes fill with despair. "Will we?"

Hazel wants me to reassure her, to promise that we'll be okay, and we'll get out. But that's not a promise I can make any longer. And I'm scared that Hazel will never forgive me for getting us into this. She is like a second sister, and I can't lose her, too.

"We'll stick together and figure out how to keep fighting." Whatever *it is, we're going to be fighting it.*

Hazel either doesn't recognize my reluctance to offer any promises or she doesn't want to admit to herself why I won't.

"Do you want to look around?" Theo asks.

I nod. "Absolutely."

The door Hazel and I just came through can't be the only way out of here…can it?

I get to my feet, and Theo is the only other person to stand. The other three must know every inch of this space, even if Hazel and I don't.

"Are you coming?" I ask my friend.

"No, thanks."

Sighing, I turn to Theo. "Okay, let's go. Lead the way."

He looks back at Hazel but doesn't say anything. No one can make her face this. She has to get there alone. The others stay where they are, too, leaving the talking and tour to Theo.

We go through the arch and into the kitchen. It's modern and white with clean lines. But there is no oven, only a microwave, toaster, and an electric kettle.

"What do you eat?"

He smiles. "It's basic food: toast, cereal, pasta, soup, bread, and microwave meals. Sometimes they send in pizza."

"How do they get food in here?"

"They leave it in the waiting room. The one just outside our door."

"There are too many rooms."

He nods and pain flickers in his eyes. How many times has he been in one of those rooms? He's had to kill. I can't even imagine all that he's gone through.

I shake the thought away because it's only going to make me panic if I think about what I might have to do if I'm put in that situation.

"What's next?" I ask, trying to distract him from whatever memory he's replaying.

"Bedroom is next to this," he murmurs, striding away. I dash after him. I might not be falling apart like Hazel seems to be, but I don't want to be alone.

Theo opens a door. The room is painted a dull gray, like the color of the sky right before a storm hits. It's not a particularly big room, so the four sets of dark wooden bunk beds overwhelm the space.

There is enough room for two more people here. *Oh, God...*

"The two bunks along that wall are free. You and Hazel can take whichever one you want." He gestures to the empty bunks. There are two sets of bunks against the walls opposite each other. If I sleep on my side, I'll be able to see the others across the room. I will definitely need to know people are with me if I'm going to get any rest.

"All right," I whisper.

He looks down at me. Theo is tall, easily a foot taller than me, maybe a bit more. "What you told Hazel was right. We're all in this together. I understand your fear and your desire to get out of here, but while we're stuck in this place, we need to make it bearable. We do that as a team, okay?"

I nod. "Yes, I appreciate that."

That's surprisingly comforting to hear. I know I have Hazel's friendship for support, and I know that when it's needed, she will snap back to herself, but there are only two of us. We're a team— until we go to room zero.

He places his palm on the wall near my head. "If you ever have to go to that room, don't hold back; it'll get you killed."

I press my lips together and close my eyes. *Please, don't ever let me experience that.*

"How often does that happen?" I ask, blinking my eyes open and staring at him to gauge his response. I don't want anyone to downplay the situation. All I want is facts.

"Not very often. Since I've been here, it's only happened to me and Priya, and before that it had been months. They let the number of us…dwindle. Then in quick succession…"

"They kidnap more people." They wait until their subjects are almost all dead before taking in more people. "Wow." I shake my head. "Wait, how long were you alone here?"

He laughs, but it holds no humor. "When I got out of the shower after… Kevin was here. The guy, Max, who was with me before Kevin arrived, had been the only one here. He'd killed three people before I…before room zero. I was terrified to sleep in the same room when he told me that he'd murdered three people. He was convinced he would be the last man standing. I thought he might do something to me in my sleep, so I knew I had to be the one to walk out of room zero. He knew what Caleb, Owen, and Matt were up to."

So, Matt is the mystery friend.

"How long do you think this has been going on?" I ask.

"We're not sure since time gets messed up in here, but based on what Max had said, I'm guessing about a year to a year and a half."

Eighteen months. That's when there were suddenly a lot more *runaways*. It seems like too much of a coincidence to dismiss. "Do you think we can get out of here?"

Theo shrugs. "I've tried."

"You willing to try again?" I ask.

"You have a plan?"

"No," I admit. Well, I kind of do, but I'm not sure how much our captors can hear, so I'm not ready to talk about it…though I think I can trust Theo. But I'm working on one.

9

So, a plan. I need to think of a plan. A decent one. There are three of them and six of us, but they're bigger and stronger, which makes attacking them stupid because they have the upper hand.

Think again, Piper. And better.

The doors are strong and locked, therefore breaking them down would be pretty much impossible. Plus, there are tons of them.

One of us could pretend to be deathly ill, but that doesn't seem like something they would care about.

Okay, I'll keep thinking about it.

Theo briefly shows me the drawer of basic toiletries and sanitary products in the bathroom, since I've seen this room when I changed clothes. It has a shower, dresser, toilet, and sink. All pretty compact together since the room is small, but it's clean and stacked with towels.

"Who does the laundry?" I ask.

Theo chuckles. "You ask some odd questions given the circumstances. There's a washing machine in the kitchen."

Oh. So, we do the laundry. I wonder what kind of explosives you can make from different cleaning chemicals? I totally know that's a thing, I've seen it on TV, but I wouldn't know where to start. Hazel is way better at chemistry than I am. If we—she—can make something that will create a strong enough explosion to bust a door open, we could all get out.

Or all die from chemical inhalation.

Theo and I leave the bathroom and return to the main living quarters. Hazel is still sitting in the same position, staring off into space. Probably not the best time to question her on creating chemical explosions and the likelihood of dying. Lucie is pacing back and forth.

I sit on a seat of my own. Lucie's eyes follow me. She stops and sits beside me. Her eyes hold a thousand questions.

"You can ask," I tell her. If the situation were reversed, I would want to know. After all, it was only a couple of hours ago that I was talking to her friends.

"Who was it you saw?"

"I don't know who, but three girls and then a guy."

She presses her lips together. "Leo."

"The guy is Leo?"

"Yes. We were friends. I like him more than a friend, though, and I never had the opportunity to tell him."

I want to tell her that the feeling appeared mutual when I met him, but that seems cruel since she's stuck in here.

"You can do that as soon as we get out."

She tilts her head and deadpans, "You think we're getting out?

They've been doing this for over a year, and you think we're the ones who will escape? People have tried before."

"They couldn't have tried everything, or they would be out," I say.

Lucie rolls her eyes. "You're a fool."

"No, I'm just not giving up."

"How do you do that?"

"Not give up, you mean?"

She nods.

"I'm still breathing, Lucie, and I have people I love at home. You do, too."

"People come in here, get tortured, then fight to the death. Where are you finding the hope in that?" She sighs sharply. "Wait until you've been in one of those rooms. If you come out and retain that positive attitude, I'll join you."

She stands and walks into the bedroom.

Theo, Kevin, and Priya watch my reaction. They were listening to the whole thing. I don't blame Lucie. We all react differently, and maybe I won't be the same if something bad happens to me, but I've always been of the opinion that although I can't always control what happens in my life, I can control how I react to it.

Perhaps I'll change my mind, but for now, I'm sticking with that.

"She doesn't mean to be rude, but she was in her first room yesterday," Kevin says.

"God," I whisper. "Which one?"

He shrugs. "She won't talk about it. She didn't come out with wet hair, so not room five, and she was only in there for the day, so that rules out room four, too."

"Right," I reply. So, she was either tortured with sound, light, or temperature.

"Does anyone talk about it?" I ask. "I understand why you might not want to, but when someone else experiences the same thing, it can be helpful to discuss it."

When my sister died years ago, it helped me to talk to a boy in my class who had gone through the same thing. Before her death, I had never spoken a word to him.

"We do, yeah," Priya replies. "It helps to get through what's happened to you."

"Good." I give her a smile, and she surprises me by returning it with her own. I didn't expect that; she's been quiet and reserved so far.

Priya's eyes flick to Hazel then back to me, silently asking if she's okay.

I shrug. Right now, she's not, but sometimes it takes Hazel a little while to process things. I know how strong she is, so I'm sure she'll get there.

"Are you hungry?" Kevin asks. "I can make something."

My stomach rumbles at the thought of food. Thankfully it wasn't too obvious. "That sounds good. I mean, I'm hungry but I'm not sure if I'll be able to stomach anything."

Kevin nods. "I get that. It took me a day to start eating here, but then I was so hungry I felt dizzy. Try to eat... Hazel, too."

"Thank you."

"Sandwiches?"

Priya stands. "I'll help Kevin. We can all have ham and cheese."

"Sounds good. Thanks," I reply.

Kevin, Lucie, and Priya go into the kitchen, and it's basically just me and Theo because Hazel is still staring. I'd love to know what's going through her head, but it's almost certainly the worst-case scenario.

"How can you eat?" Hazel whispers. She's not even really talking to me.

"Do you think people will look for you?" Theo asks.

I look up at him and say, "No," but I hope he can see the *yes* in my eyes. Caleb and his friends can't know. Obviously, they will soon enough, if my parents start a full-scale search, but for now I want them to think they've won. Then I want people to notice their reaction when they find my face—and Hazel's—plastered all over town.

Theo lingers and nods. I think he got my real answer.

Finally, he smiles. "We'll all be all right. We have each other."

"You're right. Can I ask how many times you've been in those rooms?"

How often am I looking at here? One room once a week? More than that?

He dips his chin. "I-I'm not sure. I've been in all of them. Rooms one to five multiple times. You can survive them, Piper. You have to stay strong—mentally strong."

"I can do that."

"I believe you." He smiles. "You're going to be okay."

His repeated sentiment is for me only. He's still not sure about Hazel, but that's only because he doesn't know who she really is.

"What do you do to get through it?"

"Talk to Kevin and Priya. Lucie doesn't want to discuss any of it."

"No, I mean, while you're in there."

"Oh." He wrings his hands, and I know his head is back there, remembering some awful things that've happened to him.

"I put my mind somewhere else. Imagine I'm out of here. I think about what I would be doing, what college would be like."

"You were going to college?"

"That was the plan, but I never even got to apply."

"How old are you, Theo?"

Sighing, he replies, "Seventeen. You?"

"Sixteen."

"You seem older."

"I get that a lot. My sister died three years ago, it…aged me, I guess."

Before Penny's death, I couldn't really do much for myself and I relied heavily on my parents and Hazel. Not anymore. I'm confident I can do whatever I need to survive. I just never thought I would have to put that to the test. Not in this way.

"I'm sorry," he says.

"Thanks. So, where are these rooms?"

"You passed them on the way here. The long corridor off their playroom." His words are overflowing with venom.

"They're all the way back there?" We came through, like, four other rooms to get here since that corridor. That makes sense. There were six doors out there. None of them were numbered, though. How would you know which one is which?

"You don't go back that way."

"Right." I take a breath. "Which way do we go then?"

"There is another door behind you."

I twist my body and crane my neck to see it. How did I miss that?

On the wall beside a small bookcase is yet another door. This one is a natural wood color like the bookcase, so that's probably why it didn't jump out at me.

"How does that lead back?"

"There's a tiny room, and you come out in the room where you get the clothes, the one before the corridor of rooms."

I slowly turn around and exhale. "This place is like a maze."

He nods. "Yeah, and they seem to be able to get around pretty freely, so there are possibly more hallways than we've seen so far."

"Did you know any of them before this?"

"I'd vaguely seen Matt around, but that's only because my older cousin Tony went to high school with him. They weren't friends, though. I came with Matt because he said Tony was here, playing in their game room." Laughing without humor, he adds, "I thought those games would be of the arcade variety."

"Well, they do have some of those."

"Yeah," he replies. "But they also have a whole lot more."

"Is that door locked?" I ask, pointing to it over my shoulder with my thumb.

"No, but the one it leads to is. We get notified when someone is back in that corridor, so we usually meet them. And I know what you're thinking, but we're not told until they're back on the other side and it's locked again."

"What if you were to wait by that door to the clothes room?"

He shakes his head. "Don't do that."

"Why? What's the punishment for it?"

"Room zero. Straight there, no questions asked, and no mercy shown."

My body deflates, and I sink back against the sofa.

"They're evil."

What if I do end up dying in here? What if Hazel and I are sent to room zero together?

10

Theo hasn't offered to show me the little corridor that leads to the clothes room, and although there is no one in one of those torture rooms right now, I don't want to risk going there.

Priya, Lucie, and Kevin bring our sandwiches, and we eat in silence.

Hazel doesn't eat; she just stares at her food.

My sandwich feels odd, as if my body is trying to keep it out. I swallow, forcing the food down. It must be getting late now, but I don't have a watch on and there is no clock.

Everyone is so quiet, I don't want to break the silence. I can see they're in their own heads, thinking about this place, no doubt, wondering how and if we'll be able to get out.

I finish half the sandwich, and my stomach closes up completely. I put the plate on the coffee table and focus on keeping the food down.

"You okay?" Priya asks.

"Yeah, thanks."

"Not all that hungry after all?"

Shaking my head, I reply, "Not really."

"That's okay, it takes a while to be able to eat normally."

It doesn't seem right, getting used to everything that goes on here enough to be able to shake the nauseated feeling in my stomach, but I suppose it will happen. It's survival, right? People keep going through the most horrendous situations because the survival instinct is so strong.

"When do you think I'll have to go in one of those rooms?"

Now that Priya has broken the silence, my thoughts spill out.

Theo swallows and puts his empty plate down. "Some have waited weeks, others days."

Days or weeks. Great.

I hope Hazel gets weeks. She needs more time to adjust. They might see that, and if they do, they could make her go sooner.

"Don't think about that, Piper. You'll drive yourself mad. Believe me," Kevin says, shaking his head as if he's recalling his early days here.

"How do you not think about it?" I ask. My mind flicks back to those rooms about every three seconds. They sound so awful; it makes my head throb every time a room is mentioned.

"What will you do when you get out of here?" Theo asks.

He's on a distraction mission, and I'm grateful. "Lock myself in my bedroom to binge Netflix and eat junk, where I should be now."

He smiles, but his dark eyes are sad. "I miss junk food."

"Netflix and junk binge at my house as soon as we're out?"

"Sounds good," he replies, managing a slight laugh.

Hazel stands abruptly, and my heart jumps. She looks down and glares, her eyes firing daggers at us.

"Haze, what's up?"

"You're planning goddamn Netflix nights while we're stuck in here? We're going to die, Piper. Why can't you accept that?"

Taking a breath to calm my nerves, I stand and clench my trembling hands. "We are not going to die. *Stop* saying that."

"Could Hazel please come to the waiting room?" Caleb's voice calls through the speaker.

Hazel and I freeze, her body going as rigid as mine.

Theo stands and looks up at the camera on the ceiling.

"What's that? Where's the waiting room?" I ask, though I have a good idea.

"That's what they call the corridor leading to the clothes room."

"No!" Hazel shouts.

She may have been a statue when Theo and I were talking about this place, but her hearing is fine. She knows what it means to go into that corridor.

"This isn't right," I argue, stepping to Hazel's side. She grips my arm, her fingertips digging into my flesh. "She's supposed to have longer."

"Could Hazel please come to the waiting room?" Caleb repeats.

Hazel's breathing quickens. Her eyes widen to saucers. "N-No."

My heart pounds, the pulse swooshing in my ears. She's not ready. She can't do this yet. "Can I?" I shout, looking at the same camera Theo turned to. "Can I do it instead?"

"Could Piper please come to the waiting room?" Caleb says. I can hear the smile in his now musical tone. He knew this was going to happen.

"Piper," Hazel whispers.

"I'm okay." I tug my arm out of her grip and walk toward the door. No one says a word, and I'm not sure if that's because they're in shock that this is happening so soon or if they never give a pep talk.

What can you say, anyway?

I run my tongue along my dry bottom lip and push the door open.

You are fine, and you are going to be fine.

The corridor is long and turns a corner. I close my eyes. *You can do this.* Without looking back, because I can't stand to see the guilt in Hazel's eyes right now, I step forward and allow the door to close behind me.

This is it. I'm in here now.

I place my palm on the wall to steady my wobbly legs and shuffle down the narrow walkway. Caleb has gone uncharacteristically quiet. Though what more does he need to say? He told Hazel to go because he knew I would volunteer in her place. Everything that he wanted to happen is now in motion.

Swallowing a lump the size of a bowling ball, I turn the corner. There's a door, obviously, up ahead.

You're fine, you're fine, you're fine.

My hand grazes the smooth wall as I take the last few steps.

Caleb hasn't told me to go through the door but waiting here seems pointless. I turn the handle, still using my other hand to keep me vertical.

I am breathing fast as I step into the clothes room. The hooks that Hazel and I took our bags from have been refilled. Two new bags embroidered with an *S* sit in their place.

They've been in here after us, setting up for the next person.

Sick, sick, sick.

"You guys need help," I mutter.

I walk to the middle of the small room and drop my hands to my sides.

It's only when I'm waiting for instruction that my heart starts to beat wildly. I'm alone. I'm going into one of those rooms. What have I done?

I gasp, desperate to fill my deflating lungs. I want out. I want to go home. And I want my mom.

"Open the door to the corridor, Piper," Caleb instructs.

Nope. Don't want to. My earlier confidence has abandoned me, and for the first time since they locked us in here, I feel as scared as I should.

"Open the door, Piper."

My arm lifts, almost independently, my body following orders. This is what I need to do. I have to turn off, go somewhere else, so whatever is about to happen only affects my body.

I walk through the door, and I'm back almost at the start. The corridor of doors. The start of the labyrinth of horrors.

Which room?

"Room two is open, Piper."

Room two. Which one is that again? Temperature. I think it's exposure. That I can do. My town is on flat land; we get no shelter from the bitterly cold wind in the winter or the blistering sun in the summer.

I don't know which one is room two, but logic would suggest one of the doors closest to the entrance. There are three on either side.

I walk with renewed confidence to the other end of the corridor and look to my right and then my left. One of those doors must be room two. I raise my hand and push. The door to my right is locked. Turning my body, I face the door I'm about to go in and give that one a push.

It slides open.

I shuffle my feet forward, though my muscles lock, trying to keep me from entering.

Maybe they're all in on it?

Maybe Theo, Kevin, Priya, and Lucie are friends of Caleb's, too, and they're all having a joke at my expense.

Don't be so naive, Piper.

I take three steps, and I'm inside the room.

It's okay. Small, probably the same size as a standard prison cell and painted brilliant white. There is a thin mattress and gray blanket on the floor.

How long am I going to be in here?

Behind me the door closes and a loud *clank* echoes through the room. I've been locked in. It's deathly quiet in here, probably soundproof.

Caleb chuckles. It's almost as if he can hear my thoughts. "Lie down, Piper. The fun is about to begin."

Fun.

I blink tears from my eyes, stumble forward, and my legs give way. My knees hit the mattress, and my hands break my fall. Taking a ragged breath, I look up around the room. There are two black circles in two corners of the ceiling. Far too high for me to reach, of course.

The light dims, and the rattling of a fan fills the air.

11

grip the blanket in my fists as my eyes flit around the room, searching for the vent. There are two on the walls near the floor. They're white like the walls so not immediately identifiable.

Warm air hits me, and at first, it's nice. But the temperature keeps rising.

Is Caleb controlling this? I can just see him with his hand on a thermostat, laughing as the room heats.

Rolling over, I sit against the wall, equal distance from both vents. The hot air pumps into the room. It's really warm, and I would definitely be more comfortable if I weren't wearing sweats, but it's still bearable.

Dropping my head back against the painted brick, I close my eyes. *You're fine. This is okay.*

The temperature rises again, and it's close to being out in the sun for hours. How does it get so hot so quickly?

Will anyone talk to me in here? I don't want to hear from Caleb,

Owen, or Matt, but voices would be a comfort. It's so small and isolated in here. Theo said hours, right? I could be in here for hours. This isn't the sleep-deprivation room. I can handle two hours on my own in the heat.

I swat my neck as a bead of sweat trickles down my collarbone.

My eyes are still closed because the room is depressing, and I've only been in here about five minutes.

One hour and fifty-five minutes to go.

I squeeze my eyes together tighter.

You're on a beach in the Mediterranean. The sun is shining and…oh my God, it's so hot.

My eyes fly open as the air thickens to the point where I can barely breathe. My skin prickles. I grip the waistband of my sweatpants and shove them down, desperately trying to cool off.

This is what they want.

I sob, my heart sinking as I realize they're winning right now.

I want to fight back, but it's too much.

I gasp as I kick the sweats over my heels. My head flops to the side as I tug the hem of my sweatshirt. I need to get it off, too, but my muscles feel as if they've melted.

Gripping the material in my fist, I raise my arm and pull the sweatshirt over my head. I drop it to the floor and exhale.

My palms are sweating, but I don't have the energy to wipe them. I don't even care that I'm sitting here in my underwear; it's just a relief to have the fleecy material away from my skin.

My insides are boiling. I want to claw at my skin and relieve the itching that feels like ants buried under my flesh.

This is hell.

How long have I been in here?

I slide down the wall, and my face presses into the mattress. I should roll onto the floor, it's probably cooler, but my body is boneless. Every part of me is soaked with sweat. My lungs burn with each scorching breath I take.

My eyes close of their own accord. It feels as if I've been in here hours already, but realistically it's probably been about fifteen minutes.

Why do they like this? What are they getting out of it?

I'm floating. Ha, I can float. The heat is doing something, not just turning my skin pink and itchy, making me sweat and drying out my lips, but it's lifting me up. I'm weightless.

This is okay. See, I knew it would be okay.

I'm flying, floating up and up toward the cool darkness. I raise my arm and flex my fingers. I want the dark. My arm drops, thudding lightly against the mattress, and I fall into that darkness.

I wake with a start. My skin pebbling breaks me from my sleep.

I gasp, and my breath makes a little cloud in front of me. *Whoa, it's cold.*

Sitting up, I reach for my clothes. Wait. I left them right here. Leaping to my feet, I look around the floor. My clothes are gone.

Someone was in here with me. Caleb? I snatch the light blanket that was underneath me when I slept and wrap it around my exposed body. I still have my underwear on, thank God. But I hate that they've seen so much of me.

Don't think about that.

Nothing matters right now other than surviving. I have to get through this by any means. I sink to the floor and curl my arms around my knees. Tugging the blanket over my head, tightening my arms in an attempt to keep warm.

How far will they go again before switching the temperature? Will they let me pass out? Is that what happens when you get too cold?

My body is still damp with sweat. Or maybe I'm just extremely cold. I don't really know.

Am I wet? I run my finger down my icy arm under the blanket, but I can't tell. Somehow, I need to warm up. I tighten my grip around my legs, chaining myself around my own body and burying my head in my knees. The blanket is around my head, completely covering every inch of my body.

Why don't I feel any warmer?

I close my eyes.

Think about something else.

What would Mom and Dad be doing now? Besides looking for their missing daughter? They'll find me. Parents don't stop hunting; they won't give up.

So I can't, either.

But it is so cold; the bitter chill seeps into my bones.

Mom will be at home. Don't they make someone stay at home in case there's a phone call or something? She could be waiting for a ransom demand while Dad frantically drives all over town. He might be with Hazel's dad.

My teeth chatter. Why am I cold? I raise my head to see what's going on, but it doesn't move. Every muscle in my body is stiff, too weak to support the weight of my head. I can't even move my hand.

Wiggle your finger.

I try. I focus so hard, even going as far as picturing it in my head so my body knows what to do, but still I stay unable to move except for the aggressive trembling that's taken over my body.

Where am I? My head swims, heart beating slow and hard. It's the only thing I can hear. *I don't remember...*

I flick my eyes open but can only see darkness. *Your head is in your knees.*

Am I dreaming? I dream a lot, but never like this.

God, it is freezing. I close my eyes again as my mind floats. *What am I doing here? Where...*

I sink into a dark, icy abyss.

12

Groaning, I grip my pounding head with both hands and tentatively crack my eyes open. The temperature is warm. Not boiling nor freezing, but warm. Low lighting fills the small room.

Sitting up straight, I look around as the blanket slips down my body. The door is open. It's open! I slam my palms on the floor and haul myself to my feet.

My vision blurs as the blood drains from my head. I fall sideways, my body hits the wall, and my head lolls to the side.

How long have I been in here? I don't remember much, just being hot and then cold. Beyond that, my memory is a blank.

I take a minute and focus on the rising and falling of my chest, my lungs filling with oxygen, until I'm used to being vertical. When I don't feel like I'm going to hit the floor, I take a step. My legs work. On a gasp, I sprint out of the door and along the corridor.

I push the door open into the clothes room and lunge for a bag marked *S*.

This is why they have so many bags hanging up. Replacements. Will I end up in only my underwear in each room?

I tear at the opening and pull on the clothes. Once the soft material covers every inch of skin, I breathe easier. Tears sting the back of my eyes. I look up, willing them not to fall. They've taken so much out of me, I don't want them to see me cry, too.

Caleb is quiet. No one tells me to go back to the room with the others, but they don't need to. It's pretty obvious. It's not like Caleb is going to open the front door and let me go free.

I can't even promise them I wouldn't go to the police if they let me go. Not after that. I would rather die than keep their sick secret.

The curving corridor feels longer. I pad down the hall, my body shivering from the last cold snap. I think they changed the temperature six times, but I can't really remember. When it was hot, I passed out, every time. All I really know is that I always woke up freezing.

The door at the other end opens. Theo is the only person to walk toward me, but Priya, Lucie, and Kevin are behind him. My best friend is nowhere to be seen.

I wrap my arms around myself, pushing back on the ache in my stomach.

"Are you okay?" Theo asks. He stops just a few feet from me, and I do the same.

I meet his eyes. "I don't…"

Am I okay? I mean, not really. I have just been exposed to extreme temperatures. I'm weak, my body doesn't know if it's warm or still ice cold, and mentally I'm done.

They saw you without clothes.

That might even be the worst part. The indignity of having at least three pairs of eyes seeing so much of my skin without my permission. It's a stark reminder of the power they hold. I'm just along for the ride, and if I want to live, I have to do whatever they want.

"It's all right, come on," Theo says.

"It was so hot…then so cold."

"Last one was cold, right?" Theo asks.

"Yeah." So cold.

He turns away. "Kevin, can you put the kettle on?"

"The kettle?" I ask. My grandmother always says a nice cup of tea can fix almost anything. This isn't one of those things.

Theo's face twists in sympathy as he glances back at me. "It helps to warm up from the inside."

"Oh," I reply. *Maybe Grandma is on to something.*

I follow Theo back into the main room. Priya hands me a blanket and gives me a sympathetic smile.

"Thanks," I say, taking it from her and curling up on a single chair. Hazel is nowhere to be seen. Where is she?

"She's in bed," Priya offers, somehow guessing I'm thinking about my friend. "She was upset and feeling guilty that you were going in her place."

"Right." I honestly don't know what to do with that. I just need her to be here.

"I don't think she's asleep, if you want to go and see her?"

I shake my head and touch my freezing lips. The skin feels rough. "I just want to warm up."

Priya sits on the chair closest to me. "Drink your tea, and then I'll get you some lip balm."

"They're chapped? They feel it."

"Yes, always happens. Don't worry, they'll be back to normal in a day or so."

I don't want to think about that now.

"How many times do they change the temperature? I couldn't keep up."

She shrugs. "I don't know. I always pass out. The heat is… overwhelming."

Yep, that's a pretty accurate description. Knowing the heat is coming back is hell. There's very little reprieve. The cold, although torturous, doesn't last as long. It's all about the heat, about making you feel like your body is on fire and your life is slowing burning out.

"I need a shower." Hot sweats and cold sweats have left me feeling gross.

"Warm up first," Kevin says, putting a mug of tea on the coffee table. "Trust me. You're only going to feel worse if you get into a hot shower when you're still shivering."

I raise my hands and sure enough, they're shaking. "What time is it?" I ask.

"Early hours of the morning, I would guess. It's been dark a long time."

"My parents will be looking by now. They'll have the police out looking."

Kevin and Theo share a glance, their expression holding an entire conversation.

"What?" I ask.

"Well, no one has found anything on Caleb, Owen, and Matt, and it's been over a year."

"Right. But that doesn't mean we won't eventually be found."

"No, it doesn't," Theo replies, but there is nothing about his words or his flat tone that makes me think he believes them.

"God," I breathe. What if there is no evidence again? No clues as to where we could be. I didn't see anyone else when I spoke to Caleb or when he picked us up. Who is going to know?

Priya laughs. "This is what they do, and they're damn experts at it," she says, gesturing in the air. "They're not going to make a mistake and risk being found."

I dip my head, embarrassment filling my cheeks. "Right."

But I shouldn't be embarrassed to have hope.

"Sorry, I didn't mean to sound cruel," she murmurs.

"No, it's okay." I lift my eyes and give her a smile. "I'll just have this and then take some water to bed. I want sleep."

Priya's lips twitch as if she's trying to smile but can't quite make it. She doesn't think I'm going to get any sleep tonight.

I'm fine, though. I mean, I know the situation I'm in, but I'm not going to sit back and allow them to win. Somehow, I'll find a way out, and no matter what they do to me before that happens, I'll deal with it. I'm stronger than they give me credit for.

I don't give up when there is hope—not ever.

Picking up my tea, I hold it in both hands, letting the heat from the mug seep into my skin. My arms are pebbled with goose bumps still. I take a sip.

"You're doing so well," Theo says. "But remember, if you need to talk or cry or shout, that's okay, too."

"Thanks, I appreciate that, but I'm all right."

What's the point in breaking down? It's not going to help. Caleb and his crew have no empathy; they don't care if someone is hurt. They relish in the pain of others. If I fall apart, they win.

Maybe I have watched one too many true crime shows…or maybe I've saved my life by watching them.

I feel the cold deep in my bones, but the tea is taking the edge off it.

When I'm finished, I take my cup to the sink and go to the bathroom. In the cabinet are new toothbrushes, so I tear one out of the packaging and brush my teeth.

You are fine.

They may well have hurt me, but I'm still here. *I'm still fighting, bastards.*

I finish up in the bathroom and make my way toward a bed opposite the ones claimed. I don't have much energy left, but I need to get to the top bunk. My legs are weak, my body still adjusting to the drastic changes in temperature, and my head throbbing with a headache. I pull myself up, gritting my teeth as my muscles strain in protest, and slump down on the mattress.

Hazel is in the bed below mine. She doesn't say a word or even move, so I assume she's found sleep.

Curling the quilt around me, effectively making a cocoon, I close my eyes and wait.

I can see the white walls of the torture room, and my body feels red-hot. I flick my eyes open again. Okay, so Priya might be right about not being able to sleep. The image of that room needs to leave.

Think about something else. Justin Bieber. Liam Hemsworth. Becoming a super-successful detective and putting men like Caleb behind bars.

I've always been curious about people who turn to crime. I love getting a glimpse into the minds of the most infamous murderers. When I'm out of here and finished with school, that's what I'm going to concentrate on.

One day I'll be catching guys like Caleb, Owen, and Matt.

I just have to survive them right now.

I close my eyes again, repeating in my head how I'll win. This time, I don't see the room. I clutch the quilt, holding onto something real, something that grounds me to this room. I'm here, not back in there. I'm still cool but warming up. My body won't get too hot this time.

As I'm drifting, soft music fills the air. I want to listen, to place it because I don't recognize the song, but my eyes are too heavy, and my mind is drifting.

You've got this, keep breathing.

With a long exhale, I let my body loosen, my muscles relax, and I sink deeper into the mattress.

I will win.

13

My body jerks, and I wake with a start. I'm too hot, the quilt stuck to my body, creating an oven effect. Kicking my legs, I manage to untangle myself.

Where am I?

My lungs burn with the lack of oxygen as panic overrides my normal bodily functions. When I'm free, I leap out of bed, barely using the ladder, and grip the side of the bunk, my nails digging into the wood.

Oh God, I'm still here.

I draw in a deep breath and then force it out.

You're not too hot or too cold. You're fine.

My clothes cling to my sweaty body. I didn't shower last night because I was exhausted, but I need one now. I think I only got about three hours of sleep, but I can't lie there anymore.

Legs, now fully supporting my weight, spin me around, and I dash into the bathroom. Light was just beginning to peek through the small window as I passed, so I know it's morning. I've not had much sleep at all, but I don't feel tired anymore.

I strip out of my old clothes and turn the shower spray on.

I step under the stream of warm water and close my eyes.

Pressing my palms against the tiled wall, I allow a few tears to fall. But I keep my head down so even if they can see me in here, they won't see me cry.

The hot water washes away my tears. When I shut the shower off, I take two deep, calming breaths that make me light-headed. I grab a towel, wrap it around my body, and step out of the shower.

That's enough now. No more crying. Getting upset and feeling sorry for myself aren't going to help. People have had far worse happen to them and survived.

Once I'm dry, I grab clean underwear and slip it on under the towel. It's much harder when you're trying to dress while holding something around you, but the show is over. They're not getting another glimpse of my skin today.

If they're even watching right now.

They probably are, though. Won't they want to see the aftermath of my first time in one of those rooms?

Of course, they will. They'll be getting off on the fact that I cried, that I was scared. I straighten my back and let the towel drop as I shimmy the sweatshirt down over my stomach.

You assholes aren't breaking me.

I finish up in the bathroom and go to make coffee. But Theo has beaten me to it. He's waiting for the kettle to boil. Two mugs are on the counter in front of him.

He looks up and smiles, but it's more of a grimace. "How are you doing, Piper?"

"I'm good. You're up early. I don't think it's been light for long."

"Yeah, I woke and noticed you were gone."

I wrap my arms around myself. "Couldn't get back to sleep and desperately needed a shower. You didn't have to get up."

"That's okay. I'm awake now. Coffee is almost ready. Do you want to sit and I'll bring it over?"

I nod. "Theo, I do appreciate this, but I'm not going to fall apart. I really am okay."

His eyes question me as he watches my every move. "It's also okay not to be okay after what you've been through."

"Agreed, but I'm not going to pretend I'm falling apart because that's how I should be after going through that." I want to tell him that I'm still alive, so of course I'm all right, but I don't want Caleb and his friends to hear in case they take it as a challenge.

I'd like to think I'm mentally strong enough to take a lot, but I'm not that naive to believe that what they're going to do to me will be easy to get past.

I wait for Theo to make our drinks. "Thank you," I say, taking my mug when he's finished.

"Do you want to talk about it?" he asks as we sit on the sofas.

"What's there to say? It was hot and then cold. I didn't like it, and I wanted to get out."

"You're being quite blasé about it."

"What do you want me to do, Theo?"

"Be honest. At least with yourself if you can't with anyone else."

"I am being honest! Look, it sucked. Like, royally sucked, but it's done now. I'm not willing to allow it more head space than it's already taken up." Now, I focus on the next thing. I'm doing this step-by-step, day by day. I'll get past one thing and then move to the next.

"I remember my first time," he says. "I was in room five."

No. "Water right away?"

He nods.

While all the rooms sound awful, some seem like they'll be worse than others. I would rather be exposed to light, sound, and extreme temperatures than be on the brink of drowning over and over for hours.

"Caleb was there?"

"No, it was Owen. He came into the room holding a gun and strapped me to a table. While he was making sure the restraints were tight enough so I couldn't escape, he told me he'd won the coin toss."

I gasp and my heart thuds. "They flip a coin to see who will come and do the torturing"

"They did that time. I don't know if they always do."

"Sick, sick, sick."

Theo nods. "Anyway, I was lying on the table, completely unable to move, when Owen put a blindfold over my eyes. I wish he'd done that first because then I wouldn't have had time to see the buckets of water and rags."

Pressing my lips together, I curl into the arm of the sofa. I don't want to hear this. I absolutely do not want to know what's in store for me when they decide it's my turn to go in there. But I have to be prepared.

If I know what's coming, then I can keep my mind busy. I can prepare myself for what they have planned and when it'll likely end.

"My God, Theo, do you know how long you were in there?"

"There aren't any clocks; no way of telling how long it's going on for; no way of knowing when it'll end. I started by counting how many times he put that rag over my face and poured water onto it. When I got to seven, I stopped. It was too much. I had to focus on getting through it by putting myself somewhere else."

"Theo, I'm so sorry. That's exceptionally terrible. I can't imagine."

He dips his head. "For weeks after, I would wake up in a cold sweat, panicking that I was back there. When the nightmares stopped, they sent me there again."

I'm definitely not reacting to anything they put me through. Somehow, I have to train my mind to hold on to nice things, to think of the things I love before going to sleep.

I look away, dread sinking in my stomach.

"How often do they send you in there?"

"Not for a while, but I've been in there five times."

"Is it the worst one?"

His chin drops in a slight nod, jaw tight as he relives each ordeal. "By a long shot. Excluding room zero, of course. Taking a life…yeah, nothing quite compares to that. It changes your very being. The guilt and the pain of knowing what you've done is persistent."

"How do you live with it?"

"Well, for one, I don't have a choice. I suppose I also deserve it."

I shake my head, my heart aching. "You don't. We're all trying to survive."

"I hope you never have to go in there."

Me, too.

"Did you hear music last night? I was pretty out of it, but I'm sure it wasn't a dream." I can still hear it now if I think about it. It kind of started of low and slow then got faster until it stopped abruptly. I didn't recognize it, but I could pick out the melody on a piano or a guitar. It sounded like it belonged in a horror movie.

"Yeah. They play it every night. I have no idea what it is."

Creepy, that's what it is.

"Right." No point in dwelling on that. "What's the plan today?" I ask.

"Breakfast at the diner, then we'll hop on a plane to—"

"Very funny," I say, rolling my eyes. "Are you always the first one up?"

"Usually. I don't know if the others sleep in, or if they just stay in bed so they can pretend."

"Right. If you're tucked up in bed with your eyes closed, you could be at home. The second you come out here…you're *here.*" I can't blame them if that's what they do. I've never really found pretending very useful. I still know the truth.

"Something like that," he replies. "I can't speak for everyone, but not all of us pretend we're home when we close our eyes."

"Where do you go?" I can't think of anywhere else in this world I would rather be than home right now.

He clears his throat. "I'm supposed to be in Forest Oaks."

"That's pretty far away. What's there?" I don't know exactly, but I'd guess it's about three hundred miles north of us.

"My dad was from Forest Oaks, but he moved here after meeting my mom on vacation one year. They split five years ago."

"Did he move back there?"

Theo drops his gaze to the floor and shrugs. "He didn't actually tell us where he was going, but I assume so."

"I'm sorry, Theo. Are you going to try and find him?"

"Nah. It's a big place, and he was from south of Forest Oaks, so I'll avoid that part like the plague, but it's the only other place I know."

"Do you live with your mom?"

"Yeah. When she's sober enough to remember she has two kids."

I don't really know what to say about that. His home life seems harder than any person's should be. "You have a sibling?"

"Older brother; he left last year."

"Where did he go?"

"East Coast. He checks in occasionally, but he has a pretty good thing going on with some chick he met and a job as a delivery driver. I want that. Not to be a delivery driver—I haven't had a chance to get my license yet—but I mean, a chance, a future."

He scratches his jaw and leans forward, resting one arm on his knee. "I've applied to every mechanic I could find in North Forest Oaks, asking if they're hiring."

No one is looking for Theo because they think he left.

I give him a smile. "I'm sure you'll get a job somewhere, Theo. When we get out of here, you'll have the life you want."

"What life do you want?" he asks.

My life isn't bad now, although it's a little boring. But I don't want to tell Theo that I have two super-loving parents who work really hard to give me the best life they can; not after he shared his abandonment by his dad and neglect by his mom.

"I want to be in the city, and I know this doesn't sound probable, but I want to be a detective, finding murderers."

I've already found three.

Theo's half smile grows. "If that's what you want to do, Piper, you should go for it. There's no reason why you can't."

"Thanks, Theo."

"Theo to the waiting room," a voice I don't recognize booms through the speaker above us.

He looks at me, his dark brown eyes dulling with defeat.

"It'll be okay," I tell him.

"Yeah," he replies. "It has to be."

14

I stay in the same spot on the sofa for a solid twenty minutes, frozen in place, heart aching because I'm powerless to do anything to help.

Where is Theo now? I'm sitting here while he's going through something awful, and there is nothing I can do about it. And why is no one else up?

Reaching out, I numbly grab my coffee mug and take a sip of the now-lukewarm liquid. What if Theo is in room two, either boiling or freezing? My cracked lips and thudding head can attest to how awful that room is and how the effects of being in it don't end when you leave.

I sip the coffee again, my lip stinging at the slight rise in temperature the rim of the mug brings. No one else has made a peep yet, and I don't have the energy to go in the bedroom and see if anyone is awake.

I'm exhausted. I woke up more tired than when I went to bed. My body is heavy as if my muscles have turned to stone. I want so bad to close my eyes and drift off to sleep, but I don't know when Theo will be back, and I want to be there when he is. He was there for me.

My skin prickles as I think about the possibility of Theo in that room. It started hot for me. Could he be boiling now? Peeling his clothes off in an attempt to stay as cool as possible in that inferno?

The bedroom door creaks open, and Hazel peers around the corner.

Her eyes gloss over as if she's trying not to cry. It's not often that I see Hazel this emotionally weak, but over the last day I've seen her fall apart. I don't like it; she's usually my rock.

"Piper," she whispers, shuffling out the door with her head low. "Theo's had to go. Are you okay?"

"Come and sit, Haze. I'm not mad at you."

Her chest expands with a deep breath. "You should be. You have every right to be. It was my name that was called, and you took my place." She makes her way across the room in a nanosecond, moving much quicker than she ever has before.

I put my mug down. "You didn't ask me to do that."

She sits beside me, curling her legs under her. "I know I didn't, but I could have done more to stop it. When I heard what they do to us, and then when my name was called...I freaked out. I wasn't thinking, and I'm so sorry."

"Stop. It's really okay. I'm glad it wasn't you in there. And, as you can see, I'm fine." My fingers find the friendship bracelet around my wrist.

You're not fine.

"Do you want to talk about it?"

"Not especially."

Her hand covers mine, stopping me from fiddling with the bracelet. "Will you talk to me about it anyway?" she asks softly.

Sighing, I drop my hand. "What do you want me to say? It was awful. I don't remember a lot because once my body got too hot or too cold I passed out, but I can still feel the pain from the heat and then the cold."

I don't want to talk to her about how I ache and how my head feels like it's being drilled from the inside out. It'll only feed her guilt. It was my choice to volunteer in her place, and I don't regret my decision. Hazel is the closest thing I have to a sister, and she isn't dealing with being here as well as I seem to be.

Who knew I could be so calm and positive when faced with torture and possible death?

Don't go there.

Her eyes widen. "God, Piper, I'm so sorry. We have to get out of here. There has to be a way."

"I know we do." I just don't know how. There are so many doors, a building like this would have more than one exit. If it was used as a place of work, there would have to be emergency exits. I don't remember seeing any from the outside, but then I wasn't looking, and we only saw the front of the building.

She shakes her head. "How did you get through it?"

"I knew it wouldn't last forever." It helped that I went somewhere else, my body unable to handle the extreme temperatures and half shutting down. Before that it was hell, but I got through it in one piece. "I had to stay calm and get through it."

"You're amazing, Piper."

"No, I'm just trying to survive."

She shakes her head. "You're trying to help me survive, too. I don't know what's wrong. I've always thought I would be stronger in extreme situations like this. Not that I pictured this exactly, but you know what I mean? Every horror movie we watch, we talk about what the characters should have done and how dumb they are for not doing it. I don't know why, but I'm the one not doing it."

"You're being too hard on yourself, Haze. The reality of this is light-years from what you could ever imagine. You think you understand fear, but…"

"Yeah," she replies.

"Theo's gone?" Kevin asks, leaning against the bedroom door frame.

"He was called. You didn't hear?" I ask.

He shakes his head. "I was woken by the crackling of the intercom, but it must have been as it shut off."

"I don't know which room he's in," I say.

"They don't tell you until you get to the waiting room."

"I hope he's not long," Hazel says. "I'll make breakfast for everyone."

"You want a hand?" Kevin offers. "You don't know where everything is yet."

Can't say I want to be here long enough to remember where things in the kitchen are kept. I want out now.

Hazel accepts Kevin's offer, and together they make microwaved scrambled eggs and toast.

Priya is next to wake up. She heads straight for me. "How are you feeling today?"

I shrug. "Okay, I guess." How should I feel? I'm more upset about not knowing if anything happened to me when I was passed out. I can handle pain, I think, but my body is my own.

"I remember being confused after my first time in one of those rooms. It gets easier, the after part. You kind of get used to it. I've found a way to protect myself."

"How?"

"I separate it. What happens out of this room is out there. In here, I'm with friends and I'm safe. It's as if I become someone else when I walk through that door."

That sounds like a breakdown waiting to happen, but none of us can worry about the future now when the present isn't a guarantee. Priya needs a way to justify what she did to Sophie in room zero. Whatever gets us through…

"What do you do to get through being in those rooms? I kept thinking about my family before I passed out."

She smiles, her eyes sad with understanding. "I think about my siblings. I'm the eldest of four, but we're all close in age. We spoke so many times about leaving and heading to the city. I want to be a lawyer, Kamal a model, Sahana a doctor, and Zaina an accountant. When I'm in those rooms, I imagine they're all there, working their dream jobs. I know they can't be—they're too young—but I need to believe they're happy."

"I'm sure they'll get there, and when you're out, you can join them."

"Do you think we'll get out?"

From the low tone in her voice, she doesn't.

"I do," I reply. What's the point of going on if I don't? This isn't a life in here, so if there's no hope…

She wrings her hands. "I wish I could be that confident. I try to be. I don't often let doubt enter my mind, but when I think about my siblings, I'm afraid I'll never get to join them."

"Well, start to imagine that, because we're getting out somehow. People break out of prisons."

"You want to dig a tunnel?" she jokes, smiling shyly.

That's the first hint of her true personality. I think she's reinvented herself in here, too, so she can survive.

"If you have anything that will dig through concrete, I'm game."

The building must have a concrete foundation. We can't tunnel through concrete.

"I know I've taken on the role of cook; I've made or helped to make most meals since I got here, and, believe me, I'm more than happy with that. But if you ever need help with a plan or anything, you can ask me."

I've been here less time than her, but she's already assumed that I'm one of the leaders, like Theo. I'm not, though. There are different roles for different people in here, but no one can be in charge.

What feels like hours pass, and I'm beginning to get restless. As I'm about to start pacing, the door opens and Theo walks in.

I open my mouth to ask how he is, but he rushes past us, head down, eyes tight, legs moving at the speed of light. He slams the bedroom door shut.

"Don't," Priya says as I stand.

"But he's not okay."

"He needs time," she tells me. "He always needs some time after. Please respect that. He'll get out of bed and talk when he's ready. Probably tomorrow."

I lick my lips, taking one last glance at the bedroom door. "Okay," I say. "I'll give him time."

15

As Priya said, Theo didn't emerge for the rest of the night, and he was uncharacteristically late getting up in the morning.

When he did get up, he didn't speak all morning and into the afternoon.

He is sitting on one of the sofas, surrounded by people, but I'm sure he doesn't see any of us. I don't know what to do to help. Does he want to talk?

Lucie put in a DVD to watch since we don't have access to broadcast TV. The atmosphere in here is tense with Theo's mood—not that anyone can blame him for not being himself. He must have been in a really bad room. I've not seen him come back before, but the side glances Lucie, Kevin, and Priya are giving him has me worrying, too.

What did he go through? I think he must have been in the water torture room because he came back damp. How do you cope with almost suffocating, hell, *drowning*, over and over for hours?

My heart slams dangerously hard in my chest.

I can't go in there. I don't know how to get through something like that.

I chew on my lip, turning over a hundred different conversation openings. None of them seem appropriate. Theo is going through something that I can't possibly understand right now, but I want to help the way he helped me.

"Theo," I whisper.

He hears me. Though his head stays still as a statue, his dark eyes flick to me.

"How are you doing?" I almost went with *are you okay* but that's too stupid.

"I'll be okay, Piper. I just need to process."

"You're here," I say. "Everything they threw at you, everything they did…you survived and you're here."

His lips curl into the ghost of a smile, my words not quite enough to offer comfort. "I appreciate that," he replies.

It's only then that I hear the roughness in his voice, as if he's been screaming. He's been here the longest, he's done more rooms than anyone, and it still affects him like this.

I swallow.

"Theo," I whisper again, my eyes stinging with the threat of tears. I reach out and touch his hand. He doesn't flinch, so I leave it there, offering him touch that isn't full of hurt and bad intention.

"Does anyone want anything in particular to eat? We have microwave lasagna and pies," Priya asks. "I'm making dinner."

I shake my head and offer a smile. Priya has a role in here which helps her, I'm sure. She told me that she's different people in here and in the torture rooms. Here she takes on almost a mother's role. She cooks and makes sure we're all fed. Hazel heads over to help her.

Kevin says, "Whatever you want to do, Priya."

"Anything is good with me, thanks," Lucie says, sitting back into the sofa and kicking her legs up on the coffee table. I'm not really sure what Lucie's role is exactly. She's both encouraging and antagonistic.

Theo doesn't move his hand away from mine until Priya and Hazel finish making dinner. Then, he silently gets up and takes his seat around the table.

Above us the lights flicker as if they're about to go out. We all look up.

"All the bulbs are going out at the same time?" Lucie asks.

The ceiling is lined with spotlights, ten in total, so all of them going out at the same time seems unlikely.

"Err, I don't think it's the bulbs," I say. "I think it's them."

Theo snorts. "They control every aspect of this place, electricity and heating, too."

"I take it this hasn't happened before?" Hazel asks, frowning at the lights.

I'm going to get a headache if I keep watching the strobe effect going on right now. Thankfully it's not bright enough to hurt, but I definitely can't ignore it.

"Nope," Theo says. He clears his throat and blinks hard. "Let's just eat."

I know that means he doesn't want us to give them the satisfaction of reacting to the lighting. So I pick up slice of bread and take a bite.

The lights go out completely, and something somewhere clicks. Every light shutting down simultaneously? With only the small window and the sun disappearing for the day, the room is cloaked in darkness.

Sighing, I drop my food and hear it thud to the plate.

"Are you for real?" Theo shouts.

"Shh, Theo," Lucie hisses.

Can't blame him. He's already tense from the room he was in yesterday and now this. The mind games are difficult to deal with. Second-guessing everything they say and do is tiring.

My pulse hums. I lay my hands on the table and look straight ahead in the dark. If they can see us right now, I want them to see me sitting still and waiting patiently. What they won't be able to see is my heart racing and my palms sweating.

Something is going on. They're up to something.

Light fills the room.

I take a breath. Theo's eyes meet mine, and he raises an eyebrow.

I shrug, telling him that I don't have an idea, either. Beyond wanting to mess with us, I don't know why they're doing any of this.

"What was that? Do you think they're doing something to the building?" Priya asks.

"Maybe," I reply. I suppose it's better to think they turned off the lighting for some electrical work that needed to be done than to admit they're just trying to keep us on edge. "Looks like it's done now, though." I smile through the lie.

Whatever they're doing, it hasn't even started. Unless...

"What if that was a power failure? Did anyone notice if the microwave turned off?" I whisper, my voice barely audible.

"What difference does that make?" Hazel snaps.

Really? Could she be that obtuse?

Theo smirks, his eyes now losing all of their earlier tension. Voice low, he says, "The doors."

I nod. "The locks are controlled centrally. Electronically. In the event of a power failure, will the doors be unlocked?"

"Do you think so?" Kevin whispers.

"I don't know if they would just stay locked or if it would trip something, but the next time the lights go out, we need to try that door."

Theo nods eagerly, the renewed hope my idea has given him unlocking his bunched shoulders. "Nice one, Piper."

Maybe it's a dead end, and maybe *they* turned the lights off. Maybe a generator kicks in when the electricity cuts to prevent the building from losing power. But maybe it's a chance.

I want it so badly, I can taste it. When I think of escape, I can smell corn growing in fields around town, and I feel the warmth of the sun on my skin. It's June now, still summer. My parents will be taking some time off soon, the same as every year. We don't go anywhere because they don't have much spare cash, but we do have a *staycation*, doing something fun each day like trips to the beach, a theme park, or a museum.

But they won't be doing any of that now. They'll be spending every second looking for me.

Hazel folds her arms. Her lips are pursed the way they are when she's silently protesting something. It was the same look she had in school when the principal tried to implement a uniform like the private schools in the area, or when her parents told her they wouldn't allow her to go to my house if she hadn't finished her homework.

She doesn't think the doors will be unlocked, but she's not going to say it in case it works.

Theo picks up on the negativity and frowns at her. It's so hard to be around people who have already given up.

"Everyone eat up," Theo says gruffly.

He's had enough, too. Theo and I are more alike than the others.

What's the point in fighting so hard to free people who already think we're dead?

The rest of the meal is silent, and no one wants to stay up after dinner, so we get ready for bed early. When I climb into my top bunk, I let myself cry through the creepy bedtime music played through the metallic speakers.

16

I wake up after a rough night's sleep with a renewed determination. I couldn't stop thinking about how Hazel has checked out and how Lucie doesn't seem to believe there is any hope. I don't believe there is, either, and last night I was getting closer to falling apart.

But at least I still have fight in me. Theo has his again, too. Hazel and Lucie are done. Kevin and Priya aren't proactive, but at least they're trying to be positive. At one point during the night, I got so frustrated I almost woke them up to yell.

I'm glad I kept myself in check, though, because that would have added to their hopelessness.

There's no chance of me going back to sleep, so I get out of bed and tiptoe past the others. Hazel is still sleeping peacefully on the bunk below mine. I don't know how she can sleep after deciding that she's going to die in here. I certainly wouldn't be able to.

So much damn negativity!

I grit my teeth, pulse racing with irritation at the situation. She's my best friend, and she's usually so tough. No one breaks Hazel. Or they didn't used to.

"Piper," Theo whispers as I get to the door.

I turn my head. "Yeah?"

"I'm getting up, too." He slips out of bed and follows.

I close the door behind us and head to the kettle. I need coffee. A really big hit of caffeine to cheer me up. When someone is moping around and scowling, I find it super-hard to be near them. Even when my sister died and my world fell apart, I still strived to get out of bed and live my life.

This place is too small to step on eggshells because someone is in a bad mood.

I stop in my tracks on the way to the little kitchen area.

The door to the hallway to hell is open.

Open.

We didn't leave it open last night, and as far as I know, no one was up in the night. Has it been unlocked since the lights went out yesterday?

No, it couldn't have been. Even if the door was unlocked, it can't open by itself.

I step closer, my heart rate quickening. Did Caleb, Owen, and Matt come in here? Do they do that? The thought of them watching all the time is bad enough, but knowing they could have been here, so physically close, makes my stomach churn.

"Theo," I call.

"What's up?" he asks. I hear him step closer.

"Did you leave the door open when you came back in? Did you hear it lock?"

"What the…? No, it was definitely closed and locked." He shuffles closer to me, his arm touching mine as he looks around the room.

They must have come in during the night.

"Why would they come in here? Everything we need, food, toiletries, and all that stuff gets left in the hallway to hell," he mutters.

Okay, I really hope they can't hear because he just mentioned our nickname for that hallway loudly.

"And why leave the door open? They wanted us to know they were here. Why?" I ask the questions, but I don't expect him to have the answers. We can speculate, but the only people who truly know are the crazy trio.

Theo shakes his head. "The mind games are evolving."

"The rooms aren't enough for them anymore," I whisper. They're not content to just watch and send us to be tortured; they want more interaction. They want even more control and to have us constantly on edge.

He draws in a deep breath through his nose and puts his hand on the small of my back. "It's okay. We can still do this, Piper."

I nod numbly. It's one thing to be sent to those rooms, I know what's going to happen there, but to never be sure what could happen while I'm asleep? How will I get any rest at all?

At the moment, I'm barely getting four hours of sleep at night. My parents would be shocked to know that I rise with the sun. Not that I see the sun much through the one tiny frosted-glass window above us that is half covered in leaves and moss.

"Hey," he says, stepping in front of me and holding my upper arms in his strong hands. "Don't do this to me or yourself. No second-guessing yourself. We had a pact, remember?"

"Yeah." My spine straightens with determination. "I'm here. Should we go in there?"

He looks over his shoulder at the open door. "I don't know…"

"What do you think is going on?"

"Maybe it's just a food drop-off," he says, but we both know it's not.

"We have to go, Theo. I'm not going to be scared of an open door!"

I pull back out of Theo's grip and walk toward the doorway. He follows like I knew he would; he'd never let me go alone.

We stop by the threshold, and I look around the corner. Gasping, I step into the hallway. "Theo, it's open!" The door on the other side is wide open, too.

What's going on?

"Is this some sort of test?" he muses.

"Probably, but we'll never know if we don't see how far we can get."

He grabs my hand, stopping me from getting farther than two steps. "You sound like you've lost it, Piper."

"Yeah, well, that seems to be the theme around here. Maybe to survive this prison you need to be a little off-kilter."

His eyebrows pull together. "I think you should have some coffee before you do anything. Clearly you need the caffeine to get your brain going."

I tilt my head to the side and fold my arms. "Are you coming or not?"

Groaning, he looks to the ceiling and closes his eyes. That's a yes.

"Fine, but if this goes wrong, it's your fault."

I shrug. It's not like it can get much worse.

Theo walks ahead and extends his arm to his side, making sure I stay behind him. I appreciate the gesture, but I don't need protecting.

Still, I'm not about to make a big deal about it right now. We have more pressing issues.

We enter the clothes room and my nerves ignite. The next door is open, too.

"Something isn't right," he mumbles. "You know this is a trap, right?" he adds as we take small steps closer to the next door.

"Yep," I reply.

"Do you want to go back? I'll do this alone," he offers, slipping his hand in mine.

I grip tight. "I'm going."

"Thought you'd say that. So stubborn."

We walk through the clothes room into the place where we were told all about this little house of horrors. Black and white squares dance over the TV screen. They've left that on, but it seems about as accidental as leaving the doors open.

They're trying to ratchet up our fear.

It's working. My heart pounds, but I keep my face emotionless. They'll be watching this for sure.

Theo and I move farther into the room and head for the next open door. We're almost back to the long corridor. What if the door to their *man cave* is open? That's the only thing stopping us now. Their room has large windows; we have escape options there. It'll be so much easier to get out.

"Theo?" I whisper as we approach the door. "Should we have woken the others?"

"Whatever they have planned here isn't going to be fun or easy, Piper."

"But what if that's the test? What if they want to see if the first people awake, always you and me, will go and leave the others behind?"

He stops near the threshold. "This isn't our escape, Piper."

I lower my voice again. "They're obviously not letting us go, but that doesn't mean we can't try."

His dark brown eyes look conflicted. He wants to share my optimism, but he doesn't believe it could be this easy.

I don't think it will be this easy, either.

I turn away and walk along the corridor. The door at the end is open.

Rooms zero to five are on either side of us. My skin prickles with heat as I recall what I've endured in room two. I breathe heavier, trying to inflate my lungs to stop my body from curling up when faced with the memories.

I hate this corridor. It holds nothing but pain and despair.

"Piper, look!" Theo says. I whip my head around just in time to see him run past.

My feet move faster, rushing to him as he runs through the door into their game room. "The front door is open!" he shouts back.

"Theo, wait!" I call, pushing myself as fast as him, straight for fresh air.

This is too easy!

The soles of my feet thud against the hardwood floor as I dash past their pool table and arcade games. Theo doesn't wait even for a second; he launches himself through the open door, and he's out.

I hesitate, slowing for a second, but then I'm outside. The thick, dry air is unforgiving, clawing at my throat with every breath.

"We're out," he says, his dark eyes wide.

"I can't believe it. But we need to get the others." I look around. "Where are those guys? Why have they let us go? This isn't the end, Theo."

The front door slams behind us. Theo and I jump and turn around. I grip his arm as we watch Owen smiling from behind the glass window in the door.

"No," I whisper. The others are still trapped in there.

Owen's grin widens, and he mouths *run*.

17

We make it to the back of the building, where the woods are thicker and the trees will hide us.

They've let us go. Why have they let us go? They haven't.

Of course, they haven't!

The realization slams me in the face.

"It's a trap," I say, digging my fingers into Theo's arm as I plant my feet. Owen is the only one of them I saw. He told us to run, but he won't let us get away. Somewhere Caleb and Matt are waiting.

Theo's black eyebrows knit together in the middle. "Who cares? We need to try!" He yanks his arm from my grip.

"We can't do this, and we can't leave the others in there!"

"What choice do we have, Piper?"

I turn my head, my body following suit as I do a one-eighty to check the surroundings. Trees line the yard, the building nestled nicely in the middle. Matt and Caleb are somewhere in those woods, waiting.

This is just one more part of the game.

There is something square on the metal siding of the building. A window? It's too far away to see properly, but it could be a window. Where is it? Looks like it's down at our end of the building, but we certainly don't have any accessible windows.

"We have to go back in," I tell him. The door is locked, so through the window, maybe. They won't expect that. But we don't know where it leads or if it even opens.

He grips my upper arms, his chocolate eyes pleading with me to listen to him. "If we get away, we can get help for the others."

The world whizzes past as I spin around. "We're not going to get away. Can't you see that?"

"We'll split up."

Worst idea ever. "It's still one-on-one. They want to hunt us, Theo. You know they'll kill us before we get to the road."

He still has hold of me, but I manage to swing my arms around his and place them on his strong shoulders. He's a lot taller than me, but then most people are. "I want to run, too, believe me, I do, but we have to be smarter than them. They want us to run, so we can't run."

"But we may never get a chance like this again, Piper." Gripping my arms tighter, he bends his head so we're on the same level. "Come with me. We can take them on together. We can do this."

"This isn't a chance to escape," I whisper, my eyes filling with tears at the impossibility here. "They want us to run. They want to hunt, and all we'd be doing by taking off now is giving them what they want."

"We'll be smart about it."

"You don't think they haven't considered all the options here? If we escape, they're going to prison." I blink away tears before they have the chance to fall. "Theo," I say fiercely. "We will die today if we run."

"We could die if they put us in room zero."

Can't say he's wrong, but I don't want to invite death.

"Please, Theo. I want us to go back inside, but if you run, I have to as well."

I let go of him.

He blows out a long breath through his full lips. "Piper, you're putting a lot on me right now." Dropping his hands from around my arms, he steps away, giving me some distance.

"Please, come with me."

"You want to walk back inside that hell?"

"I did use the word *want*, didn't I? That's not exactly correct. What I *want* is to be home, but this isn't the way. We have to go back inside."

He closes his eyes, his posture collapsing in defeat. "Fine."

"Come on. Let's try the front door," I say, turning around.

Theo's footsteps trudge behind me heavily. He wants to go back in there about as much as I do, but although he understands what's happening, what they plan to do, he still wants the chance.

He's only heading back to hell because of me.

My stomach turns to ice as we round the building and head to the front door.

I haven't seen any other doors yet, but we've only seen three of the four sides.

"Theo," I whisper as movement in the woods catches my eye.

"Keep walking, Piper," he murmurs, nudging me toward the door. Suddenly he's eager to get back inside.

Caleb steps out from between two trees. He's about ten yards away. His head is tilted to the side, sleek styled hair not moving an inch under the gel.

He lifts an arm and points a sword toward me and Theo with a wide, toothy smile on his face. The blade reflects a small slice of sun peeking through the leaves above. He has a sword!

We have to get back inside—right now. We back up, moving slowly toward the front of the building, and I grip Theo's hand. Theo looks over his shoulder. "It's open again," he mutters.

Owen closed the door when we left. Where is he now, and why did he leave it open? Because this is what we're supposed to do. They want us to run, but to survive, we have to go back in.

"Go!" Theo snaps, shoving me through the door. "This is not how you die."

We stumble into the game room. I thought this place was so cool when I first stepped into it. I was impressed with what they'd done here, imagined myself hanging out with Caleb more.

My face heats with stupidity. How naive to believe he was genuine and actually liked me.

I stop, and my breath catches in my throat. Owen is standing tall, holding open the door to the corridor of hell. In his other hand is a gun, and the barrel is pointing at my head.

I gulp.

His green eyes shine with amusement as he lowers the gun and tilts his chin in the direction of the door. "We'll have to do that again and see if anyone else wants to play," he says.

Ignoring him, I step forward, pressing my side into Theo's as we walk past him. The gun follows us, and although my heart is racing, I try to stay calm. Shooting us right now isn't going to be part of their game. How anticlimactic would that be?

Six doors line the long, dark, narrow corridor. A shiver runs the length of my spine as we pass room five and room zero. I pray I never have to go into either of those.

Theo places his palm on the small of my back, fingers digging in just a little too much. His jaw is set hard. He's angry with me still.

He saw Caleb waiting for us with a damn sword, and Owen had a gun. How can he blame me for being back in here? We had to! Somewhere out there, Matt was also waiting and who knows what weapon he was carrying.

The doors in front of us click as we dash back through to the main room. Is Matt pulling the strings instead of waiting in the woods? Or did Owen leave the door and go back in to do this? Maybe there are more of them. I've only seen three, but that doesn't mean there isn't anyone else.

Not that it matters how many are involved. Two against one isn't good odds when that one is sporting a massive sword.

We enter the room again and it's eerily quiet, even for this hour.

I turn to Theo, wringing my hands. "Do you want a cup of tea?" I ask.

He freezes, side-eyeing me and clenching his jaw.

Still mad, then.

"Theo, talk to me."

"There's nothing to say. I'll put the kettle on. I need something to do."

He storms past me, narrowly missing running into me completely.

Things could get fun in here if he's going to stay angry. There are four rooms, one a bathroom, so it's not like we can avoid each other until he gets over it. If he honestly believed we could have gotten away, he wouldn't have followed me back in here.

But it's obviously all going to be my fault.

We don't have access to broadcast TV, but we do have DVDs, so I stick *Hocus Pocus* on and take a seat on the sofa.

Theo slams the kettle down, slams the mugs on the counter, and rips the silverware drawer open so hard it bangs.

I wince at the fury in his actions. This isn't good.

"Hey, what the hell is going on?" Kevin asks, rubbing his eyes as he stumbles from the bedroom like he's drunk. I think in reality, Theo has woken him, but he's still half asleep.

"Nothing," Theo grunts. "Sorry. I'll make you some coffee."

Kevin's light eyes linger on Theo for another second, his eyebrows pulled together. I don't think he believes Theo.

Deciding not to push Theo, Kevin walks toward me and sits.

"Hey," I say, doing a much better job of being cheerful than Theo. "How did you sleep?"

He shrugs. "Not too bad when I actually fell asleep."

"You're having trouble?"

His eyes widen like a deer caught in the headlights. "I…"

"Kevin, I know you're the big, strong, sports-loving guy who works out, but that doesn't mean you can't be scared in here. This affects us all."

He laughs humorlessly. "Yeah, it does. I hate feeling powerless."

"You're not. You're super-strong." I lower my voice. "We'll get our chance to escape one day."

He cracks a smile and nods. "I can't wait to face them."

The speaker crackles. "Kevin to the waiting room," Owen instructs.

Did they hear that? Is Kevin getting his chance to face them now?

Without looking back, Kevin stands and heads out of the room.

I watch him go, watch the door click locked behind him, and my heart tumbles to the floor. Hazel walks into the room, her eyes fixed on Kevin.

My heart leaps again as the familiar sound of crackling echoes through the room. "Piper," Caleb says, a smile highlighted in his voice. "Come to the waiting room."

Is this punishment for earlier? Because I didn't run like they wanted.

But Theo isn't being summoned, and he was the one wanting to take our chances. Why would I be the only one going into a room? Not that I want Theo to, but it doesn't make sense that they wouldn't send us both.

None of this makes sense!

Theo glances my way, his manner somber. He might be angry with me, but he doesn't want me to go in there.

"Pipes?" Hazel says as I stand. She shakes her head.

"It's fine," I reply. It was my idea to come back in here and not take a chance, and although I believe it was the right decision, I have to face the consequences.

Hazel and Theo's eyes are on me as I walk to the door and open it.

"Oh God, Piper!" Hazel shouts.

I spin around just as the door slams shut and locks.

The hairs on my arms stand with goose bumps at the terror in her scream. They want me to go to room zero with Kevin.

I brace myself on the wall and breathe.

This wasn't supposed to happen. I can't fight someone to the death, and I certainly can't fight Kevin. He's big and strong.

The door at the end of the waiting room clicks. It's now unlocked, and I have to move.

18

Which room?

I suck air into my lungs, but it's like trying to inflate a punctured tire.

Where are they sending me?

It can't be room zero. Not already.

I stumble forward, my legs like lead. My palm hits the door first, and I push it open.

Get it together, Piper. You can do this.

The lighting is low through the rooms, and the smell of bleach stings the back of my throat. Caleb, Owen, and Matt cleaning this place doesn't seem to fit somehow. But they must do it. It's not like they can have a cleaner come in.

I press on, ignoring the speakers and cameras on the ceiling as they watch me make my way to whatever torture they have planned.

Opening the door to the hallway to hell, I lean against the wall and take a second to compose myself.

Whatever this is going to be, I can do it. I'm not going to die in here. I'm not going to leave my parents with another child's funeral to plan. *I could really use you with me right now, Penny.*

The first door on the right is open.

I sob in relief, my eyes closing. It's not room zero. One is sound. It's going to be loud, but I can cover my ears to hopefully muffle the worst of it. I can do sound; it won't kill me.

Underestimating. That's what I'm doing on a major scale. It's going to be awful.

Opening my eyes, I walk to the room and gently push the door until it opens enough for me to slip inside. The room is the same size as the temperature room, but this one is framed with round speakers at the top and bottom of the walls.

In the middle of the tiled floor is a thick, black pillow in the shape of a square. It could be a dog's bed or one of those outdoor beanbags. Inside, I burn. They haven't left that on the floor for my comfort, and I refuse to curl up like a dog.

Spurred on by a surge of adrenaline, I stomp forward and kick the pillow. It flies across the floor and hits the wall. I can imagine Caleb chuckling at that, but I don't care about his reaction.

Folding my arms, I look up at the camera in the corner, challenging them, although I know it's foolish. They don't need encouraging; they're going to do this with or without my cooperation.

The door behind me clangs loudly, locking me inside the small white cell with all the speakers.

This is it.

I sit in the middle of the floor, where the pillow used to be, and cross my legs. My pulse drums and my palms sweat, but I keep my face straight, absolutely determined not to show any fear. Which is super-hard to do when all you feel is fear.

Closing my eyes, I place myself anywhere but here. I go back seven years when my parents took me and Penny on our first vacation. It was to a crappy hotel on the coast because we couldn't afford to do much. We did get to spend days on the beach, go on rides at the fair, and eat ice cream for breakfast. We had the time of our lives.

It was the only week in my childhood that I didn't feel as if I was missing out. It didn't bother me that other kids had yearly vacations because I'd had one, too. We didn't manage to get away after that because the house needed repairs, and Mom lost her job and needed to find another one, but I'll always have that week.

My body leaps, heart stalling as a piercing foghorn sound penetrates the room. I curl my back, pressing my head into my hands. The noise is gone as quickly as it started.

Okay, take it one sound at a time.

I raise my eyes and look up as if I'll be able to see when the noise is coming. There is nothing in this room but me, a lot of speakers, and what is possibly a dog bed. What am I looking for?

Dropping my hands from my ears, I place my palms on the floor. Whenever I can, I need to show them that I'm still fighting.

I am stronger than they think.

The next sound that rattles through the room is so high-pitched, I fall to the floor and curl in a ball with my palms over my ears and my head tucked low. The sound slices through my eardrums, making me scream in red-hot pain.

It hurts so bad, I'm sure my head is splitting in two.

"Stop!" I scream, but I can't even hear my own voice over the noise.

It ends abruptly, and I bow my head, heaving. My body shakes, hands trembling in front of me like I'm freezing.

I want to move, but I'm too afraid they'll start it again.

There is a ringing in my ears that adds to the throbbing pain, taking my breath away.

Have my eardrums burst? The pain is so intense that I can't lift my head or move my limbs, but there is no sound in here now, so I can't tell if I can hear or not.

It's not long until I get an answer and assume the fetal position again. A low-pitched, booming sound thunders through the speakers. *Boom, boom, boom*, over and over again, loud, low, and punishing like having something constantly smashing into the side of your head.

I cry out, my throat dry and raw with the rips of screams that I can't hear over the booms. They come thick and fast, so powerful that I feel them vibrating through my body and into my bones.

Squeezing my eyes closed and pressing my hands to my ears so tight I feel my tendons pop, I scream into the oblivion.

It stops and starts. The process turning over and over until I wish I had run when I had the chance.

All of a sudden, silence swirls around me, almost as painful as the noise. The contrast between the two making my ears throb in agony.

I wait. And I wait.

A minute later, or it could have been seconds, I dare to open an eye. Is it over? The booming sounds went on for the longest time imaginable.

My headache, feeling like a full-blown migraine now, prevents me from moving an inch. My body is paralyzed with pain.

I don't know how long I've been lying on the floor curled into a ball, but it's been a while.

Time means nothing in these rooms, but I bet I was in here at least an hour.

My head lolls back, and I look toward the door.

Is it over yet?

Groaning, I lift a heavy hand and run it over my face. My ears hurt so bad, I feel the sting of tears. They've already made me wish I'd run; they won't have my tears, too.

Get it together. *Mom and Dad are out there waiting. Be strong for them.* Don't make them have to grieve for another child. I look up to the ceiling and blink until I've regained control.

I am getting out of here.

The door clicks. *Oh God, it's over.*

Planting my palms on the floor, I push to my feet. The world seems to tilt to the side, and I stumble. I slam into the door and grab hold of the metal to stop myself falling. I reach for the door handle, but the door doesn't open.

What? I heard the lock. Even with the ringing in my ears, I heard that clearly. It's not a noise I could miss.

Gripping the handle, I shove it down harder.

"Come on!"

Please open. Please!

The door clangs again, and I fly out of the room. I fall on my knees with a painful thud.

I look back at the door. That was the second time I heard it unlock. But that's not quite right.

The first one was the door locking.

At some point during the torture, when I couldn't hear anything other than the boom or high-pitched screech, they unlocked the door. I could have gotten out earlier.

I stumble back to our room to four pairs of eyes on me as soon as I step through the door.

"Piper!" Hazel says, leaping up and grabbing me into a tight hug. I wince at how damn loud she is. "I was so worried."

"Shh. I'm okay," I reply in a monotone whisper.

She steps back and, lowering her voice, replies, "Sit down and rest."

I take a seat on the sofa and fiddle with my bracelet.

Theo clears his throat and, without looking anywhere near me, asks, "You okay?"

He's still angry. And after that room, I almost can't blame him.

"I'm fine. I need to take a nap." Turning away, I lie down on the sofa.

With my eyes closed I can pretend, for a short time at least, that I'm not here.

19

I manage to nap for an hour, but my rumbling stomach wakes me up. Priya has laid out a plate of sandwiches and chips. My head is killing me, pain radiating down to my shoulders.

"How long was I in that room?" I ask.

Everything is so loud, it hammers my head.

"I think around an hour," Priya replies softly.

I haven't told them where I've been, but they know. From the second I shushed Hazel when I got in here, they knew where I'd been… because they've been in there, too. Except for Hazel, but someone probably filled her in since she's not asking me a thousand questions.

We finish eating the rest of lunch in silence, and Theo avoids all interaction with me. Lucie, Priya, and Hazel know something isn't right. I don't miss the many exchanged looks they keep giving each other.

I clear away the plates, my eyes meeting the tiny window above us. It's bright, so I think it's somewhere around midday.

Kevin has been gone a long time.

That doesn't mean anything. A lot of the rooms take longer.

If he's being deprived of sleep, he could be gone for days.

He'll be back soon, and he'll be fine.

He's not sleeping well; it's beginning to really get to him, a voice argues in my head.

"Piper?" Priya's hand flashes past my face, making me blink.

"Huh?"

She takes a plate out of my hand and puts it in the sink. "Are you okay?"

"Yeah. I'm fine. Sorry, I totally spaced there." Part of me is still back in that room, and the other part is just trying to recover as quickly as possible.

The headache is still there, but food helped, and it's bearable.

"I'm worried about Kevin," she admits. "But the last few days, he's withdrawn and been quiet and pretty defeated."

"We'll make sure he's okay when he gets back, get him to open up so we can help," I tell her.

She turns the tap and fills the sink with soapy water. "Yes, he's not good at talking about his own feelings, but he needs to."

I help Priya wash up and then we join Theo, Hazel, and Lucie on the sofas.

That's how we spend the rest of the evening, watching DVDs, volume down low.

No sign of Kevin and no music yet.

Theo is still very mad at me over our missed chance of escape this morning. Deep down, I hope he understands we never would have gotten away. They would have killed us if we got close. I think they wanted to hunt us and then bring us back here to prove they can do what they want, that they have ultimate control.

But we didn't give them the satisfaction. It was a win for us, even though being back in this hell doesn't seem like much of a win at all.

I try to make eye contact with Theo. We are the only ones around the kitchen table since Lucie, Hazel and Priya are still watching DVDs.

"Theo, I'm sorry."

He lifts his eyes to me, and from the lowered angle of his chin it looks like he's glaring. He may well be. "Let's not talk about it, Piper. It's done."

"I don't want you to stay mad at me. We both know coming back was our only choice."

"We'll never know, will we?" The bitter edge to his voice makes me flinch.

He's not usually this cold.

Dropping my half-eaten slice of bread on the plate, I lean my arms on the table. "Look, I understand why you're angry, but you can't honestly believe that we had a chance out there. You know what they stand to lose if we'd escaped."

"They would never let that happen, Piper. I know that."

"What's going on?" Hazel demands, scowling at me and Theo. "Why are you two whispering? And Theo looks like he wants to kill you, Piper. I don't know about anyone else, but I'm totally over the tension, so spill."

Priya and Lucie's eyes slide toward us, waiting for a reply. Maybe everyone has noticed how off Theo is with me. We're usually the chattiest ones, especially with each other, so of course the others were going to pick up on the rising tension.

"You want to tell them, Piper, or shall I?"

I shrug. "I don't mind. I haven't done anything wrong."

"I'm not saying you have."

"Doesn't sound like that to me. Even though you just claimed you understand."

"Hey!" Hazel snaps. "Tell us what's happened!"

Theo blows out a long breath that whistles between his teeth. "This morning, the door was open. And not just the waiting room door. Piper and I ran to see what was going on. We thought maybe we'd find a way out."

"Did you?" Priya asks, leaning forward on the seat.

Theo shakes his head. "No, but we did find all of the doors open. We ran outside, and there was no one there. We were going to come and find you guys, but when we turned around, Owen was inside. He closed the door and mouthed for us to run."

"We couldn't, though. It was a trap. Caleb and Matt were nowhere to be seen, and we suspected they were waiting somewhere in the woods for us," I add.

Theo's jaw hardens. "I wanted to try anyway. I thought if we managed to get away, we could get help for all of us. This nightmare could be over."

Lucie, Priya, and Hazel stare with their mouths parted, each of them with the same look of disbelief.

"You left?" Hazel whispers, her eyes on me.

"No, I didn't. We went as far as we could. I wouldn't have left you behind, Haze. Not any of you."

Lucie folds her arms. "How do you know you wouldn't have made it? Maybe that was our chance and you two blew it! You didn't even wake us up and let us decide for ourselves." She stands quickly. "How could you take that choice away from us?"

"Because it wasn't a choice," I say, rising to my feet. Her anger is understandable, but I won't be intimidated. "If they allowed us to get away, they would be sent to prison. They probably got bored and wanted to try killing for themselves rather than forcing us to do it." The thought sends a jolt down my spine.

Could they evolve to that?

"Still not your decision to make. I would rather die running than in that room!" Lucie shouts.

I wince as her words rub like broken glass against my skin. "Lucie, I'm sorry, but when we get out of here, we need to make sure we get out alive. This wasn't it. Before we run, we have to at least have a one percent chance. Them letting us go is them controlling it."

Much to my surprise, Hazel comes to my defense. Her eyebrows are still tucked together showing her disapproval, though. "Piper is right. I might not agree with how they went about it, no one has the right to make decisions like that for the whole group, but if we all ran, we all would be dead today."

"Yeah, Lucie," Priya says. "Think about what our captors have at stake here—they're well known and loved, their families constantly donate to charity, they work hard to make improvements to our town, all while doing whatever they want here, feeding whatever darkness is deep inside them. Do you think they would give that up willingly?"

"That's not the damn point, Priya! That was my only chance to decide how I die, and they took it from me. One of you is going to kill me, and I would have much rather it be one of them!" she screams, pointing to me and Theo as her face reddens.

"Lucie, calm down," Priya coos. "We can talk about this rationally."

"No, we can't! Theo and Piper have no respect for us. They're trying to take on the role of leaders, being the strong ones with all the ideas, making choices they have no right making! You've been here two minutes, Piper, and you think you can boss me around, make decisions for me, and do whatever the hell you like!"

"I don't think that! Will you chill out and look at this rationally? You know what Theo and I did was right. We're trying to give us all the chance to leave here alive. Isn't that what you want?"

"What makes you more qualified to decide how that happens?" she snaps.

"Logic. It's clear for anyone who gives it more than a nanosecond of thought. If we run when they leave the doors open, we die."

A low growl rattles in her throat. With balled hands, she lunges. Priya catches her around the waist with her arm before Lucie gets close. But I tighten my muscles, ready to defend myself.

"Get off me!" Lucie shouts, thrashing under Priya's grip.

The speaker crackles. Over the noise Lucie is making, we all hear that dreaded sound that makes my skin break out in goose bumps.

"Lucie to the waiting room," Caleb orders.

Lucie's face falls, her jaw getting longer. They witnessed the whole thing, of course, and now she's going to be punished.

"It's okay," I tell her. "You'll be fine. You'll be back here soon."

She turns, keeping her head down and shuffles slowly toward the waiting room door.

Oh God, what are they going to do to her? Will they punish her more than the torture rooms do already? Their plan could still be to have me face Kevin in room zero.

The door clicks shut behind Lucie. It's now locked. She's on her own.

Above us, the speaker crackles, then, "Priya, turn on the TV."

"What?" Hazel asks. "Have they ever told anyone to do that before?"

Theo shakes his head, his suspicious eyes on the TV already. "No point. It only plays DVDs."

Priya does as she's told.

The four of us gasp in unison as the hallway to hell flicks on the screen. Lucie is there, walking slowly, prolonging this part as much as she can. Going in there is inevitable.

"Which one is she going in?" Hazel mutters to herself as much as anyone else.

I don't want to speak the words and jinx anything in case I'm right, but all I can think is that Kevin is also out there somewhere, in those rooms over and over maybe, and they need two people for room zero.

Lucie is much smaller than Kevin, both in height and weight. She's petite and skinny, where he's built like a rugby player.

I move closer to the screen, following Priya, Hazel, and Theo as they also go in for a better look. "Will they show inside the room, too, do you think?" I ask, my stomach turning at the thought.

"I don't know. I hope not," Priya replies.

"We all agree that we turn the thing off if they try to?" Theo says. "No matter what punishment would come, we agree that we can't allow them to do that, right?"

"Agreed," I say.

Hazel nods, and Priya says, "Absolutely."

It's one thing for them to watch it, but to force us to see a friend being hurt like that—that's horrific. I would hate the thought of someone else watching me in there, seeing me at my most vulnerable.

Lucie braces her hand against the wall in the slightly grainy picture on the screen. She must be so scared right now, anticipating which room she's being sent to. At the moment, she's not in the right frame of mind. She's angry and thinks she was robbed of a chance to escape. I don't know what that means for her; if she'll be more or less able to handle what's about to be thrown at her.

Come on, Lucie.

"Where is she going?" Hazel whispers.

I feel Lucie's fear. Earlier this morning, I experienced it.

God, this day needs to end.

She's halfway down the corridor now. The room on the end at the left is room zero. Please don't be open. From the high angle of the camera and the poor picture quality, it's impossible to tell which door has been left open an inch.

No one else has picked up on the room zero possibility yet…or, like me, they're too scared to say it aloud.

Lucie shuffles farther down. She's almost at the end; she's going into either room five or room zero.

My heart stutters as she takes another step forward.

The screen goes black.

"What!" I snap.

"No! Lucie!" Priya shouts. "Oh my God, why would they do that?" She turns to me like I have the capability to answer her question.

"They're evil," Theo says. "That's all there is to it. Which one of them do you think will come back?"

20

think Kevin will end up killing Lucie. But I'm not going to say it.

"What do you mean, which one will come back?" Priya asks, frowning at Theo.

"Come on, Priya. Kevin has been gone a while, and now they call someone else in," he says. He sounds annoyed that she's even asking, but Priya doesn't think like those monsters. She doesn't see the opportunities they have and what they could do with them.

I envy her that. I constantly think about how they could make things worse for us.

Priya shakes her head. "No."

"Oh my God!" Hazel gasps, finally catching on to what we're talking about. "They're both going to room zero!"

That's what it looks like. Maybe Kevin really has been waiting in there this whole time.

Priya turns from us, dipping her chin. "You're wrong."

Possibly, but we never get the best-case scenario here.

What is happening with Kevin? Is he still alive? Where has he been? Did they open the front door for him, too, and he failed the test? There are too many possibilities and none of them are nice. He hasn't managed to get away, or the cops would have raided this place by now.

"I can't lose either of them," Priya confesses. "Lucie was the first girl in here in a while. We bonded even though we're nothing alike. And Kevin…"

"I know," I say. "Priya, remember, we don't know for sure yet. Okay? We're just speculating."

"Because there's a reason to!" she cries, spinning back around to face me. "You think that's what's happened. Why else would Kevin still be out there somewhere? They were waiting to see who they wanted to go into that hell with him!"

My stomach sinks. Now she is thinking like them, and it's all our fault.

I hold my hands up as the vein in her neck protrudes. "Priya, calm down. Let's not freak out when we don't know. Okay? They could have him for another reason. Nothing they do makes sense. Let's not try to think like them; we're nothing like Caleb, Matt, and Owen."

Sucking in a breath, she takes my hands and grips tight as if she's about to hit the floor.

"Are you okay?" I ask.

"One of them might die. They might be fighting right now and…"

"No, Priya, don't think like that. Let's all keep our heads. I'm sure she'll be back soon."

"Everything is falling apart," Hazel comments.

Snapping my head in her direction, I give her the look. The look that she often receives from me when she opens her mouth before thinking. It happens a lot; most of the time it's inappropriately funny. However right now, it's just plain unhelpful.

But I can't deny that she's right. We haven't been here long, but already things have changed, shifted. There's a heightened nervous energy, all of us trying to outthink them, to look ahead and see what new hell they can inflict upon us before they do. Like if we're prepared, we can somehow stop it, as if it would be better if we knew what was coming.

You never ask the fortune-teller when you're going to die.

I can feel it, in the way the others look at each other, at the joy in their voices when our captors call us, the taunting tone that they revel in.

Something is coming. Every moment in here is building up like a pressure cooker, and I don't know when it's going to explode. I only know that an explosion is inevitable.

"Nothing is falling apart," Theo says. "I'm making a snack. Everyone just sit down and chill the hell out."

Priya and I sit on the sofa, and Hazel perches on the arm of the sofa. She looks ready to run if needed.

"Is it okay if I leave the TV on? I'll turn it off if it shows something awful, like we all agreed. But in case…" I ask. They might show us more. Not that I want to see what Lucie and Kevin are going through, but I do want to know if they're okay. I want to know if Kevin is still alive.

The throbbing in my head begins to intensify. I wish I had some painkillers.

"I think we should leave it on," Priya replies, wringing her hands. "Piper?"

I lean back against the sofa and face her. "Yeah?"

"Do you think I will see Kevin again?"

If he's in that room with Lucie, I do. If Lucie is in room five, I fear that Kevin is already gone. They want to murder. They've had over a year of watching people, and now they're starting to get hungry for the kill. They could easily have started with Kevin.

"I really hope so," I reply, not wanting to lie.

Nothing is certain in here, and with each passing day, I can feel the negativity seeping into my pores.

I hate it. I'm positive. I always have been. Even in our dead-end town, I see the bright side. But it's difficult to see a bright side when you're surrounded by darkness.

"Do you think when Kevin or Lucie comes back in…*if*…we should try rushing the door?" she whispers. Her lips barely move, trying to conceal her words in case they can lip-read.

Hazel leans closer.

"I don't know," I reply in a whisper, so we're not overheard. "We'll only be through one door. There are four more locked doors before we're out. I don't know if we'll have the collective strength to get through them all quickly enough before they catch up with us."

Priya's shoulders slump as she moves closer. "There have to be windows."

"Wait, you're right. There is a window along the wall that faces the woods. I saw it when Theo and I were out there. It was near the back, probably somewhere along the waiting room. They must have built a wall in front of the window."

"So if we knock that wall down, we can get out the window?" Hazel asks.

Well, she just made that sound easy.

"In theory," Theo says quietly, crouching down in front of me and Priya. "But it depends on the wall. If it's just a stud wall, plaster-boarded, we could be through it in minutes."

I helped my dad move a wall that separated our kitchen and dining room a couple years ago; it was super-easy to do. But we had tools, and there were no psychos watching and waiting.

"Maybe. Did you get a look at the window? I didn't see bars or if it was boarded up, but that doesn't mean it wasn't. I only remember the location and the green window frame around it, but not if there was any glass," I say, keeping my voice quiet.

For all we know, it could be bricked up.

But if we're going to consider something this dangerous, we need to do a little recon first. We need to find out if that wall has just been built out with a bit of wood and plasterboard. That means one of us needs to go to a torture room soon, so we can get into the waiting room.

I don't think there will be any volunteers, and I have a suspicion Hazel and Priya wouldn't know what to do to figure out what the wall is made of.

"I didn't notice a window at all," Theo confesses.

Oh great, we're going solely on my word, then. What if I didn't see what I thought I did? No, I know what I saw.

"There is definitely a window. Or there definitely was, at least."

Theo shakes his head. "They would have blocked it up, surely? They need to keep us in; they wouldn't have a means of escape only barricaded with a bit of plasterboard."

I lean in a little closer, so we're huddled together. We can't afford for Caleb and his friends to hear this. "Yeah, but we were never supposed to see that side of the building. They're getting cockier. This could be the mistake."

I'm getting my hopes up. Like, through the roof. Psychopaths usually make mistakes when they get complacent. They think they're invincible, and then they overlook something huge.

They let us see the exit.

Priya gasps and grips my hand. Her eyes are wide and fixed on the screen, which flicked back on. Lucie is in room five, strapped to a bed.

Caleb stands over her, holding a towel. By his feet is a bucket of water.

He looks up, straight into the camera, and grins.

21

As quickly as the image appeared on screen, it disappears again. I am so grateful the picture quality is bad in here. I couldn't see Lucie's face properly; her head was facing the opposite wall. Caleb didn't hide from the camera at all.

"She wasn't facing us," I say. "Do you think he told her we were watching?"

Theo scoffs. "Yeah, I think that's exactly what he did."

Jesus. He is pure evil.

"It's usually a day in there?" Hazel asks.

"Yeah," Priya replies. "Do you think they'll keep showing it?"

"We agreed to turn off the TV," I say, standing. "We're not watching Caleb torture Lucie." I jab my finger on the button and turn the damn thing off. There's no guarantee that they won't switch it back on, but I have to try.

Theo looks up at me as if he thinks I've made a mistake, but he doesn't say a word because we all agreed.

No matter what, we don't watch each other.

If the TV is turned back on, we could just leave the room. We don't have to watch this.

"Do you think there will be backlash?" Hazel asks.

I shrug. "Maybe. We need to get into that waiting room anyway."

"I don't want to get in there!" she snaps, clenching her teeth. Hazel's dark eyes fire bullets. She's so petrified of going into a room. We've all gone multiple times, and she hasn't done any yet. I think part of torturing her is making her wait, getting her so anxious about her name being called. They make her stress and worry every day that her turn is coming up.

"No one *wants* to get in there!" Theo says. His voice is hushed, but he's clearly irritated. "Suck it up, Hazel."

Someone needed to say it. Hazel needs to be a team player right now. We all do.

"Shut up, Theo," she whispers. "This has nothing to do with me. You and Piper are the ones wanting to knock down walls."

"So if we manage to do it, are you going to stay in here or are you going to leave with us?"

Priya and I sit back. Usually I would be the first person to jump in and defend Hazel—she's my best friend and I have a lot of practice sticking up for her—but Theo is right. She can't take a step back and do nothing to help.

"You can't force me to do something I don't want to do, Theo!"

"Shh!" I hiss. "Lower your voice again, please. The last thing we need is for them to hear what we're saying."

Hazel snaps her mouth shut and folds her arms. She's acting like a spoiled child and annoying me to no end. We're all going to have to do things we don't want to for the greater good.

I need to be ordered to one of those rooms soon, so I can check if there's any sign of a window.

Better still, I need to get back outside to double-check there actually is a window we can get access through. But going outside again seems unlikely. Unless they want to see if anyone else will run. We're going to have to have a conversation about how we go forward, get everyone to agree that we can't run, but we can check out the outside of the building and report back.

The speaker above us crackles. "Piper, turn the TV on," Owen says, his voice rattling over static. "You're not going to want to miss this."

No.

"I can't," I say, looking up at the camera. That's what they're waiting for. If they wanted us to watch, they could turn it back on themselves. They want *me* to do it. Do they have no empathy at all? Is there nothing human about any of them?

"Piper, turn the TV on, or Lucie will be waiting for you in room zero."

Priya gasps. "Just do it, Piper. No-watching pact is over! I would rather be watched than forced to kill or be killed."

She's right.

I swallow a thick lump clogging my throat and pick up the remote.

My eyes are glued to the screen as it pings to life.

Lucie is still lying on a gurney-style bed. But now there is a second one in the room.

"What the...?" Theo whispers.

"Why do they have two beds?" Priya asks. "Has that ever happened before?" she asks Theo.

Theo shakes his head slowly, his mouth slightly parted. "Not that I'm aware of."

"Do you think it's for Kevin?" Hazel asks.

No, I think it's for me.

My heart rate rockets to the point where it's all I can hear, and I'm sure the others must be able to as well.

No one has been in any of those rooms, beside room zero, with another person before. Isn't part of the torture that you're in solitary confinement? We only have ourselves.

Why would they change things up again when it's been this way for more than a year?

"Piper, please come to the waiting room."

My heart freezes as they confirm my fear. Twice in one day. No, this has to be a mistake. I can't do it again.

Yes, you damn well can!

Hazel grips my arm. "You can't do that room."

They're testing me. Two rooms in one day is too much for anyone. But what choice do I have except to fight them at every turn? They know I won't give up, so they're going to keep pushing until I'm as timid and afraid as Hazel.

They want me to believe that I'm going to die down here.

Well, I'm not.

I stand, my vision blurring, and tug out of Hazel's grip. "I can," I reply.

Take Priya's coping mechanism and become someone else.

My legs wobble as I step toward the door. Theo, Hazel, and Priya don't make a sound, but I know they're with me.

This is the one I feared most, and it's finally happening. It's happening just hours after room one.

You can get through it. Soon it will be over.

I place my palm on the door, and when it clicks, I push it open.

Caleb is going to torture me with water.

The door closes behind me, clicking locked as Owen ensures that I can't go back. I couldn't anyway. Not with the threat of room zero, knowing that things around here are changing, and fearing that Caleb, Owen, and Matt are developing a taste for killing.

Will they start killing us in the other rooms? Or will they let us outside the building again, giving us the false hope of escape?

I'm certain they would like the hunt. Where is the glory of killing someone locked inside a room?

I know that Theo, Hazel, and Priya wouldn't give them the satisfaction of running, but I'm not at all convinced that Lucie, even knowing what they want, wouldn't run anyway.

She said she would rather die trying. But she wouldn't even be trying because there is no hope.

The wall, Piper. Check the damn wall!

I glance to my side and lean against the wall. Hopefully to them, it will just look as if I'm panicking. I can see the slight ridges where the joints of the plasterboard sheets have been taped and filled, and where they then painted the wall white.

Pushing myself back off the wall, I make sure my knuckles knock against the plasterboard and hear that sweet sound I was hoping for. It's hollow behind. They have built the wall in front of something, and odds are, it's the window. Why else would they need to build it out if there wasn't something in the way, like the frame of the window sticking out just past the metal siding of the building?

Ignoring the fact that there could well be something blocking the window and preventing it from opening, like bars, I suspect we could potentially get out this way.

I walk toward the empty room, and the door in front of me clicks. Owen is watching me head to Lucie, unlocking doors as I go.

He has all the control here. I bet his smile is wide, his heart racing for the opposite reason mine is.

My mind doesn't take anything in as I walk, too busy thinking about what's about to come and what I've found in the waiting room.

There is still the big question of *how* we would get out. It's unlikely they stay overnight here since they have homes and families. People would miss them. There are periods where things are quieter than others, like mornings, but that doesn't mean they're not watching or that they don't take shifts.

I stop at the door in front of me. Beyond it is the corridor to hell, lined with doors to rooms that hold nothing put pain. I take a ragged breath as the air around me thins, like I've just climbed a mountain. Stepping forward, I reach out and twist the handle.

The hallway to hell stretches out in front of me.

Room five's door is open wide. I've only been along this corridor three times, but the doors have only been open an inch before. As if they like to make us open it ourselves.

I straighten my back and walk to the room with my head held high. They will *not* get the better of me.

On the outside, they will see me as calm. On the inside, I'm hit by a wave of nausea. I press my hand to my stomach as I round the corner into the room.

Two pairs of eyes settle on me. One full of fear and heartbreak. The other burning with delight.

"Hi, Piper," Caleb drawls with a smirk.

22

The little room has only enough space for the two beds and a short gap running between. Along the ends of the beds is enough room for buckets of water that line the side and a pile of towels and jugs stacked in the corner.

Everything Caleb needs.

I clear my constricting throat. "Hello, Caleb."

His smile widens, knowing I'm not going to fall apart in front of him. I don't care if he likes it or if he doesn't. For me, I need to keep calm. I can't control what he does to me, but I can control how I react to that.

"Would you care to lie down?"

My eyes fall on the bed beside Lucie, her tortured eyes and wet hair, and my heart stalls. I don't want to play his game. I want to scream and fight, but I have no choice.

The only thing I can do is to show him the fear he so desperately craves.

Swallowing, I reply, "Sure."

It's not like he's going to let me go if I say no. I walk past him, keeping my gaze on the bed, and I sit down on the edge.

"You okay?" I ask Lucie.

Her hair is soaking wet, eyes puffy and rimmed with a red line where she's been crying.

She doesn't speak; in fact she presses her lips together so hard, they disappear. I don't know if she's still mad at me or if she's scared to speak.

"We're not here for a conversation, Piper," Caleb says.

"No? What are we here for, then?" I ask, looking at him over my shoulder.

He folds his arms, his muscles protruding. I wonder if he has always been into working out or if he did it to get strong enough to overpower others.

Doesn't really matter.

"You know what we're here for."

"Ah, right," I mutter. "We're here because you're lacking something in your life and need to make yourself feel better by harming others."

"Now, now, Piper, let's not get personal."

"Personal? You watch me in the bathroom." I lie down, ignoring the hammering in my chest. This is who I need to be in these rooms.

"I can assure you I don't *look*."

"Your assurances mean very little, Caleb, but thanks for clearing that up." I grab the straps attached to the side of the bed. "Are you tying me to this or not? I mean, it's obviously more fun when someone is strapped down..."

I'm taunting him, and it's likely to be a bad idea, but I can't help it. This version of me is harder. I'm not afraid to stand up for myself, but this is something else.

"You want to be strapped down for me, Piper?"

"I'd rather be home, to be honest, Caleb."

"You don't feel at home here?" he asks, tilting his head to the side.

"Let's get on with this. You're boring me now."

Caleb's smile grows wider and wider.

Sick asshole.

"Sure. We can go ahead and get started if you like."

The sooner it starts, the sooner it's over. Like going to sleep early on Christmas Eve. Except when I wake up tomorrow, I'll still be in hell.

"Do whatever you want, Caleb," I say, clenching my trembling hands. *Get that under check; he can't know how petrified you are.*

I close my eyes and blow out a breath as if I'm getting comfortable, about to take a nap. *You will be fine.*

For some reason I don't think I'll be sleeping while I'm in here. Unless I pass out.

Don't think about that!

"Oh, Piper, I plan on doing what I want. Isn't that right, Lucie?"

Lucie doesn't reply, but she grips the straps tight in her hands and whimpers through clenched teeth.

I don't want to look at her again because her eyes are haunted. Right now, I need to be able to pretend that everything is okay. And it is because this version of me is stronger.

"Get on with it, Caleb," I snap, turning his attention back to me.

Lucie has had enough, and honestly, I owe her for not giving her the chance to run.

Sure, she would be dead by now if she'd run, but that wasn't my choice to make.

"Oh, Piper, I think you're my favorite so far."

"Why? Hasn't there been anyone else unafraid of you?"

He steps closer. I can't see him because my eyes are firmly shut, but I can hear the quiet footsteps and feel his presence.

"You're not afraid of me?" he asks, his voice light and playful.

He's crazy.

"No, Caleb, I'm not afraid of you," I repeat.

It's a big fat lie. If he were to check my pulse right now, he would know the truth.

"Well, let's see if we can change that, shall we?"

I slow my breathing as my heart races faster. He's going to go in harder on me because he thinks that I'm not scared.

Caleb moves to the side, and I hear the clanking of metal. The buckle on the strap? A hand clamps around my wrist.

You're fine, you're fine, you're fine.

Leather. Caleb wraps the strap around my wrist and pulls it tight. My hand judders as he buckles the strap. Next, he wraps a strap around my head and tightens it across my forehead.

I swallow.

His footsteps, almost inhumanly light, pad behind my head and to the other side. He is going to tie up my other arm. My legs, too? Lucie's are tied, so I don't see why he wouldn't give us the same treatment.

If he doesn't, I'm pretty sure I could throw my legs up over my head and kick him in the face. I don't think that would do me much good in the long run, but I would prove that I'm not scared.

Although you are.

Caleb buckles my other wrist, pulling so hard the leather pinches my skin. I grit my teeth at the stinging, but I swallow any cry.

He is going to try and get a reaction, it's what feeds him, so I'm going to have to try and hold it in.

"Let's get this show on the road!" he cheers.

I look up as a white towel blocks my view. The thick material lands on my face and panic claws at my throat.

Gripping the side of the bed where my wrists are strapped, I curl my toes and brace myself. His footsteps, suddenly heavy on the cheap laminate floor, thud away from me.

With my eyes closed, I can hear better, smell the floral scent of the fabric softener the towels were washed in.

The very thought of them washing these towels is strange. Why do they care that they're clean? What does it matter?

Lucie's fast breathing synchronizes with mine.

Caleb rummages around, and the sound of plastic hitting plastic fills the air. Then pouring water.

I grip the bed harder.

Caleb whistles a tune I don't recognize as the water stops. He has filled a jug, and now he is coming for me. There is nothing left for him to do. Everything he needed to do to prepare me has been done.

It's time.

I can't see anything. My eyes are closed and covered by a towel.

Caleb has gone quiet. I don't know if he's standing over me or if he's still over by the far wall.

My pulse and heavy breathing are all I can hear.

Where is he? When is he going to start?

Stay calm, hold your breath, don't panic.

There is no doubt in my mind that I can get through this. I have to be strong.

In here, I'm not Piper Willis. I don't really know who I am, but I know that I can get through anything they throw at me.

A heavy weight presses down on my shoulder. Caleb's hand.

He's here, right here.

This is when it begins.

The first drop seeps through the towel and hits my lips, pattering onto the towel like a raindrop. But it's not raining, it's about to storm.

Another drop hits. My heart slams against my rib cage. I curl my fingers into the thin foam mattress covering the bed.

Heat blows against my ear.

Don't react.

Caleb's head is beside mine, his breath grazing my skin and turning my stomach.

"I'm going to enjoy this." His voice rattles through my body, shaking me to the core.

"Bring it," I rasp.

Don't bring it!

Shut up, what are you doing?

He chuckles and then the warmth is gone. He's stood upright again. How much longer is he going to mess with me?

In no time, Caleb dumps a jug of water on me. The towel caves in, molding to my face, the weight pushing my head into the mattress. I hold my breath. The jug couldn't have been big because it's over in seconds.

Far too easy to be as bad as it gets.

He's still playing with me. Caleb is going to take his time, make me suffer and try to break me down. It's him against me, and I have no intention of losing.

23

I wait with my heart in my mouth. The room is eerily silent, like everyone is holding their breath. Where is he? Caleb doesn't make any noise when he moves anymore, as if he's some sort of deadly ninja. It's a stark contrast to how loud he was preparing a minute ago.

I swallow against the churning in my stomach as acid rushes up my throat. *Keep yourself occupied!*

Count.

One. Two. Three. Four. Five…

Three hundred and forty-eight seconds.

My face is cold, the water icy and getting colder the longer it sits on my skin. The towel is still covering my face, heavy and damp.

Lucie hasn't made a sound. In fact, nothing has. For all I know, Caleb has left the room. But that seems unlikely since he's set on making me hurt.

I want to call out to Lucie and see if she's okay, but I'm scared that he will use the opportunity to pour more water on my face. To get through this, I need my eyes and mouth closed and to hold my breath as water hits me. If I don't, I'll get into some serious trouble fast.

My fingers ache as they curl harder into the thin mattress of the bed. *Breathe in. Breathe out.*

Caleb hums low and deep, sending a shudder racing up my spine. My pulse thuds in my ears. *I'm okay.* I don't recognize the tune, but it's creepy, like it belongs in a horror movie right as the killer is about to pounce.

"Hmm hmm. Hmm, hmm, hmm, hmm. Hmmmm."

I squeeze my eyes together tighter.

The first thing I feel is a weight slamming into my face. It feels like someone has dropped bricks on me. The next thing is the temperature. Ice cold.

Water seeps through the towel at an unimaginable rate, gushing against my skin. I hold my breath as a steady stream follows the initial downpour. I keep holding my breath.

Please stop. Please be over soon!

Cold water continues to drum on my face, hitting my mouth and nose. How is he doing this for so long? The water is never-ending.

My lungs burn.

He needs to stop. I need him to stop.

Caleb, no!

My hands cramp.

I'm going to die.

My lungs deflate. I can't take a breath, but I need oxygen. I have nothing left.

"Hmm, hmm, hmm," Caleb hums as the water comes to an abrupt stop.

I turn my head the best I can in the restraint against my forehead, and it's just enough to move my mouth from directly touching the towel. I take a deep breath.

My eyes sting with unshed tears. I know that Caleb wouldn't be able to tell if I was crying with the water already on my face, but *I'll* know. *You will not break me.*

Beside me, I can hear Lucie cry quietly. I focus on her. I'm not alone. I have someone else going through this with me.

Water slams into my face again. I clamp my mouth shut and stop breathing.

It keeps coming and coming and coming.

I dig my heels into the bed and scream so loud in my head that I'm sure Caleb will be able to hear it.

He doesn't stop. Water whacks my face, drilling into my mouth. I clamp my lips closed harder and swallow a sob.

My legs shake, hitting the mattress as my lungs scream in pain.

I want this to end. *Stop! He's going to kill me. This is my punishment for challenging him. Oh God, this is it.*

My legs go heavy. The water continues to pour onto my face.

I'm never going to see my parents again.

Every muscle in my body relaxes; my hands drop their grip and my feet fall to the side.

Caleb moves back. Air fills my lungs in a big rush that makes me light-headed. If I weren't already lying down, I would have hit the floor by now.

My body is done already. But Caleb isn't. Chuckling, he begins humming, and water hits my face again.

●　　●　　●

Time passes so slowly. I feel the agony of every second. My chest aches heavily, fingers numb from holding on so hard.

Caleb hums again as he removes the restraints around my head, wrists, and ankles. The freezing towel is still on my face. He hasn't told me not to move, but it's kind of a given. And anyway, I'm not sure I can right now. I'm spent, emotionally and physically. The last thing in the world I want right now is to have any kind of conversation with him.

So I lie still and wait.

Caleb rips the towel from my face. I blink at the sudden assault the bright light has on my eyes. I avert my gaze, not giving him the satisfaction of any kind of communication. But he's not even looking at me.

He unbuckles Lucie next, and she rolls onto her side, away from us both.

I don't move my head, but I do follow him with my eyes. He chucks an empty bucket to the side and heads out the door.

The door shuts, and I try to jump to my feet. Gripping the edge of the bed, I close my eyes as my vision blurs and wait for the head rush to pass. Every inch of my body hurts.

One, two, three, four…

I get to eleven before my head stops spinning. I open my eyes.

Lucie hasn't moved. Her restraints are undone, but she's lying in the same position as if she hasn't realized Caleb has released us and left.

"Can you get up?" I ask her. Caleb hasn't touched her in hours, or what I assume to be hours, so I don't know why she's not getting up. She's had time to physically recover.

"I don't want to," she murmurs, staring up at the ceiling. Her red hair has dried, but it's still stuck closely to her head. It must have been a while since Caleb paid any attention to her for her hair to be bone-dry.

Mine is dripping.

Sniffing, I shove my hair over my shoulders, ignoring how the water seeps lower into the fabric of my top.

"Lucie, please, you need to get up," I plead. She can't fall apart right now. We need to go. I need to get back. I have to see Hazel, see something good from my life outside of these walls.

"Go back, Piper. I'm going to see if they'll let me run."

My eyes bulge. "No, Lucie! Don't think like that. Come back with me and sleep on it. We'll talk in the morning."

"What's the point? I won't feel any different tomorrow. I've had enough, Piper. I'm done."

I grab Lucie's hand. *That's it. I've had enough. She has to get it together!* I'm tired, my chest hurts, my throat is raw, and I just need to curl up in bed and be the other version of me.

She needs to get it the hell together long enough to get back in that room where we'll be locked in and she can't make any dumb decisions.

"Don't, Piper," she says, tugging her arm. But I don't let go. "Seriously, I—"

"Save it and get up." I pull, and she swings her legs over the side before she falls off the bed.

"What are you doing?" she demands.

"Good, you're up. Let's go."

Narrowing her eyes, she snaps, "Are you stupid? You heard what I said."

"I heard. Now, let's go."

"Piper!"

"No!" I shout. "Stop being a bitch and get back to the room now. If tomorrow you want to offer your head on a platter to them, so be it, but right now, after what's just happened to us, you need to come back." I widen my eyes, trying to tell her there's been a development. That we might all have a chance of getting out of here alive.

Lucie frowns, tilting her head to the side like she's trying to figure something out.

Yes, get that I'm telling you something. Trust me one last time.

"Fine, but if I still feel like this tomorrow…"

"Then you do what you need to. Okay?"

She dips her chin in agreement and we both stumble to the door. Most of the water was on my face, but the neckline of my top is damp and cold. I don't care enough to stop and get fresh clothing.

Lucie and I run out of the room with unsteady legs and almost slam into the wall in the corridor. I place my palms on the wall and take a breath. Lucie sobs and slaps her hand over her mouth. "Piper, I want to get out of here."

I'm not sure whether *here* refers to this hallway or the building as a whole, but I agree that we need to keep moving. I take her hand

and push away from the wall. My legs, weak from either the water torture or shock, carry me slowly along the hallway to the door of the orientation room.

We press on, clinging to each other like we'll fall if we let go, and pass through the clothes room, the random empty room, through the waiting room, and back into our space.

We're here.

I tug the door shut behind it and wince as it slams. Not two seconds later, it clicks locked. My shoulders sag.

24

Theo jumps to his feet a nanosecond after we enter the room. "Are you two okay?"

My eyes, stinging from the water attack, find the TV. It's on, and the room we just ran from is still on the screen. Everything is where it was, the buckets, the beds, the towels. They haven't been back to tidy yet.

I turn around, not wanting to see that room ever again.

"They kept turning the TV on," Theo adds. "We were told to watch and feared what would happen if we didn't."

They all saw what you went through.

I hold my hand up. "I understand." *They could have been sent to one of those rooms for not watching—how could I be mad at them?*

"Lucie, are you all right?" Priya asks.

"No," Lucie replies and curls up on the sofa. She buries her head in her knees and ignores everyone.

Priya sits next to Lucie, far enough away to give her the space she so clearly wants, but close enough so Lucie knows she's there for her.

"You were amazing, Piper," Theo compliments. "You didn't show any fear."

"Could you hear us?"

He shakes his head.

"So do we think the surveillance is image-only or they just didn't allow you to hear the sound?" I ask.

Maybe they can't hear us in here.

Theo shrugs. "I'm not counting on anything."

I sit on the sofa that's next to Lucie and Priya. Hazel and Theo follow and sit on either side of me. I grip the string of my friendship bracelet and spin it around my wrist. Sinking back against the cushions, I tuck my legs under myself.

Hazel lays her hand over mine, stopping my fiddling with the bracelet. She knows I do it when I'm nervous or anxious. When my sister first died, I nearly wore it out. "Are you really okay, Pipes?"

"I'm fine," I reply, removing my hand as her touch makes my stomach squirm. I don't want anyone that close to me again for a long, time. Her tender touch doesn't feel right to me. I'm waiting for pain, though I know she wouldn't hurt me. "I don't really want to talk about it."

What happened in that room happened to the other Piper. That wasn't me.

She nods. "Okay, whatever you want."

I lower my voice and say, "The wall in the waiting room has been built out. I think because of the window."

Theo's eyes widen. "Really?"

"It sounded hollow when I knocked on it, and it moved slightly when I bumped into it. Definitely not solid."

That makes Lucie glance up. "There's a way out," she whispers, her empty eyes now lighting with hope.

"Looks that way," I reply, careful not to make any promises. This is all my opinion. I could be wrong. I'm not a builder. I have pretty limited experience with construction work, and I'm by no means qualified to make the call I've just made. But my dad did teach me a few things, and the wall definitely sounded the same as it did when we knocked on our old kitchen wall.

"Let's go, then."

"The door is locked, Lucie," Theo points out. "We can't do it now."

"We can't do it when they're here because they'll be watching us," I say. "There are times when it's quiet, and I think they've gone. They have to leave to keep up pretenses at home. What's the day? The hospital fund-raiser is on August fifth. They're always at those events. I know we can't be sure that one of them won't stay behind, or that there aren't more people involved, but I think it's the best chance."

"I think tomorrow could be August fifth," Priya. "I'm not positive, but I've been counting sunrises since I got here."

I've tried hard not to dwell on days and dates. It's too depressing to tick by days while being stuck in here. I don't want to know exactly how long I've been in captivity.

But I think it's coming up to a week.

My parents have been looking for me for almost a week. Are they now fearing the worst? Do they believe I ran away?

I'm a homebody. They know that. They have to know that I wouldn't take off.

"Tomorrow it is, then," Lucie says, pinning her gaze on me.

I frown. "I'm not against this, Lucie. I just want the best chance. The event starts at midday. They begin at the country club with golf and tennis, then onto the formal part in the evening of speeches and thank-yous to the donors. They're always present for that."

Theo snorts. "They wouldn't miss the praise."

"Psychos," Hazel grumbles under her breath.

"You're sure they'll all be there?" Theo asks.

"Hazel and I are forced to go to these things by both our parents."

"Caleb and Owen have been to them all before. I don't remember seeing Matt with his friends there, but he could have been with them," Hazel confirms. "This is our chance."

Maybe. It's a chance. Albeit a slim one. We don't know what other security they have here, if any. We don't know if they watch us from an app on their phone. I would imagine so, but we would still have enough time to escape. I hope.

"Is everyone in agreement?" Theo asks.

Lucie, Priya, and Hazel agree immediately.

But no one has thought about one other issue.

"Before I agree, what do we do about Kevin?" I ask. "If we escape, they might find out and come back here before we can get help."

Priya's face falls. "They'll kill him...if they haven't already."

"They'll either do that, or they'll run to avoid being caught. Do you think they would risk coming back?" Hazel asks.

"Yeah, I think they would come back to try and stop us. We can't use the road, but we can't be too far from it or we'll get lost." I reach across and grab the remote. My shoulders feel lighter as I turn it off and the room disappears. Who knows how long that will last before Caleb, Matt, and Owen switch it back on?

I don't need to watch them clean up after torturing me and Lucie for hours.

"We can't leave Kevin," Priya says.

"Priya, I don't think we have a choice," I reply. "We don't know if he's even still here, and if we get caught while trying to find him, this will have all been for nothing."

Shaking her head, she closes her eyes and allows a fat tear to roll down her cheek.

"I understand," she whispers.

"We will do everything we can to get help for him." If he's still alive.

I want to help Kevin if we can, but we can't screw this up trying to rescue a potential corpse.

"So…tomorrow." I take a breath as the enormity of the task we're about to take on washes over me like a tsunami.

Theo wrings his hands. "We'll have to use whatever we can to get through the wall. The kettle and toaster. Anything."

"I don't think that'll be a problem; it's only plasterboard and we really want out," Priya replies. "I'd do anything."

She's not the only one. Besides, don't you find extra strength in situations like this?

"Let's get some sleep," Theo suggests.

We're going to need all the energy we can get, and honestly, I need to sleep. I'm exhausted.

Lucie and I pick ourselves up off the sofa with a lot more effort than the other three. She shuffles to the bathroom. We all let her go first since she was in room five for longer. Caleb did delight in taking a break from Lucie to torture me, though.

It seemed like he spent all his time on me. I didn't hear him go back to Lucie at all. But that might just be because time stood still whenever water hit my face.

I can still feel the hot burning of my lungs as I held my breath. *I need to lie down and pretend it never happened.* This isn't something that I will easily forget, though. Or ever.

After I get ready for bed, I climb into my bunk as Hazel, Priya, and Theo take their turns in the bathroom. Lucie is already curled up on her mattress. Her body is as still as a statue, but somehow I don't think she's asleep yet.

Tugging the quilt over me, I snuggle down, leaving only my head out. I want to be covered, protected, invisible.

Caleb could be watching. He likely is, wanting to witness how he's affected us, wanting to see how broken we are.

So I won't cry. Not one more tear will be shed from me inside these walls.

I close my eyes and listen to the others getting ready for bed.

It takes only a few minutes, but the room falls deadly silent. I think everyone is tucked in, trying to sleep as they think of our escape tomorrow. It feels too soon, too rushed. We're too unprepared. But it's our best chance. I don't know when any other events are planned. I only remember this one because my mom bribed me with a day out shopping with her if I attended. They always gave away a limited number of tickets to locals. Mom and Dad volunteered with local organizations so were always chosen.

I never like going to fund-raisers. They're full of rich people who have every door open to them, every chance and opportunity to have the best life. They hand away lots of money without a second thought, as if it's nothing.

I don't even know if I'll be able to go to college because I have no savings, and my parents always end up having to spend theirs on car repairs and other things that crop up too often.

My family works so hard for having such little spare cash.

But that doesn't matter right now. Nothing but getting free matters, and these *look how much money we have and how much we care by donating* parties may actually work in our favor now.

The room is so silent, I feel like I've gone deaf. It's eerie how quiet a place can be with five people in close proximity.

I lie awake, staring up at the ceiling in the dark. I can just about make out the shapes of a few patches on the white paint. One is a bumpy pyramid like a piece of candy and another resembles a half moon.

My eyes move from shape to shape, trying to form something else. I'm tired enough to fall asleep, and my heavy limbs are glued to the bed, unable to move an inch. But my mind isn't willing to give up the fight.

What if I dream about it?

I can still feel the cold, soaking-wet towel on my face and the water pounding down as Caleb poured more and more and more.

When I'm awake, I can force myself to think of something else, but when I sleep, I'm not in control. If I wake up upset from a nightmare, they might see and then they will win. I'd rather be tired. At least my body is resting here, I can do without switching off completely for one night.

By tomorrow, I could be out of here anyway.

I bite my lip and the seconds tick by, rolling into minutes.

Across the room, Theo enters into a deeper sleep and starts to breathe heavily. The sound, usually a bit irritating, is comforting tonight. I know there are other people in the room with me. I'm not alone, but I feel it more now that there is some noise.

I'm kind of jealous at his ability to fall asleep that fast. I've never been able to do that, not even before this, not even when sleeping was safe.

I don't dare look at Lucie. She's on a top bunk across the room, so I could easily see her if I glance over. She's traumatized by room five and was ready to give up then and there. She's only here because I wasn't going to leave her. So how soundly is she going to sleep tonight?

Is she lying there awake, too scared to close her eyes in case she's back in that room, having Caleb pour endless amounts of icy water over her face?

There didn't seem to be much reprieve, either. He reveled in keeping the torture coming thick and fast. When he removed the towel, his empty eyes stared dead, mouth curled into a smile.

Evil.

I want to get off this bunk and go to Lucie, but how can I do that when I can't even move my head to look at her? She's mad at me for not letting her run when Theo and I had the chance, and she's mad that I made her come back in here.

That's a whole lot of anger aimed in my direction, and I don't want to piss her off any more than I have already.

I tap my fingers on my stomach under the cover.

Water is everywhere.

No, don't go there!

I can't start thinking about it. I can't let it in…because it didn't happen to this Piper.

Yeah, how long is that one going to work?

It actually only needs to work until tomorrow. I can almost taste the freedom.

We have to get out.

Above my head the speaker crackles and our nighttime song begins to play.

I close my eyes and feel a single warm tear trickle down the side of my head.

25

I wake to the sound of banging. What the…?

Sitting, I look around the room, disoriented, as my eyes haven't quite caught up with my brain yet.

"What the hell is going on?" Theo asks, leaping out of bed.

I look around the room, scanning each bed. "Where is Lucie?" I ask, gripping the quilt and shoving it off. I swing my body around and scurry down the ladder.

Theo and I bolt out of the bedroom at the same time, Hazel and Priya just starting to get out of bed to follow.

"Lucie!" I shout.

My heart drops when I see the waiting room door open. Lucie is escaping! How did she manage that? Did they leave it open?

No, it definitely locked behind us. Didn't it? Was this a mistake? Too caught up in the high of a double torture that they forgot to lock up? Not that we would get far—the place is like a fortress.

I stumble toward the hallway, slamming my hand on the edge of the door frame as I lose my footing. "Lucie!"

Her hair is wild as she thrashes at the wall, hammering a plastic knife into the plasterboard. She has already made about a dozen deep slashes, dust covering the floor.

"What's wrong with you?" Theo shouts, grabbing her wrist.

"Get off!" Lucie yanks her arm out of Theo's grip, the knife thudding to the ground. "I can't stay here another second. I can't…I can't…" She takes a deep, ragged breath that rattles and sounds like her lungs have been punctured. Her eyes are wide as saucers and flick wildly between me and Theo.

I watch the two of them in horror. What can we do about this? How can we clean this up enough so it's not noticeable on their screens? It's too early. They might come here before they go to the charity event in the afternoon. They might be watching this.

"What were you thinking?" I snap. "You've ruined everything!"

"You did that!" she shouts, pointing at me and glaring. "I could be free by now. Room five might never have happened if you and Theo had let me run!"

"Enough!" Priya orders, her voice carrying through the hallway like a foghorn. "We need to figure out what to do now."

"We keep going," Lucie snarls.

"How did you get in here?"

"I woke up in the middle of a nightmare. I couldn't breathe. I ran to the door and it opened. I'm not going to pass up a chance like this. If you help me, we'll be out of here faster."

I shake my head. "What's the time?" I ask, dread lining my stomach.

"It looks like sunrise," Hazel replies. "They'll probably be here soon."

"God. We have to go through with this now," I say. There's no way the slices in the plasterboard will go unnoticed, and we don't have anything to vacuum up the dust on the carpet.

They will notice, and we'll get punished.

We *have* to go.

The speaker above us crackles, and ice slides down my spine. They're watching.

"Lucie, Lucie, Lucie," Caleb sings. "You've been a very naughty girl."

Lucie turns slowly, terror filling her eyes. "No," she whispers.

He chuckles, and the horrible sound makes a shudder rock my body. "Piper, Theo, Priya, and Hazel, back to bed."

Will they kill her now? She was trying to escape, after all.

Theo backs up, pulling me with him. I let him because there is no other option. My eyes stay with Lucie as she braces herself against the wall. Theo moves me back enough for the door to close.

Lucie's heart-wrenching sob is the last thing I hear before the door clicks locked.

26

It has been a little over forty-eight hours since Lucie was taken. Three days for Kevin.

Not knowing what happened is eating away at me. Where are they? What are they going through? Questions I may never get answers to.

Caleb, Owen, and Matt have been deathly quiet, too. No one has spoken to us since we were ordered back into the room, and nothing was showing on the TV when we turned it on. For the last two nights there hasn't even been any music, and we've had full control of the lighting.

Something isn't right.

We don't know what's happened with Lucie, if she's okay, what they plan on doing with us, or anything. The waiting is excruciating; so much rides on what they choose to do. My heart hasn't slowed since they took Lucie.

I just want to know.

Priya is making soup for lunch, Hazel is hovering around helping her by divvying out rolls, and Theo and I go over a hundred scenarios. None of them are particularly great. The best ones are that they will keep her in those rooms for a while as punishment. It's what we assume has happened with Kevin.

The worst scenario is that she's dead. They have two teens they want to get rid of. Room zero is a strong possibility.

That being said, we still don't know if Kevin is alive.

We don't know anything!

Theo grits his teeth, his jaw hard and eyes tight. He's been angry for the past two days, believing that Lucie has ruined our only chance for escape, and he is quite possibly right.

There is no way they would keep that window as it is now.

All yesterday we heard banging, drilling, and other odd noises coming from the hallway. Possibly even welding noises as they make sure no one can ever get out through that window.

"The building is going to get a security overhaul," he growls.

I hold my palms up. "Theo, chill. I know what this means, and I'm angry, too, but we can't let them see us arguing. Remember what happened last time there was a fight in here?"

Lucie was sent to room five, and I was sent to room five. Then Lucie got caught trying to escape. We have to be smarter.

Theo slumps back in his seat and blows out a breath through his teeth. "Okay, I get it. But what are we going to do now?"

My heart plummets as I admit, "I really don't know."

There isn't going to be another way out. Not unless they leave the doors open again, and that's an ambush waiting to happen.

But that ambush is looking like our only chance now.

What else can we do from in here?

The door from the waiting room clicks. I leap to my feet as Lucie stumbles through. Her legs give way, and she crashes to the ground. Hazel is closer and bends down to pick her up.

"Lucie, are you okay?" Theo asks, sweeping her up in his arms like she weighs nothing. Her head lolls back, her eyes closing.

"I'm tired," she whispers.

That's where she's been. For the last two days, she's been tortured with sleep deprivation, loud noises waking her whenever she almost drifted off.

"Take her straight to bed," Priya says. "I'll get her a bottle of water in case she wakes thirsty."

I follow Theo as he takes Lucie into the bedroom. I feel a little useless. She might have screwed our chances by acting so rashly but she didn't deserve that, especially not straight after room five.

Lucie is already asleep as Theo lays her down on her top bunk.

"She'll be okay," he says, rising to his feet.

I don't know if she will. She was already emotionally done and ready to die if she couldn't get out now. That room wouldn't have helped matters.

Think, Piper.

Maybe there is a skylight in the roof from the time the building was used for something other than this. It's not like I can request the blueprints, though.

"Theo," I whisper, tugging on his arm. "Come with me."

Hazel and Priya pass us as we leave the room. They have a bottle of water and a couple of packaged snacks to leave for Lucie. She won't have much energy to get up, not until tomorrow I wouldn't think.

I pull him into the main room and over to the corner of the kitchen area.

"What, Piper?"

"When someone dies in here, they have to take them out, right?"

His dark eyes consider my words for a minute before he tilts his head. "You mean if something happens in this room? Yes! Oh my God, you're right. They'd have to do something… One of us needs to play dead."

"That's what I'm thinking…but what do they do with the bodies? I mean, if they set them on fire…" An ice-cold shiver ripples down my spine.

"No, fire in the woods wouldn't be a good plan. Besides, someone would see smoke eventually. It would get unwanted attention."

"So that leaves burial. The river running through town from the lake isn't deep, so they would never be able to hide bodies there."

"You volunteering to be buried alive, Piper?"

I frown. No, not really. "Good point." Who is going to do this? Not only do we have to play dead, but we have to stay calm while they bury us. "Wait, they might transport us, though. I can't imagine they would bury anyone that close to the building, so they'd need a vehicle."

He bites his lip.

"Come on, Theo. I fully appreciate it's a flawed plan, but it's better than waiting for them to open the doors. At least this way, they're not expecting us to run. They won't be waiting in different locations in the forest," I whisper.

Nodding, he sighs. "All right. It's worth a chance. We still need a volunteer."

Yeah, that's where the plan hits a small setback. It's basically suicide. The chance of pulling it off is slim, like, ridiculously slim. But it's a chance.

"I'll do it," I tell him. "Next time I come out of one of those rooms, I'll collapse back here and pretend I've died."

Would they check thoroughly? I can hold my breath, but I can't do anything about my pulse.

"Piper, it's dangerous."

"Yeah. I'll take a crappy plastic knife in my pocket, or something I could use to defend myself in case it goes wrong. Better than nothing, right?"

He blinks slowly as if he's thinking *when* it goes wrong. I don't want to think too much about it because then I'll chicken out.

"I should do it," he says. "No offense, but I'm stronger and stand a much better chance against them."

"This was my idea, Theo, and it's a pretty bad one."

"I know the risks. I've been in here too long, I won't be controlled anymore. I won't let them continue to win. I want out, and the time is now. I'm doing it."

I hope I haven't just set him up to be killed.

27

'm unbelievably bored with watching the same movies, but there is very little else to do, so I sit with Theo, Priya, Lucie, and Hazel. It has been three days since Theo and I came up with our dangerous plan, and we've not yet heard anything from Caleb, Owen, and Matt.

But we still get food, so they haven't abandoned us. I'm not sure if that's good or not.

Murdering each other or starving to death? It's a toss-up really.

Kevin's absence still weighs heavily in the room. The spot where he usually sat is vacant and has been since he was last here.

I don't want to spend all my time stressing or overthinking about what happened to him, but I can't shake the sinking feeling in the pit of my stomach.

But there is no one else in room zero with him right now, we're all still in here, so he must be somewhere in this dungeon alive unless they've killed him themselves.

Theo said it's not the first time someone has been taken into solitary confinement for a longer stretch of time. But the fact that it's happened before does nothing to ease the worry. I just want Kevin back, so we can carry on as normally as possible in here, waiting and secretly plotting.

No one voices their ideas for fear of being heard, but they must think about escape on a daily basis, too.

"Where is your mind?" Theo asks, scooting to the empty cushion beside me.

"On Kevin and the escape," I admit softly. "I know you said to not worry, but I can't help it. Something isn't right about Kevin's disappearance, Theo. I can feel it."

"I agree that it's concerning, but this has happened before. Two guys have gone missing in here, I've heard Caleb and Matt talking about it when I was in room five. It's just another way for them to control us, another game to play. And as for the escape, it'll be okay. Don't allow them to win, remember, Piper?"

I nod, though I'm not quite able to shut my mind off the way he seems to be able to. Maybe that's because he has had more practice. "I remember."

The door in the waiting hallway clicks. I leap to my feet, steadying myself by grabbing the top of Theo's arm as he gets to his feet, too.

Priya gasps. "Kevin?"

No one moves closer to the door by the bookcase, but we all stare at it.

It has to be him, but what condition will he be in? It's been six days, I think. Was he moved from torture room to torture room? The only way I deal with being in those rooms is knowing that I'll be back out with the others soon.

The door opens, and I grip Theo's arm tighter.

The guy, tall and a little on the skinny side, drops to his knees. His dark, tortured eyes regard us one by one.

"Who are you?" Lucie asks.

He looks traumatized, his chest caving with each ragged breath.

I take a step forward, but I'm stopped by Theo. His fingers curl around my wrist, and he shakes his head. I know we don't know this guy, but he's clearly been harmed.

"Don't, Piper. Look at him. Something's wrong."

I tug my wrist out of his grip. "Of course, there is! Can't you see he needs help!"

What has happened to him? He looks like he's been to battle.

"We have no idea where he's come from, Piper."

I gasp. "Yes, I do," I whisper, looking into this guy's wild eyes. He has dark circles and is wincing like the light hurts. His hair is damp, clothes fresh and new. *He's been here.*

Turning to Theo, I tell him, "You said yourself, people have gone missing in here. I don't think they've been missing. I think he's been held somewhere here, or they've been moved from room to room, constantly tortured." I turn back to the guy on the floor.

The guy grips his messy brown hair in his fists and squeezes his eyes closed like he's fighting something in his mind. Memories, no doubt. I know how that feels.

No one stops me as I take a few steps closer and crouch down. "What's your name?" I ask.

He stills, muscles bunching under his sweats. Letting go of his hair, he stares up at me like I'm an alien. How long has it been since he's spoken to another person? "Evan," he replies, his voice rough like he's been screaming.

I don't remember ever seeing his face on a missing poster, but then not everyone is reported as missing or having run away.

"Hi, Evan. I'm Piper. How long have you been here for?"

Shrugging, he sits back. "I don't know. I was taken in February."

I suck in a breath. "It's now August."

He's been here for six months.

"August," he repeats.

"Have you ever been in here?"

He looks around and nods. "Not for a long time, though. I tried to escape with another guy, and they…"

They took them out of here and kept them in the torture rooms.

"I'm so sorry, Evan."

"I'll get him a drink," Priya says from behind me.

Evan must have received food and water, but his eyes are sunken, and his clothes a little baggy. He should have picked up a size smaller than usual.

"Are you hungry?" I ask him.

He nods. "They only gave me bread, soup, water, and the occasional piece of fruit."

Almost six months of only bread, soup, fruit, and water. They are so cruel. My eyes prickle with unshed tears.

"Come and sit, Evan. We'll make you something to eat."

He slams his palm on the wall and rises to his feet. "Who are all of you?" he asks the others.

Theo's jaw tightens.

"That's Priya, Lucie, Hazel, and Theo," I say, pointing to each one so he can put a name to a face. "Theo has been here the longest… Well, besides you. Hazel and I have only been here for about eleven days."

"You were taken together?"

"Yes," I reply. "I don't know if that was their intention since Caleb was talking to me alone earlier in the night, but when he drove past later, Hazel was with me."

"Was it just him? There were two of them when I was jumped."

"Owen was there, too. You were jumped?"

"I was at a party they were throwing. When I left, two of them jumped me and threw me in their car. I think my drink might have been spiked, because I don't remember much about it."

Evan stumbles a little as he walks to the sofa.

"Are you okay?"

He looks over his shoulder. "Hungry. My body feels so weak."

Slumping down, he lays his head back against the cushion.

"Sandwich okay?" Priya asks. "I could make you microwave pasta if you'd prefer, but it'll take a little longer."

"Sandwich sounds great, thanks," he replies.

I can't imagine he wants more bread, but Priya is right, he needs to eat now. We can cook something more substantial in a little while.

"Do you drink tea or coffee?" she asks.

He chuckles. "Coffee sounds like a dream right now."

She smiles. "Coming up."

Hazel folds her arms. "Are we just ignoring the fact that he came in here looking like he's been attacked and Kevin is still missing?"

Evan frowns. "Who is Kevin? I haven't seen anyone else recently."

"He's our friend and he's been…somewhere here for the last five or six days. Where is your friend?"

Shaking his head, Evan clenches his hands into fists.

"What happened to him, Evan?"

His eyes lock with mine. "Room zero."

I gasp. "He's in there? Kevin could be, too!"

"No, he's not there with Kevin."

"How do you know that? They need two to fight to the…" I take a breath. "They now have two."

"I'm telling you, Kevin isn't in room zero."

"You can't know that!"

"Yes, I can. I've just come from room zero."

My heart hits the floor. "Oh."

"Your friend…"

Evan's chin dips to his chest. "I had to. Three days they kept us in there, no food or water. They kept saying things to him, telling him how I was going to attack soon so he should do it first. I tried telling him I wouldn't, but in the end it was too much for him." He takes a breath. "He ran at me, and we got into a fight. I don't want to talk about the rest."

Evan is a murderer. He didn't want to, and he's clearly torn up about it, but that doesn't change the facts. He's taken a life, just like Theo and Priya.

I want to ask questions. There might come a time when I'm forced into that room, and I don't know how I will cope or what I will do. Both parties refusing to hurt the other isn't an option, not for long anyway.

Asking everything I want would be selfish. Evan isn't going to want to talk about it, not yet anyway.

All that matters right now is taking care of him physically.

Priya hands him a plate with two sandwiches on it. He thanks her and inhales the food. Lucie takes three trips to bring hot drinks to all of us and an extra bottled water for Evan.

I try not to look at him while he eats, so I focus on the others instead. Hazel and Theo sit on one sofa with their arms folded, totally closed off to Evan. It would be super-dumb of me to blame them or call them out when they're only trying to make sense of this whole thing, too. We don't know Evan. We had no idea that he was in the same building, and we don't know why Caleb has let him come back in here now.

There are so many questions.

Priya and Lucie are much more open to Evan. Priya is one of the sweetest and most caring people I have ever met, so I don't think it would ever occur to her not to be kind, until she becomes someone else in one of those rooms. She has such a genuine love for people; it will be a double tragedy if she doesn't get out of here.

Lucie kind of looks done. She's neither caring nor uncaring. She's in survival mode, doing what she needs to do.

Evan puts the plate on the coffee table. "Thanks, that was good."

Priya gives him a smile in return and sips her tea.

"Are you feeling any better?" I ask Evan.

"Less hungry. I see James every time I blink my eyes."

"James? That's your friend?"

"Yeah."

"What happened when you were fighting?" Theo questions.

His voice is tight. He doesn't care that it's probably superhard for Evan to talk about his friend. I understand that Theo's concerned for Kevin, and I think Evan might know what's happened to him, but he's not being fair.

"I…" He inhales and then reaches for his coffee. "There were two knives. He was holding one, and the other was on a table. James's eyes were vacant. I have never seen him like that. We've been tortured for months, taken to the brink of death, only to be brought back and tortured all over. He always stayed positive, even in the depths of hell. But that moment, he was gone."

Evan pauses to take a long sip of coffee. "I didn't want to hurt him, but he was going to kill me. It was instinct. I saw the whole thing unfold in front of me, almost as if I were somewhere else. I grabbed the knife and…"

"And?" Theo prompts.

Evan glares, his knuckles turning white as he grips the mug hard. "You can guess. I'm not going into details of how I stole the life from a guy who's kept me sane in this asylum."

Is that what Evan has done to Kevin, too? No, there is no reason for him to lie. We all do things in here that we don't want to.

I shake my head at Theo, signaling him to cool it. His loyalty is appreciated. I love that he's trying to protect us, but Evan isn't the enemy here.

We have to be united against these rich psychos.

Theo's jaw hardens again. It might take him a little while to trust Evan, but he'll have to.

We're in this together.

28

I t's been two days, and Theo still hasn't warmed to Evan much. Hazel is better; she'll actually talk to him now.

We've not heard a peep from Caleb, Owen, and Matt, like the time Lucie tried to escape. I don't know where they are or what they do between sending us into those rooms. Can they get any joy from watching us just sit around?

They're planning something.

Whatever. I'm not complaining or overthinking. When we're left alone, I can almost pretend we're all here because we want to be. Like one big sleepover. It's nice to have those moments, even if they're not real.

Theo, Priya, Lucie, and Hazel are asleep still. I envy them for being able to sleep past five in the morning. But at least now I'm not alone drinking coffee; Evan can't sleep, either. Theo, for the first time ever, isn't up yet.

Evan and I are on the sofa, both holding a mug of strong coffee in silence. For being here as long as he has, Evan seems to be doing okay. He's certainly not falling apart the way you would expect. He doesn't seem broken. Or maybe he's pretending, too.

He stares into the distance, the dark expression in his eyes aging him. He might act okay, he might even be okay, but his eyes are haunted. He's been through a lot, seen a lot.

"Evan? What do you think will happen?"

He swings his head toward me. "What do you mean?"

"Here. Will they do this forever? Will they get bored? What happens if they decide they've had enough tomorrow? They can't let us go, so will they kill us all?"

"Piper, it's sunrise. Can I wake up properly before you ask the heavy questions?"

I don't even know where to begin with helping him deal with the last six months. He doesn't want to talk about James anymore, so all we know are the facts.

"Sorry."

"It's okay. I don't know what will happen, but at the end, whatever that looks like, we'll fight."

"There are more of us than them."

He smiles. "See? We can take them. We have more to lose, and in situations like that, you have twice the strength."

"Is that what it was like for you?"

"I don't know. Probably. I just reacted, I didn't think, and the whole thing was over so quickly. That's a small mercy. James didn't suffer."

"What is that room like?"

He lowers his mug. "It's dark, painted a midnight blue, but the lighting is bright. The room is bare besides a table where the two knives sit."

"Have they only sent you in there once?"

His eyes wince with painful memories. "No."

"How many times, Evan?"

Averting his eyes, his Adam's apple bobs as he gulps. "Four."

"Four?"

"Three times before I was kept in the other rooms. Once after."

"You weren't in here long before you were taken out, though."

"No." He smirks. "I didn't play by the rules, and I tried to break down doors and organize escapes. They thought sending me in there would make me give up, but I couldn't, Piper. I have to find a way out of this hell. This is bigger than any of us. I want to bring them down."

"Shh!" I hush, my eyes flying to the camera on the wall.

"What?" He follows my line of gaze. "No, I don't think they can hear us."

"How do you know that?"

He shrugs. "Tested it. I told them I was going to flood the bathroom. They only intervened when water started pouring over the tub. But when I shouted that I was going to smash it, they had no reaction."

"They can't hear us," I mutter. The revelation fills my lungs. I didn't think we had any privacy. My body is on show to them, and I can't do anything about that, so it's comforting to know that my voice is still my own.

"Nope, you can say whatever you want in here."

"Good. I have a lot to say about *them*."

He taps his finger on the side of the mug. "Narcissistic psychopaths."

"Sounds like a pretty accurate description. There has to be something wrong with them to want to do this, right? I mean, there was a lot of planning, a lot of remodeling the building to do all of this. They must have had meetings about it, discussing what they were going to do and how to do it. Which one of them thought of the different rooms?"

"How do you even go through that process? Planning the torture and murder of other people?" He shakes his head. "I bet it was Caleb who started it. He's always had the air of authority about him. I've only seen him with Matt and Owen once, but he was definitely the boss."

"Yeah," I reply. "He was the one who picked me and Hazel up. Owen was with him, but he was more a bystander."

It makes total sense that Caleb is the ringleader. He is the one we hear on the intercoms most. He is the one who found me; he was driving the car; he convinced me going with him was a good idea. He's charming, beautiful, persuasive, and deadly.

"He's the one we need to take down," Evan says.

"Take down? You want to take them down? How would we even do that? We're locked in here."

He dips his head. "Okay, I haven't gotten that far yet. But when the times comes, we go for Caleb."

"Do you think we will get a chance? They don't come in here, and if they did, it certainly wouldn't be all three of them. They couldn't risk that. They always need someone out there in full control. It's how they make us do what they want."

"We'll have to make them. There's always a final showdown, right?"

"We're not in a movie, Evan."

"How do you know? They're watching us. They might be recording it, streaming it on the deep web."

My mouth falls open. Now that he suggested that, I can't unthink it. "Why would you say that?"

"Because it could be true…and because I've seen one too many movies. Look, it doesn't really matter what's happening, all that's important is what goes on inside these walls."

I shake my head. "Stop."

He sighs. "I'm sorry. I've been here too long. I know I'm very matter-of-fact about these things, but in my experience so far, it's necessary."

"I'm not there yet."

"I get that," he says, softening his voice and leaning closer. "I really am sorry, Piper."

"Forget it."

Evan gives me a bright smile, and his shoulders relax.

"So, when do you think I'll be accepted here?" he asks.

"They're just scared, Evan. It's not you. Can you see it from their view? We had no idea you were here."

"I get it, but from my view, I had no idea any of you were here, either. I had to come into a room of strangers, who have been less than welcoming and look at me like I'm the enemy. I'm in the same position as you all."

"Hey, you're preaching to the converted here."

His eyes soften. "Well, I'm glad I have you."

I bite my lip and look away. Evan is sincere and unfazed, on the outside anyway, by everything. He's mastered what I want to be in here, and he makes my heart sprint.

"You okay, Piper?" he asks.

I clear my throat. "Yeah, I'm fine. Are you hungry? I need to eat breakfast," I say, getting up and heading to the kitchen area before he can reply.

"Evan, how old are you?" I ask, glancing over my shoulder.

His arms are folded, and he's watching me like I'm some difficult math problem he can't figure out.

"I'm nineteen."

Okay, not too much older. Not that it matters.

I nod and go back to fixing some food.

"What about you?"

"Seventeen," I reply, popping four slices of bread in the toaster. I don't even know if he wants toast, but he's getting some.

I don't look around because I'm trying to be cool, which is super-hard to do when I'm so uncool, but I hear his footsteps. "Want some help?"

My breath catches as I feel the warmth from his body far too close to mine.

"I'm fine," I say, my traitorous voice breaking.

Way to stay cool.

"Will you go and sit, please?"

I turn, taking a small step back as I do. "But I'm making breakfast."

He chuckles, shaking his head. "You're not making this easy. Will you sit so I can make you breakfast? I mean, I'd like to thank you for welcoming me back with open arms. You were one of the first to reach out to me after I got out of those rooms and not assume I was a monster."

"I don't need any thanks." Honestly, I would accept anyone. We're all in the same position. We need each other.

"Piper," he says on a sigh.

I hold my hands up. "All right. Sorry. I'll go and sit."

Stepping around him, I walk back to the sofa. But I can't relax because that would be impossible here.

"Piper!" Hazel shouts, darting into the room. Her eyes fall on Evan first, and she only relaxes her posture when she sees me. "There you are," she says.

"Where did you think I was?"

She shrugs. "I was just talking to Theo last night."

Great.

"I'm not here to hurt anyone, Hazel. Why can't you understand that?" Evan says. "I've been stuck between rooms, kept in some for days at a time sometimes, before being allowed back in here."

She bites the inside of her cheek and nods. "Was it constant?"

Hazel doesn't elaborate but it's clear she's asking about the torture.

"No. I got days of reprieve, but it was solitary *all the time*." I can't imagine what that was like.

He shakes his head, his chest expanding with a deep breath. "All I'm asking is for a chance, like everyone else in here." He swallows and blinks heavily like he's trying to blink away the memories. "Just a chance."

Hazel nods, thawing further.

"It's going to be okay now, Evan," I say.

His eyes quickly find mine, and he gives me a warm smile that I return.

"Will you tell me about yourself?" I request. "I don't really know anything."

"Sorry," he replies with a shake of his head. "I'm not used to talking; it's been a while."

"No, it's okay. But I would like to get to know you better."

"I used to be an open book, but I've not had the opportunity in such a long time. Ask me anything, Piper."

"Where do you live?"

"My mom lives on the edge of town, close to the decent side but not that close. Our house is small, but Mom has a lot of pride in it. She spent ten years renovating it all by herself. My dad moved away when I was ten, and I haven't heard from him since."

"I'm sorry to hear that."

"It's no loss."

"Do you have siblings?"

He looks away, something passing through his eyes that steals my breath.

"Evan, what is it?" I ask softly.

I think he has siblings. Or had.

"My brother is two years older than me, he lives in the city but checks in regularly. Well, I assume he still does anyway. But my sister died when she was five."

"Oh God, I'm so sorry."

He laughs bitterly. "My dad left before her funeral. He told us it was too much, and he left. Me and my brother, Luke, weren't enough for him to stay. I was ten and Luke twelve. I've never felt so low and worthless as I did that day. Elliana was the only kid he wanted."

"That's awful."

He clicks his tongue. "It's done now."

Somehow, I don't think it is. You don't get over the death of your sibling or the rejection of a parent, not completely.

"Evan, you are enough."

He sucks a long breath in through his teeth. "No one has ever said that."

"Not even your mom?"

"At the time, she was too buried in the grief of losing Ellie. By the time she resembled my mom again, I was doing okay. Luke and I got through it together."

"You were only ten."

"I grew up fast."

"No one should have to grow up fast like that."

"Piper," he breathes, closing his eyes. "Can we not talk about this anymore, please?"

"Of course. I'm sorry."

"No." He opens his eyes. "It's not that. You're not hurting me, you're healing me, but it's too much."

I bite my lip, my heart light with the knowledge that I've given him some peace, even without trying. I wish his mom were able to tell him that his dad was wrong at the time.

"Okay." I sit straighter and smile, shifting the mood. "What's your favorite food?"

He grins. "Burgers from Lyle's. You ever been?"

"No, but I've heard good things. It's just out of town, isn't it?"

"Yeah. When we get out, we're going."

Don't ask if it's a date.

"Sounds good to me. We like this game in here: Where would you be right now if you could go anywhere?"

"Right now, I'll take *anywhere*."

"I said that the first time I was asked, too."

He chuckles. "I guess we'd all just rather be on the other side of these walls."

"What do you want to do with your life?"

"Ah, the questions continue." He smiles. "I haven't figured that out yet. There's a lot of pressure to take any job, and I would to get some money and help my mom, but I want a career, too, you know?"

"I get that. People settle far too easily where we live, and I know there is a dramatic lack of opportunities, but sometimes you have to make things happen yourself."

"I'll drink to that," he says, taking a sip of water from the bottle.

"I've never had an alcoholic drink. Unless you count one sip of my mom's champagne last New Year's Eve. Kind of sad, right?"

"You're seventeen; you're not supposed to have had a drink yet."

"Right, but most people have."

"You are not most people, Piper."

I love how Evan sees me. He has a lot of belief in me, though I'm still a stranger. Up until now, it's only been my parents, Hazel, and one teacher who think I can do more than stay in this town and wait tables.

The speaker crackles.

Evan and I make eye contact.

It's morning, so not late enough for our creepy bedtime song.

The boom of bass makes me jump. I throw out my hands, gripping the sofa. It so similar to the noise in room one. Then, they play an instrumental song that I don't recognize, but it's loud, obnoxious, and full of constant beats that make me want to rip my hair from my scalp after only ten seconds of listening.

"What the hell is this?" Theo shouts over the volume as he walks into the room, followed by Priya.

Priya stomps toward us with a scowl. She curls up on the sofa and closes her eyes.

This is just another way to keep us on our feet and prevent us from relaxing for even a second.

Evan takes my hand that's digging into the cushion of the sofa.

"It's okay," he says, pulling me closer. I slump against his side and wait. Because what else can we do but wait for them to finish having their fun and turn it off?

Another reminder that we don't have one scrap of control in here.

Suddenly, the room is drenched in darkness.

"Everyone sit down," Evan shouts.

Besides Lucie and Theo, we all are.

"I've got you, come on," Theo says to Lucie in a voice I can barely make out under the music. She takes Theo's outstretched hand and sits down on the sofa.

"Are you all okay?" I shout.

I close my eyes to focus. When I hear them all reply, I sigh in relief. What are Caleb and his friends doing? Loud music and no light.

Can they see us? I would imagine they would be able to. They will have night-vision cameras, surely.

I lay my head on Evan's shoulder, my stomach churning and nerves frayed. What if they come in here while we're all sitting in the dark? They could do anything.

I wince as the volume is turned up. My ears ringing and throat clenching every time the bass kicks in.

This is why I don't like this music!

Evan squeezes my hand harder and runs his thumb over my knuckles. He's trying to distract me, to tell me he's here and I'm not alone. I appreciate it so much, but I don't know how I can ignore the blistering sound of that music or the way it makes me feel sick.

You're fine. Keep calm. Go somewhere else.

This isn't supposed to happen in here. They do mess with us, but they don't hurt us in this room, not directly anyway.

Why are they doing this now?

"Everyone okay?" Evan shouts. I can barely hear him over the music now, and he's sitting right beside me.

Rather than screaming back and hurting my throat, I nod against his shoulder. I'll be fine. I've survived worse by now. At least here, we're all together. We're not doing this in solitary.

Then, the music stops, and the lights flick on. I blink my eyes open and lift my head off Evan. Hazel and Priya are huddled together, their heads buried in the cushions, and Lucie is in Theo's arms. They all sit up and look over.

"Why?" Priya asks.

No one has an answer.

"Do you think they'll do that again?" Lucie's wide eyes are full of fear and rimmed with unshed tears.

I know what she's thinking: There could be no breaks. It could be room after room, only to come back here and face new tortures.

They're getting worse.

"I'm going to get us something to drink." Priya stands and heads to the kitchen area.

I give her a sympathetic smile as she walks past me. She needs to be doing something productive again.

I do, too, but I'm not exactly sure what that is in this moment. My heart is still racing at the thought of this being a regular thing. We're no longer pawns in their games in the torture rooms, but we're also players in here.

No escape. No hope.

That's what they're trying to do. They want to take everything from us, prove who holds all the cards.

I'm not stupid, I know the deal here. I know the power they have over me, even if I won't ever accept it or stop challenging it.

"You all right?" Evan asks. He hasn't let go of my hand yet. I sort of need him to keep holding it for a while; he's the only thing preventing me from trembling.

"I am now," I say, blowing out a deep breath. *Breathe long and slow. In and out.*

"What the hell was that? Has that happened before?" I ask Evan.

"I've never experienced that, but then I've not been in here long, even before all of you. And I think they're getting worse."

Yep. We're all going to have to fight a whole lot harder.

29

n the end, Evan makes breakfast for everyone, and we kind of pretend the whole random morning music thing is no longer an issue.

Priya, Hazel, and Lucie show gratitude; Theo says thank you, but his mouth is tight. I understand he doesn't trust Evan yet, but this cold-shoulder thing isn't going to help.

Priya and Hazel clean up. Hazel is beginning to take on a role similar to Priya. Planning escapes isn't their strong suit, but they are doing what they can.

I've taken on more of a Theo-style role, being strong, coming up with ideas, volunteering for things I don't want to do. It's what I need to do to get through. I have to be working toward escape or I'll just be accepting that this is our life forever. The playing-dead idea is kind of a last resort since all they have to do is check our pulse.

There is no life in here. We're stuck in perpetual hell until the day we're free.

After breakfast is done, everyone kind of does their own thing.

Priya reads, Hazel puts a mindless DVD on, Theo heads into the bedroom, probably to sulk, and I stay at the kitchen table with Evan.

"How are you holding up?" I ask.

He leans his forearms on the table. "I'm holding," he replies. "Breakfast went well…right?"

I nod. "Yeah, I think so."

"You want to join Hazel and watch TV or…?"

"Or go for a walk outside," I say sarcastically.

"I meant cards. There's a deck on the bookshelf."

We have more entertainment than I would have thought we'd get. But making it nicer in here only makes it that much worse when we're sent into a torture room.

"What do you want to play?"

He grins. "Poker."

"You'll have to teach me."

"That I can do," he replies, and rises to get the cards.

As it turns out, he cannot teach me, because I suck beyond belief. Poker isn't my game, and if we'd have been playing for money, I would be broke.

But I laughed. For the first time since I was taken, I laughed. A lot.

It's so nice to feel human again. My heart is a fraction lighter, my mouth curved into a smile. It's an odd feeling considering where I am, but for now, I'm enjoying it.

I lean back in the seat and throw my cards into the center of the table. "I'm awful!"

Evan chuckles. "You really are. I've taught a lot of people how to play, but I'm throwing in the towel with you."

I shake my head. "Sorry."

"Evan to the waiting room," Caleb says over the crackling speaker.

Evan's smile falls. He's only just come in here. What if they keep him away for months again?

"No," I whisper.

Evan covers my hand with his and my heart falters. "It's okay. I'll come back as soon as I can."

He's only been here a little over two days, I'm not ready for him to go yet. He made me laugh!

"Whatever it is, you can do it."

"Piper to the waiting room," Caleb calls next, his voice musical.

Evan looks up at the camera in the corner and scowls.

"Piper, not again," Hazel says, gripping my arm. Her eyes are wet with tears.

I can't see that right now. There is no room for weakness where I'm about to go.

"It's okay, Hazel. I can do it."

Evan moves his hand, but only to hold onto mine. "We've got this, Piper."

Standing with him, I try to smile as my stomach churns with nerves. It's too soon, I wanted more time after room five.

Oh God, we're going together, what if Caleb wants two people in there again? *What if Caleb wants two people in room zero?*

Nope. Nope. Don't think like that.

I walk with Evan, not missing the wounded look Theo gives us. I don't have the mental capacity to even go there, so I don't. We stop at the door until it clicks.

Evan is the one to push it open.

The speaker crackles again.

"What the…?" I mutter as Mozart is played into the room. This is a new song. They've not played this before.

"Music?" he asks, squeezing my hand.

"They didn't play music when you were in here?"

He shakes his head with a frown. "No, that's new."

There seem to be a lot of new things.

I bite my lip and then say, "Well, it doesn't matter. Let's just get through this, okay?"

Click.

The door at the end is unlocked.

"Evan…"

He looks back as he starts to walk into the empty room in front of us. "Yeah?"

"If it's room zero?"

Before I can blink, he spins around, facing me, his body almost pressing into mine. "You don't need to worry about anything, Piper. You won't be dying in that room, I can promise that."

"You've known me two days," I remind him.

"That feels like a lifetime when you bring sunshine into this dungeon."

I couldn't have put it better myself. I thought I could get through this because I have Hazel, but she hasn't been herself at all. Theo has turned frosty with me. I've been alone. Until now.

30

"Room three," Evan says as we stop in front of the door. It's open an inch.

I haven't been in this room before. Light. Room three. And room four, sleep deprivation. Those are the only rooms I've not been in. Oh, and obviously room zero.

Hazel hasn't done a room once yet.

I guess I piss them off more than Hazel does. But they won't drive a wedge between us, it isn't Hazel's fault.

"You've done this one?" I ask, squeezing Evan's hand tighter. Somehow having another person with me is making me more nervous. Or perhaps that's just the unknown. I don't know what to expect in here.

Evan nods. "Too many times to count. We'll be fine, okay?"

My heart is racing as I reply, "Okay."

Taking the lead, Evan pushes the door open with his free hand and leads us into the room. There is nothing in here; it's a white box. On the ceiling is one big light, like the whole thing is a light.

I lick my lips. While I don't think bright lights will be the worst room, I'm not naive enough to think it's going to be easy. I get headaches from being in the sun for too long, and I'm going to have to spend some time in this room with what I would imagine is super-strong lighting.

The door clicks locked behind us. Evan turns to face me. He's calm, like he knows what's coming. He does, and he's survived this.

Though I can't see how room five could ever get easier.

He takes my other hand and steps closer. "You can do this, Piper."

"Don't let go," I whisper as the room is cloaked in darkness.

Gasping, I step closer to Evan.

"It's okay. It's always dark first. Close your eyes, Piper, and keep them shut."

I don't ask why I would need to close my eyes in a dark room, but I have a feeling that if I don't do what said he says, I'll regret it.

I blink my eyes and squeeze them shut. "Are your eyes closed, too?" I ask him.

"Yeah. Don't open them."

How bright can it get?

My heart hammers, and my breath is shallow.

"Calm down, Piper," he soothes. "Breathe deeply."

I take a deep breath and relax my grip on Evan's hands as my lungs fill with oxygen.

"Good." He lets go of my hands and wraps his arms around my back.

This is rather intimate, but he's not doing it because he wants anything to happen between us. This is support. He's doing everything he can to make this as easy on me as it can be. I really, really appreciate it. Being strong and upbeat all the time is exhausting; it's nice to be taken care of the way we take care of Lucie and Hazel.

I hold on to Evan and press my face into his strong chest.

The light switches on with a loud thud and floods the room. It's bright. It's impossibly bright, and my eyes are closed and buried in Evan's T-shirt.

"Evan," I whisper. The light burns, my eyes sting, my skin prickles.

His body tenses, and he bows his head against my shoulder. "I know." His fingers dig into my back. "Keep your eyes closed."

I couldn't open them if I wanted to. The light burns as it is.

"It's too much," I whimper. My throat is dry from the heat the light is giving off, my head pounding from the brightness.

Evan's knees give out, and he takes me to the floor with him. We don't let go of each other. I'm scared to move because I know it will only get worse if nothing is shielding my eyes.

They've cut the lights four times already today, and they've been doing it for days. Each time it comes back on, it's like being hit by the sun.

"You've got this, Piper," he whispers.

I don't know how I would have done this alone. I thought it would be better than the noise and heat, but it's not. It's so much worse.

The lights go out again, and we're cloaked in darkness. It offers only a small amount of comfort. The damage has been done; my head pounds so hard, it hurts to blink. I need some pills and water. Nothing else will help now.

"How long have we been in here?" I whisper.

"Hours," he replies.

It feels like weeks.

"How long is it usually?" I ask as the light clicks. I hold my breath, but this time it doesn't hurt. The light is dim, like it was when we first came in.

Evan looks up at the same time as I do, both of us squinting our eyes. "It's over," he says. "And that was about how long it lasts most of the time."

"Most of the time?" I ask.

"Sometimes it's longer," he replies. "Don't think of that now. Come on."

Pushing to his feet, he offers me his hand.

I place my hand in his and rise to my feet. "Thank you," I say. "I don't think I would have been able to do that without you."

"You would have. You know you're strong, but I don't think you know how strong. You're going all the way, Piper."

"All the way to what?"

The door clicks unlocked but Evan doesn't move.

"The end of this."

"We don't know what the end is going to be."

"No," he says, brushing hair from my face, "but I know you'll be there." Dropping his arm, he takes a breath. "Let's get back."

We make the short walk back to our room, grabbing a bag of new clothes in the clothes room as we go. The heat from the light has made me a sweaty mess. I need aspirin, a shower, and to lie down.

Hazel, Priya, and Theo are sitting on the sofa when we get back. Where is Lucie? Sleeping, maybe.

"Are you two okay?" Hazel asks.

I nod and pain slices through my forehead. Damn, that hurts so much. "I need…"

"Sit down. I'll take care of it," Evan says.

"Hey, no, you sit, too." Priya leaps to her feet. "You need a glass of water, right?"

"Thanks," Evan replies and follows me to the sofa.

When my headache has ebbed a little, I'll go for my shower.

"Was the camera on?" I ask.

Hazel nods. "You two were amazing, though. So strong."

"What camera?" Evan asks.

"When Lucie and Piper went into room five, they showed the live feed in here and made us watch," Hazel says quietly. With the constant threat of room zero looming over us, it's understandable that we do what we're told.

Evan shakes his head. "They really do that?"

"Yep," I say, taking the glass of water from Priya with gratitude. "I love you," I tell her.

Evan downs his pills, too, and lies back against the sofa, gripping his glass of water as if it's his lifeline.

I know the feeling.

"Do you guys want anything to eat or are you going to bed early?" Theo asks. He avoids eye contact with me, preferring to look between me and Evan.

"I can't eat a thing," I say. "I'm going to shower and sleep."

Evan nods. "Same. My head is killing me."

"All right," Theo mutters.

Things with Theo have gone from bad to worse. It started when I didn't let him run, and Evan's presence has only widened the distance between us.

I miss having him as a friend, but I'm not going to turn my back on anyone in here in order to do that. There can't be any cliques in here. Everyone is equal; everyone gets the same treatment.

Evan insists I use the bathroom first, and I'm thankful, because I don't know how much longer I can stay awake. I need to curl up in bed and close my eyes. I need this damn headache to go away.

Will there be any lingering effects from the extreme light exposure? I don't know how long you have to be exposed for that to happen. We were in there for a couple of hours, and there were moments of complete darkness, too, which only made it worse when the lights turned back on.

I think I'll be okay.

You have to be okay.

When I'm finished brushing my teeth, showering, and changing into the new clothes I brought back, I head straight to bed. No one stops me as I walk through the main room, understanding that I need to go to bed.

I'm not really feeling in a chatty mood.

Slipping into bed, I tug the quilt around my body and close my eyes. Sleep may not come quickly, but at least I can lie here in the dark and be still.

After about five minutes, or it could have been many more, I've lost the ability to count, Evan creeps into the room. I hear his footsteps getting louder, and then he climbs the ladder to the top of the bunk next to mine.

His head hits the pillow with a light thud, and he sighs quietly.

I wonder what he's thinking? Was it easier or harder for him having me there? He's done the room before but on his own. He took on the role of protector. Did that give him enough of a distraction?

"Evan?" I whisper.

"Yeah?"

I smile at the gentle tone in his voice. "Are you okay?"

"I'm okay," he replies, and I can hear the smile in his voice. "Are you?"

"I guess. My head doesn't feel good."

"No, but it'll go away."

Evan lifts his arm, flopping it over his head and into my bunk. Biting my lip as my smile grows, I lift my arm up and grip his hand. That has to be uncomfortable for him, his arm resting on the wooden side of the bunk and bent back, but he doesn't seem to care.

In fact, it only takes a few minutes before I hear his breathing getting heavier, and only a few minutes more until I follow.

31

I wake early as usual. Evan's hand is still beside my head, but sometime in the night, I let go.

Sitting up, I rub my eyes. The ache in my head has subsided, but it's still very much there. I kick off my covers and sneak a look at Evan as I turn around to go down the ladder.

He's still asleep, and I'm sure as hell not waking him up.

I go in search of aspirin and water. To my surprise, Theo is sitting on the sofa, drinking from a mug. The smell of coffee hits me like a truck. I love it, but I can't drink it with a headache.

"Morning," I say.

"How are you doing?"

I grab some aspirin, fill a glass with water, and down them. "I'm okay; head is still hurting."

"Take it easy today…you and Evan."

I sit and tuck my feet under my butt. "Are you okay with Evan now? It was a little scary knowing he's been here longer than us, but we didn't know he was there. Think about it, Kevin could be in that situation months down the line, and we would want people to accept him."

If we're all dead, that could happen.

Let's not think too much about that one.

"I get it," he replies with a nod. "And clearly you really like him, so he can't be that bad."

"I like everyone in here."

Maybe Evan in a slightly different way.

Theo smiles, but it doesn't reach his eyes. "Right."

"Are we cool? Except for Hazel, you are the first friend I made in here. And I know you wanted us to run when we were let outside, but I'd hate it if we can't go back to how things were."

"Do you honestly think it can go back to how it was now?"

I press my lips together, unsure if he means because of what's happened or because of Evan. I'd ask, but I don't want to go there with him. Awkward in here would take on a whole new level considering we can't get away from each other.

"I hope we can. You've helped me a lot."

"You have Evan for that now. He seems to help more. I saw you playing cards."

"Theo, you could have joined in."

"I'm not really talking about the card game, Piper."

Can we move on?

"Hey." Evan's smooth voice makes me smile.

Theo lifts his chin in greeting. I look over my shoulder. "Hey. How's your head?" I ask.

"Not too bad. Yours?"

"Hurts."

He gives me a small smile. "You're not used to it."

But he is, because they've sent him from room to room for months. It takes a really strong person to get through that.

Evan sits next to me, his arm pressing against mine. I don't know if it's because we got through room three together, but his touch doesn't make me cringe.

He is comfort. I feel safe.

You're ridiculous.

"Are we still on for the plan?" Theo asks, his eyes only on me since Evan wasn't here for the planning.

"Are you sure you want to do it? It's risky. Like, insanely risky."

"What plan is this?" Evan interjects.

Theo's eyes tighten. "I'm going to play dead the next time I've been in a room. Maybe I'll be able to get away and find help."

"No offense to either of you, but that sounds like a terrible plan."

Theo and I laugh. Shaking my head, I agree, "Yeah, it is."

With a frown, Evan looks between us, a little lost, like he's not sure if he's missed a joke or not.

"This is all we have now," Theo tells him.

"But you'll die."

"Theo, he has a valid point."

"I'm not disagreeing, but I can't keep doing this. Like Lucie said, I would rather die trying to escape than at the hand of one of my friends. I don't know what they think this is, but the era of gladiators ended for a reason."

"So, you just need to get in one of those rooms?" Evan asks.

Theo nods. "Lucie was called when she tried to attack Piper, so I figured I'll do the same."

I can feel Evan's eyes on me. "She attacked you?"

"Not really. She only tried. She was upset."

"And you're going to pretend to attack Piper?" Evan asks Theo. His voice is hard, like he's challenging him to try.

Can't say I hate the protective side of Evan. In fact, I damn well love having someone take care of me.

Theo laughs. "No, I think she's had enough. But now that you're here…"

Evan rolls his eyes. "Sure, attack me."

"Pretend," Theo stresses. "I'm not going to attack you. I just need to do something that will get me in a room, something that's not going to make me feel like crap."

Apparently even pretending to attack me would make him feel awful.

Evan lifts his hands. "Go ahead."

The speaker crackles, sending a bolt of fear down my spine. "Evan to the waiting room," Owens voice sings.

"What? No way, it's too soon!"

Evan shakes his head. "Don't. Calm down. It's fine. I'll be back soon."

"But it's—"

"No," he cuts me off. "Don't do anything that could get you in there again."

Evan gets up. I want to follow him to the door, but my legs feel like jelly. This isn't fair.

I watch with my heart in my stomach as he grabs a quick swig of water from the tap before disappearing though the door.

Theo moves from his seat and wraps his arm around my shoulder. I tense for a second before relaxing.

"He'll be okay, Piper. If anyone can handle going in there again, it's him."

"I like him, Theo."

He chuckles. "Duh."

32

Evan has been gone a long time, and I can't help worrying that he's been taken away for another six months or worse.

How long can you be in solitary confinement, flitting from torture room to torture room before you lose yourself completely? Evan is one of the strongest people I know, but everyone has their limits and I could see in his eyes that he was scared when they called his name.

Priya senses my stress. "It's been a good few hours now, but I'm sure he's fine."

I shake my head. "But he keeps having to do this over and over. How do you stay strong through that?"

"He's stronger than anyone. Caleb, Owen, and Matt know that, which is why they kept him in those rooms for months, Piper."

"Right. Yeah, that makes sense. They punish him harder."

Hazel scoffs. "He's probably dead. We don't know where Kevin is. They're probably in room zero."

"Hazel!" I snap, scowling at her. "If you can't be positive, then don't speak! I've had enough of this doom-and-gloom attitude you've adopted since we got here."

"Oh, I'm sorry for being realistic."

"You're not being realistic; you're being pessimistic, and it's not helping."

She rolls her eyes and flicks through one of the old magazines, ignoring me.

All our lives, she's been so upbeat. Whenever I had a freak-out that I'd done badly on a test or essay, she would talk me down. I hate what this place is doing to my best friend. I miss the old her so much.

There is nothing I wouldn't do to be back in my room with her, eating popcorn, watching some stupid rom-com, or trying to pick out the killer in a mystery movie.

Hazel never guessed right because she always overthought it.

I probably shouldn't have snapped at her, but her attitude is crappy. Constantly hearing the worst-case scenario is bringing us all down. I'm not naive. I know what they're capable of, but I can't let my mind constantly go there. Hope is all we have.

I turn back to Priya. At least she's trying to make the best of things here until we figure a way out of this mess. "You're right. Evan's probably just being kept in there longer. I hate that he's been treated worse because he tried to escape. I mean, it makes sense for them to do that, as a deterrent to the rest of us, but it sucks. Royally sucks. We would all escape if we could," I say.

"We can," Priya whispers. "Remember, there is a way out of here. We just need to figure out which way is most likely to work."

Any new ideas would be welcomed.

What if Kevin and Evan are in room zero?

The door in the hallways clicks, unlocking. Priya and I jump to our feet. Lucie dashes out of the bedroom, and Theo puts down his plate to walk closer.

It's either Evan or Kevin.

Evan walks through the door, rubbing his forehead.

There is no blood on him, no injury or sign of a struggle, and he's carrying a bag of clean clothes. His brown hair is still disheveled in that purposeful way.

He hasn't been in room zero. But his head is hurting.

"Sound?" I ask, my shoulders now free of stress. He's safe.

But we don't know if Kevin is.

Evan nods, his eyes are semi-vacant as if he hasn't been able to bring himself back from wherever he goes mentally while in those rooms.

"Yeah, sound. I'm okay, though." He drops his hand. "Everyone else all right?"

"We're all fine," Priya says. "Do you need anything?"

"Sounds like dinner is cooking," he replies.

The microwave is humming.

She brushes her long black hair over her shoulder. "Yes, it will only be another minute now."

Theo opens the fridge and tosses Evan a bottle of water.

"Thanks, man," Evan says.

The two of them are less frosty with each other, which is nice. It's not Evan's fault that any of this is happening. And it's not his fault that Kevin appears to have taken his place in exile.

"You were there a long time," I say.

He pauses on the way past. "I was?"

"Yeah. A little over five hours, Evan."

"I-I don't know if I've been in that room that long before. When you're in there…"

"Time is meaningless. I know."

Smiling, he adds, "It didn't feel like any longer than usual."

When you're in one of the rooms, it could be for minutes or all day. It's impossible to tell.

"Well, at least you're back now. Do you need aspirin?"

"I'm all right. I've gotten used to not having anything. My head isn't too bad." He flops down beside me. "What have you been up to while I was gone?"

I shrug. "Nothing. TV." *Worrying about you mostly.*

He glances over. "*The Da Vinci Code*, huh?"

"It's one of the better DVDs we have here," I reply. "Keeps my mind busy."

"What do you usually watch at home?"

"Ironically, anything crime-based. I love those documentaries about getting into the minds of serial killers."

"Really?" he asks, lifting his eyebrows.

"Yep. So, I should have known Caleb was a creep, right?" So stupid to have trusted him.

Evan throws his arm over the back of the sofa behind me. "We're all in the same position, Piper."

"Yeah, I know. I still feel like I should have seen it coming. I know not to get into cars with strangers."

"Caleb is rich and respectable. You knew who he was, right? I mean, everyone knows about those guys."

"I knew about him, yeah. But that doesn't mean I'm not an idiot."

He shakes his head, a frown marring his face. "Don't put yourself down. I think you're pretty awesome. You have no idea who you really are yet."

"Who I really am?"

"You can change the world, Piper, or take it over."

"Hmm, I don't hate the idea of owning the world."

He tilts his head back and laughs. "I knew you were going to say that. Perfect answer, and when we're out of here, we'll get working on that."

"We have to get out first."

"We will. There is no way our destiny is to die in this building."

I lean a little closer to him. His warmth is comforting, his words spurring me on, strength seeping into my pores. I'm ready to fight to get out of here.

"Thanks, Evan. You always seem to know what to say."

"I know you better than you think."

"Which is incredible since I've known you such a short time."

"You said it yourself, time means nothing in here."

It's true. Evan, Theo, Lucie, Priya, and Kevin, along with Hazel of course, have become so important to me in such a short amount of time. We've made a family in here, bound by fear, the need to survive, and the same horrifying circumstances.

But that's not to say that just because we're the heroes of the story, we'll get out alive.

"I can't wait to do normal things like going to see a movie with my mom, eating breakfast out with my dad, riding my bike, and, I can't believe I'm about to admit this, but I'm even looking forward to school again."

Evan laughs. "I need to figure out my whole life when I get out of here. College, work, everything."

"There will be plenty of time for that. What you really need to do is spend time with your family. Ultimately, that's all that matters." Being here makes me realize that I haven't appreciated my parents enough. Sure, we spend time together, but I took it all for granted. Evan after Penny died, I still assumed they would always be there. The three of us was the new constant.

I should have spent more time with them, had more conversations, and now I'm facing us being apart for the rest of my life—however long that is.

I just want one more conversation, one more hug, one more chance to tell them I love and appreciate them.

Dipping my head, I press my fist into my aching chest and bite back the tears for my parents. What's the point in crying? It's only going to feed the evil inside Caleb, Owen, and Matt.

"Piper?" Evan whispers. He leans over to me and wraps his arm around my shoulders. Shouldn't it be me comforting him right now?

"Sorry," I say, lifting my head and forcing my mouth to smile. "I'm okay."

"Where did your mind go?"

"Nowhere."

"Piper," he prompts. "Tell me."

"It's just… I was thinking about my parents and wondering if I'll see them again."

His fingers brush though my hair. "You will see them again."

If only I could be so sure.

I smile because there isn't much else I can do or say, and Evan sinks into the sofa, his hand still working through the strands of my dark hair. "You know I think it's pretty unique to have black hair and blue eyes," he tells me.

"That's what my mom says, too. She has black hair and brown eyes, and my dad has blond hair and blue eyes. I took one from each."

"It's pretty special."

Priya calls us to dinner, and we all eat in deafening silence. No one seems to look up from their plate, the sober atmosphere doing nothing to lift my mood. Without speaking about it, we have all gone into ourselves. My parents are on my mind, and I have a feeling the others are the same.

There's a sense of urgency now, with so many things changing in here, accelerating. It feels like we're getting closer to the end.

We finish our food and clean up, then one by one, we get ready for bed.

I walk to my bunk and climb the ladder. My limbs are heavy, and it takes a lot of effort to pick each one up and get into bed. But I manage it, and tug the cover up to my chin.

Why do I feel so drained?

My eyes are closing. *Something's wrong, stay awake.*

I force my eyelids to part, but nothing happens. They're stuck together, and I'm getting heavier, my body sinking into the mattress.

Why can't I open my eyes?

I want to call out, but I don't have the energy to even do that. Sleep is all I want.

No, stay awake!

No one else is saying anything. Everyone is in bed, and there would usually be a little talk for a few minutes, some whispering beyond that, but tonight there is only silence.

We've been drugged.

The speaker crackles. Our music starts to play.

A loud thud in the main room echoes throughout the bedroom.

My pulse soars, then the world turns black.

33

My head pounds so violently, I gag. I press my index fingers to my temples and groan.

I was eating in the common room. Then... God, what happened after that? I can't remember. Did I go to bed? Is it now morning?

The air is warm, warmer than the common room's temperature. They usually keep that just a fraction above cold.

Where am I?

Picking my head up, I try to make sense of my surroundings. There is something big; I think it's a sofa, but it's a different color than the one I spend so much time sitting on.

What the...?

With my palms flat on the floor, I haul myself to my knees, and my head throbs.

I was drugged. Our food was poisoned! What is wrong with them? Our room was always a safe space before, but I can't trust anything now. Not even food.

My head is fuzzy, but my vision slowly sharpens. The old-style TV and sofa. I'm in the orientation room.

Evan.

I gasp.

He's in here, too, but we're alone. Where is everyone else?

He's lying on the floor, and he's so, so still that it sends chills down my spine.

"Evan?" I whisper.

His face is pressed into the floor, but I can see his eyes are closed. My gaze homes in on his chest, seeking confirmation. Please be alive. Please, please.

His chest rises and falls.

Grimacing, I get to my feet and glance up at the camera. *You will not break me. Whatever you have planned, bring it.*

I turn back to Evan and stumble toward him. My head is spinning, legs not quite cooperating like the way I felt after having a bad case of the flu last year.

"Evan? Evan, please, speak to me."

His hand twitches.

"Evan, can you get up?"

His head turns to me, and he flicks his eyes open, but they don't focus on me. Instead, he stares ahead blankly, pupils dilated. "Evan!" I screech, my heart racing. "Come on, talk to me!" Is he in shock?

I crouch down and brush my fingers across his forehead. "Please, Evan. Look, we were drugged but we're okay now."

He blinks heavily, and his eyes meet mine. "Piper?"

I smile as a sob of relief escapes my mouth. "Yeah. Hey, it's me. Let's get you to your feet."

I wrap my hands around his waist and help him up. He leans on me and grips my upper arm. "What happened? They drugged us?" His voice is filled with disgust.

"Yeah, they did. We're in the orientation room. I don't know where the others are." They could be somewhere out of the common room, too. But unless they're in one of the torture rooms, it would be harder to control all of us out here. There are places we can run and hide and the main door we can escape out of.

News of us being outside the common room seems to perk him up, and he stands on his own and looks around the room. Rubbing his forehead, he asks, "Where are they?"

"I don't know. I only woke up a minute ago, right before you."

He grits his teeth. "Why do you think we're in here?"

Shaking my head, I reply honestly, "I have no idea, but I'm scared."

"Don't be. We're okay," he whispers, pulling me into his arms.

While I'm here with him, I can give in to the weakness inside, the part of me that fears for my life, who wishes someone would rescue me. Although we share an inner strength that I certainly didn't know I had, Evan still allows me to be weak without judgment.

With everyone else, I feel an intense pressure to always hold it together because that's who I've been, the together girl. I don't let things get to me, and I keep myself firmly in the positivity camp. But it's such a relief when I get to be vulnerable, even if it is just for a minute.

I step back after a few seconds. I'm okay now. There is a time and place for weakness, and right now is not the time. We don't know why we're here or what they have planned.

The sound of metal clanging, a door unlocking, startles me. I grip Evan's hand. We're united. Whatever Caleb, Matt, and Owen are about to do, we can get through this.

The door to the long hallway opens. Caleb and Owen storm in. Matt stands by the door frame holding a gun.

I press into Evan's side, but I don't cower.

"What's going on?" Evan asks, his voice strong but wavering at the end.

I'm not the only one who is scared.

Caleb smirks, loving doing something that we don't expect. "Come with us," he orders.

Evan's eye twitches. "Why?" he challenges.

Caleb's smirk widens. "Come with us."

Oh God, what is he doing?

Owen lunges toward me, grabbing my arm. I'm jerked forward and his death grip on my wrist bites, but I steady myself and stand tall.

Evan grabs my other arm, his eyes burning a hole in Owen. "Let go," he spits.

Caleb reaches out and grabs Evan's upper arm. He pins him to the spot with dark, dead eyes.

"You come with us or Matt will shoot you," Owen says, addressing both me and Evan.

"Just do what he says, Evan," I plead. There is no need to make this harder than it's going to be. Not when we're out here like this.

They don't physically bring themselves into these rooms unless it's room five.

They tug us roughly through the door. I gasp as I'm shoved into their room with all the games. I thought this place was so cool when I first saw it. But it's just a front for evil.

"What are you doing?" I demand as Owen pushes me down. My hands curl around the edge of the seat as I'm forced onto a hard plastic chair.

My breathing is erratic. I can feel my chest moving too fast.

Breathe slow. You can do whatever this is, too.

Caleb slams Evan down on the chair opposite me, our knees an inch from touching. I keep my eyes on him, letting his calm wash over me. He watches me, too, using me as an anchor.

I'm okay. Evan is here.

I tear my gaze from him and stare up at Caleb standing behind him while Owen works on tying me to the seat with a thick rope.

"You two have been very bad," Caleb says. His voice is strong and domineering.

I swallow bile, my stomach rolling at the excitement in his demeanor. He's light on his feet, eyes shining with possibilities.

"We haven't done anything, you sick freak!" I shout.

Caleb folds his arms after securing Evan to the seat. "That's not very nice now, is it? I give you a place to stay, provide you with food and water, and you call me a freak."

Owen finishes up with my restraints. The rope pinches my skin, causing a hot burning sensation, but I do my best to ignore it.

"Can you hear yourself?" Evan snaps. "We never asked for any of this."

"Yet, somehow, you're here."

"Because you took us, idiot!" I yell.

I can tell from how controlled Caleb always seems to be that it takes a lot to irritate him, but he grinds his teeth at the word *idiot*.

He dips his head, his eyes pinning me to the seat better than the restraints. "I knew you were going to be feisty. That's what attracted me to you when I saw you walking by the lake. Your lips were pursed, and you weren't paying much attention to your surroundings. You weren't looking because you didn't think there was any danger."

Matt laughs. "Poor Red Riding Hood."

I look up Matt and glare. "I'm not poor anything."

"You're playing with the lions now, sweetheart."

"You're not as clever as you think you are," I tell Matt.

"Time for you to shut up." He raises his arm, and I struggle against the restraints to stop him.

"Don't!" Evan shouts at the same time Matt's free hand comes down hard and heavy across my cheek. My head whips to the side. "Piper?"

"I'm fine," I reply, though my cheek feels like it's on fire. Blinking away stars, I focus on Evan.

"Are you done?" I ask Matt.

But it's Caleb who replies, "With you..."

My eyes flash to Evan, and my heart drops.

34

Tears roll down my cheeks, dripping onto my legs.

Evan is slumped over in the seat after the last blow from Owen. They've been taking turns hitting him for what seems like hours. I don't know if he's alive. Blood trickles steadily from his nose.

"Help him," I cry. "Please help him."

"Shh, Piper," Caleb says, crouching down beside me. "Let's see if he gets up."

"W-What? This isn't a game."

"On the contrary, sweetheart. Life is a game; you just have to make sure you're in control."

I turn from him, the smell of whiskey strong on his breath. It reminds me of Christmas when my dad would have a couple of whiskeys after dinner.

"You're sick. Is he breathing?"

Caleb chuckles. "I do admire how you can insult me and ask me to check on your boyfriend in the same breath."

I ignore his boyfriend comment; there's no need to address that.

"And I admire your ability to sleep at night after everything you've done and continue to do."

"Thank you, Piper," he replies.

I don't look at him, but I can hear the smile in his tone.

"Caleb, check him."

"Ooh, she's bossy," Matt says. He's leaning against the far wall, his legs crossed at the ankle, holding the gun.

Seriously, we're tied up, so what's the point?

"She is getting very bossy," Owen chimes in. "I like it."

"We all like you, Piper," Caleb says. "So I will check Evan for you."

"He's breathing," Owen says. "I can see his chest from here."

I sigh, my muscles loosening.

Owen is sitting opposite Evan, watching him like a hawk. I don't know why Owen feels he needs to watch Evan so closely when Evan's all tied up.

"There you have it, sweetheart," Caleb says. "He's all good."

"Why?" I ask.

Caleb laughs again, and the dead tone to it sends a shiver down to my toes. "Why not?" he replies.

There is no point in me pursuing this. It's not going to get me anywhere. I'm not suddenly going to get any satisfactory answers. They're doing this because they can and they want to. It's as simple as that.

They all need a lot of professional help.

Evan splutters beside me and his back shudders.

"Evan!" I whimper. "Evan."

He turns his head, and I gasp. His eye is swollen, lip cut, and nose steadily dripping blood.

"I look that good, huh?" he rasps.

"You still look good to me."

My face is on fire. Why did I say that?

"Well, that's nice to hear," he replies. Then he looks at Caleb. "Finished, or do you still have something to prove?"

He's provoking them, and usually I wouldn't talk back in this situation, but he's weak and clearly in pain. He doesn't need them to start on him again.

"Matt, ensure Evan and Piper get back okay."

"I don't think we'll get lost," I snap.

Caleb laughs and cracks his knuckles. "See you soon, Piper."

Owen unties us while Matt moves the barrel of the gun between us, making sure we don't try to do anything to Owen. I don't have a death wish, so I have no plans to aggravate Matt while he's holding a gun.

We're so close to the door. I can see the outside world through the windows. The trees look greener than they did before. I long to walk outside there and feel the breeze on my face.

If Matt didn't have a gun, we could try running. With Caleb gone, we'd have a chance. But there's no point in letting those thoughts in; Matt does have a gun and we can't get out now.

The rope around my wrists drops to the floor with a thud.

I flex my fingers and roll my hands.

Owen moves behind Evan. I keep my eyes on Evan. His eyes are tight, and he pants when he breathes.

Owen steps back with Matt, and I push myself to my feet. I grab

Evan the second we're free. He's unsteady on his feet, his body weak from the beating, but he doesn't lean on me. Even though he's in pain, he still won't lean on me.

"It's okay," I tell him, stepping closer.

The metallic smell of blood stings my nose. God, he's in a bad shape.

With his pretty eyes staring ahead, he gently shakes his head.

"Always the strong one," I say as we walk through the door, me a lot steadier than Evan. He won't accept help, so he is shuffling along with one eye almost completely swollen shut.

I place my palm on his back because I know that's about as much as he's going to allow me to do. "Are you all right?" I ask as he braces himself against the wall with his hand.

"Yeah. Are you? They didn't hurt you, right?"

"They didn't," I reply. Not physically, but watching someone you care about being hurt is difficult. Evan's grunts of pain and the twisted expression on his face will stay with me forever.

I follow a step behind him, and as we walk through the clothes room, I grab us both a bag. My clothes are fine, but I don't want to wear the same things I have on now. Evan's top is covered in drops of blood from his split lip.

"We're both okay. That's great," I say.

He smiles. "We're the same, you and me."

"Hurry it up," Matt mutters from behind us.

I push the door open and the next and the next, being sure to slam them behind us. Then we're back.

Hazel is on her feet the second she sees us. "Oh my God! What happened?"

Theo stands stiffly, his eyes wide and fixed on Evan. Evan's face is shocking; what they've done to him is brutal. He's going to be in pain for a little while, with his eye in particular.

"Get some wet towels," Theo commands.

"His lip might need stitches," Priya says, walking over from the kitchen where's she's microwaving something.

They take over completely, which I am grateful for because I feel like I'm holding on by a thread, my heart thudding in my chest too fast.

Evan could have died. I thought he had at one point.

I take in a deep ragged breath and let go of him.

"I'm fine," Evan grunts, hating the attention.

"Sit still, they're trying to help. You look awful, bro," Theo says.

I stumble backward and grip the edge of the counter. Evan is getting looked after now, so I need to take a minute away. My ears ring.

Hazel's hands grip my upper arms just as my head feels light. "Are you okay? You've turned pale as a ghost."

My vision blurs the way it does when I stand up too fast. My blood pressure has always been low, and at times when I find eating hard, like when Penny died and when I was kidnapped, I'm even more prone to dizzy spells. "Hazel, I thought they were going to kill him," I whisper.

"Oh, Piper." She pulls me in for a hug, and for the first time since we got in here, I want nothing more than to hug my best friend. I want the same comfort she gave me when I lost my sister. She never let me lie down and wallow for long. I lay my head on her shoulder and hug her back. "He didn't die, though. He's here and the others are going to fix him up."

"The deepest scars are the ones you can't see, Haze. How is he going to get through all of this?"

"The same way the rest of us will, with help from each other."

I nod against her shoulder, for once being the pessimistic one, and I hate it.

"What happened to you guys?" I ask, still holding her tight.

"We woke up groggy, and minus you and Evan."

"I'm glad you were here."

"Where did they take you?"

"To their game room. They tied us to chairs and beat Evan."

She pulls back and her wide eyes stare into mine. "But they didn't hurt you, right?"

"No, I'm good."

Her pupils home in on my cheek. "There's a mark."

"I was slapped. It's nothing, Hazel."

"The bastards," she grinds out.

"Drop it. Let's focus on what's next."

Dropping my arms, I step back, and Hazel lets me go. "You're really okay?" she asks, moving her head closer to judge my reaction.

"I'm okay. I promise."

Something in my voice or my expression makes her believe me. This is the first day in here that I feel helpless. I want to know why they took only me and Evan. What was the point in hurting him? Why force me to me to watch? It doesn't make sense that it was only us. Like it doesn't make sense that Theo and I were let out. We were always the first ones up, so they had to know it would be us.

35

Two days later and Evan is looking a lot better. His bottom lip is still slightly swollen, and he's sporting a pretty decent black eye, but it doesn't hurt him as much to move around. There is no more wincing when he gets up, although he is walking a little slower than usual.

Right now he is sleeping, something he's done more of these last two days. His body needs time to heal, and I think his pride does, too. There is no shame in being beaten up, especially not when you were tied down.

Priya is the next best thing to a nurse and has fixed him up as best she can.

My cheek is almost back to its usual pale color, too; the mark left by Matt is nearly gone. The physical scars of that day are healing. But when I lie in bed and wait for that music to play before I sleep, all I can see is Evan's broken body slumped over in the chair.

They made me watch my friend being hurt. I don't know what I would have done if it had been Hazel in Evan's place. It's hardly a secret that the stress of this situation has meant Hazel and I haven't been as close as usual, and I've spent a lot of time with Evan. Is that why they chose him? If it is, I'm grateful for the distance between me and my best friend. I will keep it that way if it stops her from being hurt.

Or maybe this has nothing to do with me at all. Though why would I be brought out there to witness Evan's beating if it didn't?

There's another unanswered question to add to the ever growing list.

It's midafternoon, a particularly boring time in here when lunch is done and we've exhausted good conversation in the morning. There are very few new subjects to discuss since we're stuck in this small room.

The speaker above me crackles, and my spine stiffens. Caleb's voice echoes through the room. "Evan to the waiting room."

"No," I whisper.

"Again?" Priya says, shaking her head. "Why do they keep picking him?"

"He'll be okay," Theo replies.

Ignoring them, I walk toward the bedroom. Evan opens the door just as I get to it. His jaw is tight, posture hunched.

"I know, but I promise you, you've got this, Evan," I tell him, willing him to find strength in my words.

Swallowing, he nods and his eyes find the waiting room door. "I'll see you soon, Piper." He smiles, but it doesn't reach his eyes.

After the beating, he has been more withdrawn. We haven't laughed in a while. I understand, but it scares me because he's been rock solid since I met him. He's the one who's given me more courage to face whatever is coming. He makes me believe I can survive in here. After all, he has been doing it for months, and most of that time he's been alone.

"Soon, Evan," I say as he walks away from me.

The door clicks twice, once when it was unlocked for him and then again as he disappears through it.

He's on his own now.

"Piper, you all right?" Theo asks.

"I'm fine," I reply, pressing my hand against the ache in my heart. How much more can he take? I need to focus on something else, or I won't be able to handle waiting for Evan to come back, thinking of the worst-case scenarios that could be happening.

Kevin might be somewhere in the building, but we don't know for sure he's alive. Caleb, Owen, and Matt might have got up close and personal with him. Or Evan could be sent to room zero with Kevin right now.

No, don't think that. Distract!

Hazel. She is sitting down watching TV, her elbow resting on the arm of the sofa, finger tapping against her chin. I've seen her do that a million times before. Every exam at school, every time a cute guy in our class would talk to her.

She's nervous. In here she's never not nervous, but this is something else. She hasn't moved in an hour.

"Haze," I say, scooting a little closer to her. "What's going on?"

Still looking at the TV, she shrugs the shoulder closest to me.

"Talk to me."

Priya is the only person sitting close enough to hear us, and she won't interfere. Lucie and Theo are playing cards at the kitchen table.

"Hazel, please, I'm worried about you."

Her eyes slide to mine and well with tears. Her voice, rough, whispers, "I'm going to die in here."

"Don't think like that."

"Why haven't I been in any rooms? Everyone else has."

"I think they're trying to drive a wedge between all of us."

"But why me? Why use me?"

Okay, good question. "I'm not sure why."

Wouldn't it make more sense for them to do that to me? Though apparently, I give good reactions when I can't shut up, and I stand up for myself. Could they be saving Hazel for room zero? But what would be the thinking behind that? Surely the stronger a person is the better for the...show? Would they not want it to last, watch people fight for longer, not knowing the outcome?

Maybe I'm trying too hard to think like them. There has to be a reason but it's unlikely we'll understand it since we're not certifiable.

"See? We know there's something coming, and I'm being treated differently," Hazel says, shaking her head.

"You're not the only one getting different treatment. Theo and I have done a lot of rooms, and Evan and Kevin have been taken away, Kevin still is gone."

"Fine. I'm the only one treated in a different way: *solo*."

"That doesn't necessarily mean anything, and we don't know something big is coming, we only assume it because of the changes in their behavior. But maybe this is part of their plan."

"Piper, we're in different positions here. Let's not try to pretend otherwise."

Why is she being so hostile? It's not as if any of us are in a good position, but it's not a contest over who has it worse. Evan would win that hands down; he's been here the longest and done more rooms than all of us combined probably.

"This is what they want," I tell her. "We can't be divided in here. We might not have the same experience, but we're all trapped."

She shrugs. "That's all we share."

I bite my lip. I don't know how far to go with this. Hazel is either talking through pure anger and fear, or she's letting them get into her head and believes that she's going to die here...soon.

Honestly, I would never think she's going into room zero.

Not all of us are in here to fight. There is a purpose for everyone.

I would ask Caleb when I see him, but I don't know how helpful it would be to know, kind of like knowing when you're going to die. Some things are best left unsaid, and my purpose for being in this dungeon is definitely one of them.

"Do you want to play cards?" I ask her. It's been a long time since we've done anything together. God, the last time might actually have been the night we went to the lake.

She turns her head at that, her mouth hanging open. "Did you not just hear me?"

"What?"

"We're not the same, Piper."

"I'm lost, Haze. Just because they see something different in us and treat us differently doesn't mean we're not the same. This is still you and me. I'm your best friend no matter where we are, no matter what anyone does or doesn't do to us."

"You're friends with Theo and Evan. I'm friends with Priya."

Jesus, she is not getting this.

"Hazel is right," Priya says.

Damn it, not her, too.

Hazel and I glance over at the same time, but our expressions are polar opposites. She is relieved to have someone backing her up. I'm irritated that they're both believing the crap Caleb, Owen, and Matt want us to believe.

"No, she's not! Come on, surely you can see that they want us to think this. Don't give them that. We're all the same."

Priya rolls her almost-black eyes. "I want to believe you, Piper, but if they were to put us all in room zero, we know the three left standing would be you, Evan, and Theo."

Throwing my hands up, I exclaim, "I'm not going to kill anyone!"

"Not right now, but you will. Theo and I have, and so has Evan. Let's not pretend like we have a choice when we go into that room. It's instinct," Priya rants, her face reddening.

I sit on the sofa, my back sinking into the cushions. "Priya."

Sighing, she gently tugs on the bottom of her long hair, twirling strands through her fingers. "I'm sorry, but let's not pretend here. We're not getting out alive, not me, Hazel, or Lucie anyway."

"And you think what? That they'll let me, Theo, Evan go? Because that's not going to happen. Maybe we won't die the first time we go into room zero, but taking someone's life is going to destroy us anyway."

The door from the waiting room opens, and Evan walks back in. He braces himself against the wall and looks over.

Our eyes connect, and he takes a ragged breath.

"Are you okay?" I ask, getting to my feet.

He straightens his back and drops his hand. His moment of weakness is over, and now he's back to his strong self.

"I'm fine."

"Where were you?" I ask, walking over to him. Though from his wet hair and sweatshirt, I already know.

His eyes find the floor. "Five. I'm tired."

I follow him into the bedroom. "Was it Caleb?"

He looks over his shoulder. "And Owen."

"Both of them?"

"Yeah. They took turns." He spins and wraps his arms around my back. Burying his head in my neck, he whispers, "There was hardly any time between."

"Evan," I murmur, hugging him back so tight, I'm scared I'm actually hurting him. But he doesn't complain.

Caleb and Owen tortured him with water together. It's one thing to have two of us in that room, but something else entirely to have two committing the torture.

"It's okay now. You're here and you're safe."

"You believe we're safe here?" he whispers in my ear.

"Right this second, I do."

Evan steps back and brushes my hair from my face. "I really needed your positivity, Piper. Thank you for following me in here."

"Of course. Do you need anything?"

"Just for you to be up on your bunk again." He smiles shyly, like he's just shown me his journal.

"That I can do," I tell him.

We climb our respective ladders and lie down. I stare up at the ceiling and wait. A second later his arm flops over and onto my pillow.

With a big smile, I reach up and take his hand.

"Good night, Piper," he says softly into the dark.

"Night, Evan."

36

spent most of the night tossing and turning. In the morning, we all get up together. It seems no one slept well.

The reason? The damn roasting bedroom.

They turned up the heat.

So that's new.

Theo, Hazel, Priya, Lucie, and I are all on the sofas, drinking coffee like it's going out of fashion. Evan is in the bathroom.

The temperature is back to normal now, but the damage has been done. We're going to spend the day tired and hope they don't do the same thing tonight.

I felt like I was going to burn to death in the dry heat last night, with nothing to cool me down.

Wait. Fire. *That's it!* We could set fire to the place.

Great, and actually burn to death.

But…would they let us burn in here? The fire department would come. Even if they don't call, someone would see a lot of smoke in the woods. They'd think it was a forest fire.

244 | NATASHA PRESTON

Caleb, Matt, and Owen couldn't leave us because firefighters would find our burned bodies and start to ask a lot of questions.

They would be forced to act. They would have to let us out of here. The transportation of captives is the part where the kidnappers are most vulnerable; there are factors outside of their control.

We can escape.

"We need to set the place on fire," I say.

Theo, Lucie, and Priya look at me with wide eyes.

"What did you just suggest?" Hazel asks.

"That's too dangerous!" Theo growls. "We'll die."

I shake my head. "No, I don't think we will."

The four of them look at me like I've lost it completely. I haven't. Not completely anyway.

Unless I have, and I just don't know it. Either way, it's a plan that could work. It's better than playing dead since Theo and I aren't getting called into any rooms.

For some reason, we're getting a break. For how long? Every time that speaker crackles, my heart takes a dive and my palms sweat.

That's probably why you're getting a break. To drive you crazy always fearing it.

Evan walks into the room from his shower. His messy dark hair is damp. His eyes lock with mine as soon as he turns around, always to me first, as if he's checking to make sure I'm still here and I'm okay.

He frowns, sensing the tension in the room. "What's going on?"

"My best friend has finally lost it. That's what's going on," Hazel tells him.

He walks to the sofa and sits. Ignoring everyone else, he says, "This should be fun."

"I've thought of a way out of here."

"No, Piper, you've thought of a way to kill us all at once," Lucie says, cutting in.

Evan looks at her, frowning. He leans more on the positive side, like me, so I appreciate that he's at least willing to hear me out.

"What's your idea?" he asks, tilting his head. I can tell he's half-amused, but I have a feeling my idea will wipe away his smile.

I look at him dead serious and say, "We set fire to this room."

He stares for a second, and I can see his mind working overtime. "Fire? Really?"

"Yes. People will see the smoke, and the fire department will come. Caleb, Matt, and Owen can't leave us in here to burn because the officials will find our bodies and a lot of questions will be asked. Don't you see? They have to let us go for their own survival. And while they're opening the door for us, we have a chance of getting away. Six on three, it's not bad odds."

It's not great odds, either, but there isn't much we can do about that.

His mouth curls into a grin. "God, I love how you think, Piper."

"Are you kiddin' me?" Theo yells. "I know you back her on everything, but this is ridiculous!"

Evan's head snaps to Theo. "We can't break out. There are too many doors and they're always locked. What else would you suggest? She's right, Theo. This is the only way. They can't let us burn in here; they have to let us out. It's our best chance."

Silence cloaks the room like a blanket.

I chew on my lip while they all consider our chances. This is the best way.

It's the only way.

What else can we do that would force them to let us all out at the same time?

They don't care about us, so we can't pretend to be sick. But they do care about self-preservation, so they'll open the doors to save themselves from a lot of questions the police would have if they found charred bodies in here.

Priya takes a breath, tears welling in her eyes. "I hate to admit it, because I'm scared, but I think Piper is right."

"Yes, I'm right," I say. "There is nothing else we can do, at least nothing that will get us all free at one time."

"No, Piper is not right. Piper is insane!" Hazel exclaims.

Evan ignores her. "When are we doing it?"

"Now." My heart is beating out of my chest. The rhythm so fast that I feel dizzy. But I can't wait. I can't stop and think about this because there is a good chance I'll talk myself out of it. I mean, it's the best plan we've got, but I won't deny it is dangerous.

"What the hell?" Theo snaps.

I look up at tiny window. "It's light outside; they'll be here. Regular as clockwork. We have to do it now."

Standing, I head to the kitchen. We don't have a lighter or matches for obvious reasons…but we can make a fire in the microwave.

"Piper, we should talk about this more first," Evan says. He follows me to the kitchen area and grabs my wrist.

I turn around and frown. "You agreed that it was a good plan."

"No, I agreed that it was a plan that could work. There's a difference, babe. A massive difference."

When we're safely out of here, I'm going to obsess over the fact that he just called me *babe*. Right now, I need to convince him of my side. It's all or nothing. We can't keep waiting.

"Okay, but I don't see what difference it's going to make in an hour or even a week from now."

"I'm not suggesting we wait a week, but we've given this about five seconds of thought. That's not enough."

"Evan, I need you to back me up right now."

He tugs me closer. "I'm on your side, but I'm also thinking about everyone else here."

"After last time, we said we'd all be in agreement," Hazel says, folding her arms. She's joined us in the kitchen with the others.

"Yeah, and then Lucie attacked the wall with a tiny plastic knife."

"Don't bring me into this," Lucie snaps, scowling at me.

"Okay, enough," Evan says, frowning at Lucie. He turns back to me. "Piper, think about this."

"I have. You know we need to act fast. You all do. Why will no one admit what needs to be done here?"

Evan takes a breath and shakes his head. "Okay."

"Okay, like we're doing this now, okay?"

A slow grin stretches across his mouth.

My shoulders sag. "You think I've lost it."

"I know you have. I just happen to like it. Let's set this place on fire."

"Whoa, whoa, whoa," Theo interjects. "I'm not saying no, but can we at least take a second to think through how we're doing this? They come in and open the doors…then what?"

"Six against three," Evan replies. "We arm ourselves with the teakettle and toaster—that's about all we have in here. They might not cut through drywall…or a chest cavity, but they'll do some damage if you go hard enough."

It's better than nothing.

Theo nods. "Can't say I'm overly confident, but I am so ready to get out of here." He turns to Lucie and Hazel. "We die trying, not in a room fighting."

"Ooh, we should all get tattoos of that when we're out."

Five pairs of eyes slide to me.

"I was just trying to lighten the mood."

Evan shakes my comment off. "Let's do this. Make sure you have something to fight with, everyone. I'll light a fire."

"You're doing it?" I ask him. Here I was fully prepared to torch this place since it's my idea, but I have to say, I'm glad Evan is volunteering so it's not all on me.

"Have you ever set a building on fire before, Piper?"

"No, have you?"

He laughs. "I'm sure I'll figure it out. Get a knife and wait by the door."

I do as I'm told and follow Theo, Hazel, Lucie, and Priya to grab a knife, then head to the door.

You are certifiable.

Evan grabs the aluminum foil and stuffs it in the microwave. He looks back at me for a second before jabbing his finger on the button to start the microwave.

I watch as the foil spins and then catches fire. The microwave pops, and fire spills from the door, alighting the cupboards.

Evan watches the fire as if it's the most interesting thing he's ever seen, golden flames flickering in the reflection of his eyes.

"Evan," I prompt.

He blinks, and his eyes snap to mine. "Sorry." He steps back in line with us.

The flames grow as they spread toward the kitchen table and sofas. The wooden table is consumed by a bright orange blaze.

My eyes widen as the soft fabric of the sofa succumbs in seconds. They swallow it, raging across the sofa and spreading to the rough carpet.

I watch the inferno consume the room, growing at an alarming rate.

The heat the fire is giving off prickles on my skin.

Evan turns and walks over to me, putting his body just in front so he's between me and the door.

"Are you ready?" he asks.

"Not in the slightest," I reply. Just because I'm all for this doesn't mean I'm ready for the fight.

"I've got you," he whispers.

I cough as smoke begins to fill the room, rising to the ceiling.

Oh God, why aren't they here yet?

Lucie takes a ragged breath. "What if they don't open the doors? What if they decide to leave us to die?" Her eyes widen at the sight of the fire raging, obliterating the chair next to the sofa and the bookcase filled with DVDs behind it.

"They'll come," Evan tells her.

He sounds sure. I am, too. They'll come. We just don't know what will happen from there.

This is only the first part of the plan. We still have to get past them and then get back to town.

One step at a time or my head is going to explode.

I grip my plastic knife in my fist and reach for Evan with the other hand.

He rubs his thumb over my knuckles, and my lungs open, breathing easier.

"Haze, you okay?" I ask my best friend.

"Nope. I love you, Pipes."

"Back atcha. But no goodbyes. We're getting out."

Behind us the fire rages, and smoke begins to fill the room.

Come on. Where are you guys?

Evan squeezes my hand, the solid muscle on his forearm tensing.

Oh God, they're not coming...but the fire is.

37

There is nothing to do but wait and hope. It's a different kind of feeling than what I've grown used to in here. There is an urgency to this hope. If they don't come, we burn to death.

Flames grow higher, and the room clogs with smoke.

"Piper!" Priya screams.

Coughing as my lungs fill with smoke, I drop to my knees. "Get on the floor!" I shout, and we drop to the ground, covering our mouths and noses with our sleeves and collars.

The door clicks. *Oh my God, it's worked!*

Evan's eyes find mine. He can't quite believe it, either. I mean, we knew they would have to, but they're so sick and it wasn't an impossibility that they would leave us to burn.

I turn around as Theo shoves the door. "Let's go!" he shouts.

I watch the black smoke at the top of the room pour out the door as the fire roars. It's only been one minute, but it feels like an eternity.

"Go now!" Evan orders.

Pushing myself to my feet, I grab Hazel and tug her along with me. Theo and Lucie are ahead with Priya behind him. Evan is last, his hand on my back, pushing me forward. We hit the door at the end of the waiting room and it opens.

We run through the clothes room as the fire rages behind us, creeping up like it's personally trying to get us.

"Hurry," Evan shouts.

God, the fire is growing so quick. How is it so fast?

Theo bashes into the next door, and we're through the clothes room, the empty room, and the orientation room. Then the hallway to hell.

I sprint after the others and make it through the game room and out into fresh air. We did it. I turn to Hazel to make sure she's okay. Evan grips my hand.

Where are Caleb and his friends? They're not here. My eyes desperately scan the area for signs of them waiting. Are they somewhere in the woods, hiding with their gun?

"Which way?" Theo says.

"Near the road, but stay in the woods," Evan replies.

There's no time to worry about them—we have to go.

We sprint. My pulse is all I can hear.

I'm tired already, but adrenaline has taken over, coursing through my veins, spurring me on. We're miles from town, and they might get up any minute, but we have to focus on running.

My feet thud on the dry, compacted dirt. "Go!" Theo shouts, pushing Priya and Lucie in the direction we need to run.

We don't get far.

A gunshot echoes through the air, freezing my spine. We stop. All of us plant our feet.

I turn. Caleb is standing outside the door, arm in the air, gun pointing to the sky. No. Matt and Owen stand a step back from him.

"I don't think you want to run another step," Caleb says.

Evan lets go of my hand and laughs.

"Don't," I whisper. If Evan tries to take them on alone, Caleb will kill him. I can't watch someone die in front of me, especially not someone I care about.

Caleb moves in closer and his groupies come with him.

Hazel, Priya, Lucie, and Theo move in, so we're solid against them. But Evan is still in front.

"Evan," I call.

He takes two more steps closer to the three of them.

What is he doing?

Caleb watches Evan, but I can't place his expression. He looks unsure.

Inside the building, something smashes. Glass? No one pays much attention to the fire behind us; we're having some sort of standoff. None of us willing to back down.

"Where do you want to be, Evan?" Caleb asks.

"What? What does that mean?" I whisper. Are they willing to let him go? Why?

Evan is going to get himself killed. We're supposed to all get away. I don't want him being the martyr.

"Evan!"

"Man, come on!" Theo shouts.

Evan's eyes lock with mine, and for the first time, I have absolutely no idea what he's thinking. I can usually take a pretty good guess, but right now, he's closed off.

I step back, willing him to come with us.

"Don't do this, come on!" I plead.

Caleb laughs. "So dumb."

Evan turns around as Caleb, Matt, and Owen close in. Oh God, Evan, move!

They stop a meter behind him, and Evan tilts his head to the side. A slow grin spreads across his lips.

My mouth falls open. "No…"

"Come here, Piper," Evan says.

I shake my head, my vision blurring with tears.

No, no, no, no.

My heart falls to my feet. This can't be happening.

"What the hell is going on?" Lucie asks.

"He's with them," I whisper. All this time, he's been one of them. "I don't understand…"

How can he be with them? He went in those rooms; he did one with me; he was there for me. Caleb beat him. He sat there and took that. This can't be real. Why would he do all of that?

What is *wrong* with him?

"Babe," Evan says, holding his hand up. "Don't be mad."

Caleb chuckles behind Evan.

Don't be mad!

"You're… How?"

Hazel reaches out and puts her hand on my shoulder.

"I like you," he says.

"You don't even know what that means."

"Our Evan here gets bored easily. He's a genius, but he's not happy to sit back and observe," Owen says.

Evan's eyes darken. "I wanted to experience it. How could I create something and have it succeed if I didn't put myself—"

"Stop talking!" I snap, my heart tearing. "I don't want to hear it."

"Piper, you are the reason I came into the room. I wasn't going to. I was just going to do room zero."

I look away.

Evan continues. "But the second I saw you, I knew I had to break my own rules."

"You're sick," Theo growls. Lucie leaps to him and grabs his arm.

"Caleb," Evan prompts.

I open my mouth to scream, but I'm not fast enough. The gun goes off so fast, two shots, both ringing through my ears, and Theo falls to the ground, followed by Lucie.

"Oh my God," I murmur, my eyes wide and fixed on their lifeless bodies.

I drop to my knees, and Evan uses the opportunity to his benefit. He rushes forward, grips my upper arm tight and drags me to my feet.

"Get off!" I scream, squirming in his grip. I yank my arm, but his grip is too tight. "Evan, let go! Get away from me! You're sick, I hate you! Let go!"

I want to get back to Priya and Hazel. They're huddled together, standing over Theo and Lucie's bodies, sobbing. I don't belong with Evan. I belong with them. I have to get away from Evan.

"You're not sitting on the ground with them," he snaps, holding me close to his chest.

"I hate you! How could you do this?" I thrash in his grip, but he tightens his arms around me until I can barely move.

"You're taking her?" Owen asks.

"No!" I shout.

Evan looks over his shoulder and shrugs. "I like her. I want to keep her."

I shove his chest with my free hand, but it doesn't get me anywhere. His hold on my wrist is too tight. "I'm not a damn toy! Get off me. I'm not going anywhere with you."

"Piper," Hazel cries.

I thought he was my friend, maybe more than that one day. We had gotten close, he held my damn hand at night.

Wait. He wants me to go with him. Evan coming into the common room was an act, but we weren't.

Hope ignites in my heart.

"Evan," I plead, lowering my voice. "Think about this."

He leans closer and my throat closes up. "I have thought about nothing else since the moment I saw you. The guys are going to give me crap for this, but I don't care. I'm going to let Caleb finish this, and then you and me are out of here, okay?"

Okay? Is he really asking me if this is okay?

I don't know what to say. Evan is clearly sick. But he somehow thinks he likes me, and right now that is the only chance we have. Caleb is standing before us with a gun, waiting for instruction.

"Evan," I whisper. "I don't want you to hurt my friends. Please."

"There is no other way, Piper," he says, stroking my cheek with the back of his index finger.

I swallow down the cringe and force my lips to smile. "Yes, there is. You trusted me with the fire." That is currently spreading everywhere. "Trust me with this, too. Let them go, and I'll come with you."

"No way!" Hazel shouts. "Piper, shut up!"

Oh my God.

I look over my shoulder and widen my eyes at her, telling her to shut the hell up.

"Ignore her, she's worried about me," I say, cupping his cheek and forcing him to keep looking at me as he goes to face her. "Evan, for me?"

"He's not going to fall for that," Caleb says. He sounds bored, but he continues watching, waiting to see what Evan is going to do.

I'm not sure how far they will let Evan go. Will they allow him to let Hazel and Priya run?

I thought Caleb was in charge, but it's the guy I thought I was falling for all along.

How stupid am I?

38
EVAN

Piper wants me to let her friends go. I want to give her that. I want to give her the world and watch as she burns it to the ground around us.

She's capable of that, and I can't wait until she realizes it. There is nothing more exciting than watching someone reach their potential, but everything is so much different with Piper. It's not like watching Caleb, Owen, and Matt realize they wanted to do this, too. They don't mean to me what she does.

But I can't give her this. I can't let her friends go because as soon as Hazel and Priya go, they will talk. We'll be hunted like foxes. I won't ever be on the wrong side of the food chain.

"Piper," I say. "You know I can't do that. Your friends are going to go straight to the police."

She turns to face them, her eyes wide and pleading. "They won't. They'll make something up; they'll stagger their returns and tell everyone they couldn't cut it on their own. No one has to know about this."

Hazel nods her head fiercely, tears running down her cowardly face. She wouldn't say anything, either, because she only thinks of herself. Priya is different; she would do the right thing, bound by morals and sticking to laws. Dull. Safe. Hideous.

My money is on Priya to squeal in the first five minutes. She'll be straight down at the station before I've even had time to skip town. I'm not risking everything for these people. I don't care if they live or die. I only care that I start again with Piper and Caleb.

"Babe, you don't believe that," I tell her. "I don't want you to lie to me ever again."

She lowers her hands from my face and turns her head back to me. "Evan, I need this from you. Please just give me this."

"Don't you see? This is the last thing before we can all get out of here."

"Who is *we?*" she asks.

"Me, you, and Caleb." Who does she think it is? "Piper, the world is ours."

"I… Evan, no, this isn't right."

"Hush. I can see it in you, screaming to escape. Don't worry and don't think. I'll show you. I'll show you everything."

Blinking through tears in her eyes, she drops her shoulders. "I'm not a killer. I could never hurt anyone."

Caleb laughs. "I told you we should have sent her to room zero before you decided to bring her in on this, man."

"Shut up, Caleb!" I snap.

"I'm just saying, Evan. It would have been nice to know what she's capable of beforehand."

"I know what she's capable of. She just doesn't yet. Trust me, I'm right about this."

Maybe I should have let Piper get a taste for the kill before I did this, so she would know firsthand what it feels like to be a god, but I couldn't do it. What if she didn't win?

She's like a doll—a beautiful, petite doll who has no idea of the fierce, deadly woman hiding within. Her ability to stay calm and even crack jokes in the face of terror proves everything I need to know for now.

Piper is one of us. I can't wait for her to realize it.

"Evan, we need to go," Matt snaps. In the distance, I hear the faint sound of sirens. The fire is raging now, smoke filling the sky.

Another pane of glass from the windows at the front is smashed out. I grin.

So what if there's years of hard work being burned to the ground? It was beginning to get dull anyway. I need more. I want to do something different next. I don't even know what that is, but the possibilities are endless, only restricted by my imagination. Thankfully I have a good imagination.

It's been a hot summer; there are forest fire warnings and barbecue bans all across town. I knew the second Piper suggested setting the place alight that it wouldn't take long for the fire department to come. But that only makes it more thrilling. It's time-sensitive. We're minutes from being caught, and this isn't over yet.

Adrenaline pumps through my veins.

"I'm not leaving without her! End this and let's go," I tell him.

"No, you're insane. We can't take her. She's a damn liability, man. Why can't you see that?" Matt shouts.

I turn as he throws his hands up, shaking his head at me with disgust plaguing his face.

How dare he.

My stomach is burning hotter than the building next to me. I reach out and grab Caleb's gun. Without hesitation, I aim and shoot.

Matt falls to the ground. The wound in the center of his forehead seeps blood.

Turning my gaze to Caleb and Owen, I ask, "Either of you want to leave her behind?"

Caleb's response is immediate. He shakes his head. But Owen hesitates.

"Owen?"

"Man, I'm on your side. I always am. But there are people looking for her, so don't you think we have a better chance of getting away if the cops turn up here and find all of them dead?"

Wrong answer.

I don't hesitate that time, either.

Owen's body slams to the gravel, blood trickling from the hole in his chest.

Looking up at Caleb, I say, "Why do they have to be stupid?"

He opens his mouth and snaps it shut. With wide eyes, he stares at Owen and Matt's lifeless bodies.

"Caleb?" I prompt.

Oh God, don't tell me he's upset by this?

Shaking his head, he glances up and smirks. I get the old him back. Who cares if Matt and Owen are dead? They had no major role, merely right-hand men, there to do as they were told. It's me and Caleb who drives this. We do all the real work, the thinking. We're responsible for what we've created. Without us, Matt and Owen would be bored out of their minds, playing good little citizens and always wanting something more.

They would also still be alive, but what's the point in living if you're stuck inside a bubble of what you *should* do?

Caleb clears his throat. "Matt has always been stupid. I'm surprised by Owen, though. I thought he was more dedicated than that. While I can't disagree that it would be easier without her, we both know there is no fun in easy."

He gets it. He's always been my right-hand man. I can count on him.

"Do you want to chase them or…?"

I swing around. Piper, Hazel, and Priya are running.

Sighing, I shake my head. "My poor Piper hasn't realized she's not the lamb anymore."

"How much more of a head start are you going to give them?"

"Five, four, three, two, one." I smirk at him and step over Lucie and Theo's bodies. "Let's get my girl."

We take off, sprinting toward the woods where they're now lost. I know the forest like the back of my hand. They won't get far.

39
PIPER

Dead.

Lucie and Theo are dead. So are Owen and Matt. So much death.

This place is pure poison.

The warm wind whips around my face as we run with everything left inside of us. It's hot today, so the breeze is welcome. Every step is getting me closer to my parents. The only problem we have is that we've run deeper into the woods, rather than toward the road. We had to. If we'd gone the other way, we would have ran past them and that was too risky.

It's a miracle we got away at all, but as soon as Evan focused on his friends—if they can be called that since he showed no mercy when he shot them—we had to go.

Hazel is holding one of my hands and Priya the other.

"Which way?" Hazel asks, panting.

"We need to circle back and head to the road," I reply.

Priya gasps and lets go of my hand. She doubles over and holds her chest.

"Priya, we have to keep moving," I tell her. "I didn't hear them come after us, but I don't think they'll be far behind."

"Sorry," she rasps. "I can't keep going at this pace."

"Then you'll die!" Hazel snaps.

I glare at her and turn back to Priya.

"Okay, we can slow down a little, but we can't stop." I look around us, turning a full circle. "I can't see or hear them yet."

It's now three against two, since Evan shot half of his sick and twisted team.

"Doesn't mean they're not seconds behind us," Hazel whines, tugging on my arm.

"Okay! Come on, Priya." I grab her hand and pull her forward.

Among the trees are patches of thick bushes. We could hide in those if we really need to, but stopping and letting them catch up to us is the riskiest plan. I don't want to play hide-and-seek, I just want to get out.

We run and run until my thighs and calf muscles cry in pain. I plant my feet as we come to a circle of grass where the trees have all been cut down in the middle. It's small, so probably not enough to raise alarm if anyone were to see this from the sky.

"What is this?" I whisper.

Hazel and Priya get a few steps closer before they come to a stop.

It looks like they've made a circle of seats from tree stumps and in the middle is a burned patch of ground.

What do they burn here?

Who do they burn here?

I can't think about that.

"Come on," I say, and run across the circle and out the other side. We're back in trees. But we're not running for long.

Priya lets out an ear-piercing scream that sends a shiver down my spine.

My eyes bulge, and my hand flies to my mouth. Bumps in the ground, lined up in a row, all looking like grave sites. And Kevin.

He's been torn apart. Naked aside from boxers, he's lying on the cold, damp ground, palms in the air, chest sliced beyond recognition.

How many stabs?

They were getting ready to bury him when we set the fire; that's why they were slow to react. But who killed him?

My blood turns to ice. Evan. He'd been gone for longer than usual in the last few rooms he'd done.

"We need to go right now," Hazel snaps, tugging a sobbing Priya sharply. "Wait, shh," Hazel hushes, splaying her arms out so I stop, too.

I clamp my mouth closed and focus. In the distance, I can hear footsteps. My heart sprints faster than we were.

"Where are they?" I whisper, turning around and around. If they're gaining on us this quickly, we're going to have to hide, but we don't know how to disguise ourselves.

"Piper, come out, come out wherever you are," Evan sings.

I whip my head around to the direction I heard his voice. It's past us. How has he gotten farther into the forest than us? Unless we changed direction without knowing.

"Piper," he calls again.

My heart drops.

Oh God, he sounds like he's right on top of us.

I whip my head around. "There!" I say, pointing to a large, thick collection of bramble bushes and overgrown weeds. "Behind the bush!"

I dig my toes into the damp ground, trying to go as quick and quietly as I can. We crouch down and shuffle into the bush. The brambles scratch at my face and hands, but I shove myself in farther. Priya and Hazel do the same, and we huddle together, making ourselves as small as we can.

The thick trees block a lot of the beaming sun, so it's not too bright down here, but it's nowhere dark enough to guarantee they won't see us behind the bush.

I duck my head and watch through the leaves as Evan comes into view.

Only Evan.

Where is Caleb? I didn't hear another gunshot, so he's probably not dead.

There are so many graves here.

I can't help but look at them as I search for Caleb, too. Subtle bumps in the ground. If you didn't know what was going on here, you probably wouldn't notice at all. To us, it's glaringly obvious.

"Piper," Evan calls, drawling out my name like this is some sort of game.

To him, of course, it is. He has some delusion that I could actually still like him after this. How delusional is that? I hate him for what he's done to us all. And I hate him double for making a fool out of me by getting me to care for him.

Well, that's all over. I don't care what happens to him now, though it would be perfect karma to watch him be locked up.

Priya sobs, against the palm of her hand.

"Hello, girls."

My blood runs cold. Hazel takes off, Priya screams, and I slowly turn around. Caleb is standing above us.

"You might want to go with Hazel," he says with a chuckle.

I grab Priya's hand and drag her up with me. We take off back in the direction we came since that's where Hazel is sprinting. Two sets of footsteps thunder after us.

I move faster, my legs like jelly after all of the exertion.

"Piper!" Evan shouts, his voice hitching up. He sounds excited. This is what they wanted when the doors were left open. This could have been me and Theo.

I push harder, my lungs burning, throat dry as a desert as I pant. A stitch stabs into my side, but I press on as fast as I can.

We dodge trees, I plant one foot to spring my body around a tree, and then another and then another.

"There!" I shout. Ahead is the clearing and beyond that is the building on fire. And flashing lights.

Flashing lights! The emergency vehicles are here.

"Run!" Hazel screams.

I push my legs harder, asking the impossible of my tiring body.

Priya's hand is ripped from mine as she falls to the floor.

Gasping, I reach down and grip her upper arm. She pushes herself to her feet as I help by tugging her up. We run again, my body aching from the burst of exertion. I dodge trees, plating my feet as carefully as I can around roots and fallen branches.

We get closer. I reach my hand out, but the next thing I know, I'm slammed into the floor. My face hits dirt, moss, and twigs.

"No!" I scream.

"Shh," Evan hisses.

We're too close. Hazel and Priya run ahead.

Hazel turns around, her eyes wide as she spots me on the ground with Evan. Caleb stands above us.

"Go," I yell at her. "Go!"

She mouths *sorry* and turns and runs with Priya.

I watch them cut through the trees, and then they've made it. I can't see anything now. They're too far away and the fire is raging. But they've made it!

"Up we go," Evan calls.

I roll over as he gets off me. The first thing I notice is Caleb holding the gun down by his side, pointing to the ground.

"They're getting away!" Caleb snaps.

"We'll catch them, stop stressing!" Evan shouts. He's losing his cool with Caleb, eyes wild and pinning his equally sick friend down.

They're distracted.

This is my chance.

With my heart beating so hard it's all I can hear, I push myself onto my feet and leap up. The gun is loose in Caleb's hand, his fingers not even curled all the way around it. I snatch the gun and yank.

I have it. *I have a gun!*

Taking a step back, I aim. "I will do it," I growl. "Back up."

Evan's eyes widen. He holds his hands up. "Piper, give me the gun."

I walk toward the sirens, and they take steps back, keeping a distance from me. "No chance. You are going to walk back there with me right now, or I will shoot you both."

"Do you think that will stop us?" Evan asks.

"I'm done listening to you."

Caleb clears his throat. "We can't go there, Evan."

"Shut up, Caleb!"

I point the gun over their head and shoot. They both flinch, almost falling to their knees.

"Let's follow the lady, Caleb," Evan says with a goofy grin.

What's he doing? He wants to be caught?

Don't overthink it.

I don't need to get them to do anything because all of a sudden, there are cops running toward us. They got here quick.

Probably due to the fire department finding four dead bodies.

They storm in and grab Evan and Caleb. One stops beside me. "It's okay now. Can you hand me the gun?"

Gladly!

With trembling hands, I gesture for her to take it, and she quickly removes the gun from my grip. Another cop wraps her arm around me, but I can't focus on me because Evan's dead eyes are staring me down. His gaze is full of a promise that makes my stomach churn.

"Get me out of here," I say.

Then I'm whisked away.

40

Hazel, Priya, and I are bundled into a car and raced to the station. We sit in the back, holding hands and unable to speak.

I watch the cornfields whizz past, a sea of yellow dotted with the pretty purple weeds. It's never looked so beautiful.

Priya shakes beside me, her body rocking as she sobs. She and Hazel and I are all holding hands.

We're not too far from the station now. Soon, I will see my parents. I have never wanted to be in my mom's arms more. I need the car to hurry up. I've missed them so much. They will know by now. They get one of their daughters back. There was no hope with Penny—the infection kept getting worse and she wasn't responding to any antibiotics, we knew she was going to die.

The car slows as we turn into the station and the cop parks.

I take a breath while I wait for the door to be opened. With shaking legs, I get out and brace myself against the front window.

"It's okay, Piper," the cop says. "Let's get you inside."

Hazel, Priya, and I power walk behind the cop, practically bursting through the door.

I feel like I'm in a movie as we're led into the building. The events of today and the last month are taking their toll, and I can feel myself becoming distant. I don't want to talk about it, even though I know the cops will make me.

I just want to go home.

The second I'm inside, I spot my parents. They jump up from a seat. They got here first, of course. Our house is about five minutes away.

"Mom!" I howl, falling into her arms.

She hugs me, her arms so tight as if she's trying to fix everything that's happened in the last month.

There is no fix. No amount of time or hugs or therapy. Nothing will erase my memory, the only thing that would help, so I have to learn to be okay with that.

"It's okay, it's okay, it's okay," she chants, stroking my hair.

Dad is behind us, wrapping his strong arms around me and Mom, protecting us both.

I have been through hell, and so have they.

"No one will ever hurt you again," Dad says, his voice rough but full of promise.

"I want to go home," I whimper. Evan and Caleb are in this police station, and I don't ever want to be in the same building as them again.

"We will soon," Dad replies.

Soon means I'm not allowed to leave yet. My parents have been primed on how this is going to go down, and I'm not getting out of here before I'm interviewed.

The cops gave me, Hazel, and Priya some time together with our families, but not long enough before we were separated from one another to give interviews. Dad came with me to do mine. Hazel took her dad, and Priya's mom went with her.

In the interview room, Dad and I are given cups of coffee.

I thread my fingers together, the now-empty Styrofoam cup between my hands. My shoulders are hunched and my eyes are heavy. I'm drained, mentally and physically done with everything.

The cops sitting opposite me, two women, smile warmly. They had introduced themselves as Leah and Miranda.

Dad's face is ashen, and he hasn't said a word. He's listened in silence with his hand covering mine. As I spoke about my experiences in those rooms, his fingers curled tighter around mine.

Leah leans forward. "We're done, Piper. I'm sorry it's taken so long. You can go home."

"Thank God," I breathe. I feel like I've told them everything five times over. The clock on the wall tells me I've been here for almost two hours.

Leah and Miranda stand, and Leah takes my cup. I rise to my feet with them, stifling a yawn. I follow them back to my parents and tuck myself into my mum's embrace.

"Let's go, sweetheart," she whispers.

Hazel and Priya have already left. We're all supposed to get checked out at the hospital or at the very least with our doctor. We've been through a lot, and the cops recommended getting our eyes and hearing checked. I feel fine. I don't think there is any lasting damage from the torture, but I will make an appointment.

I'm in the back of the car, watching the cornfields whiz past again.

The car is silent, no one quite knowing what to say. They know I wasn't sexually abused and that offered a lot of relief, but beyond that, they've barely asked a thing. Dad might know what's happened, but Mom doesn't yet. I think she's scared to. Not only for me but for them.

Who wants to talk about the most difficult things? No one, that's who.

So I follow suit, more than happy not to go back there, at least not yet.

I don't want to think about any of it right now. I just want to be safe in my room, far away from Caleb and Evan, who are still being questioned at the station.

I'm not sure if the entire town knows what's happened yet, but news travels fast, so I can't imagine it will be long. I'm not leaving the house until gossip dies down.

I hope it dies down soon because all I want is to move forward, which is really hard to do when everyone I come in contact with wants to know how I'm doing. Which is just an in so they can then ask the questions they really wants to know, such as what it was like and details of what I went through. All things I would rather not discuss with anyone, let alone practical strangers.

We pull into the driveway. Somehow the house looks smaller. I get out of the car. Mom and Dad follow me closely, as if they're scared to let me more than two feet away from them.

Mom lets us in, and I head straight for my room. "If it's okay, I just want to sleep."

"Of course," Dad replies. "We'll be out here if you need us."

"If you need anything," Mom adds, her eyes wet with tears.

"Thanks," I murmur as I walk away to curl up in my room and pretend everything is going to be okay.

41
EVAN

Caleb and I are in the back of a cop car. We are being taken to a jail cell in the city since our town's station is tiny.

Piper was being taken into an interview room the last time I saw her. It was only a quick glimpse while I was being hauled from one room to another.

I have to get out of this, or I won't see her again. This is my only chance for the ending I want. Once I'm in a cell, that's it. We have two cops in the front, and we're handcuffed to the seat. We're only in the same car because the others are at the scene, cops still scouring the building—what's left of it—and the surrounding areas.

Apparently they found the graves. They told me that like it was a major find. It wasn't even hidden. Idiots.

We turn out of town, and now it's just miles and miles of nothing until we hit the city. We have to act fast and soon.

Either side of us is cornfields. There are no other cars, and this cop car has nothing to separate the front from the back. They're trusting that the handcuffs will prevent us from trying anything. They have no idea who we are.

I make eye contact with Caleb, a secret conversation passing through one glance. He dips his chin, confirming he understands and he's in. Of course he is.

We turn our heads, and both reach out.

My heart soars as I choke the cop in front of me, with Caleb doing the same to the other one beside me. I grin as I pull my hands back, the chain of the handcuffs cutting into his neck. Choking fills the air, and it's the most satisfying sound I've heard since Caleb and I shot four people earlier. The car veers off the road. We don't have long until we're going to crash, but I welcome it. I yank my hand back from the cop's head and feel the metal chain of the cuffs cut into his throat. His head lolls to the side at the same time we hit a ditch.

The car stops abruptly as it smashes right down into a ditch and falls to the side. Glass smashes, sending shards scattering through the car. My head slams into the headrest in front of me.

Shaking my head, I blink hard and remove my hands from around the cop.

With a groan, I roll my neck and turn to Caleb. His eyes are alight, grin stretched the width of his face. "All good?" I ask.

Caleb laughs.

"Fun, right?"

There is no stopping us.

"We going to get your girl now?" he asks.

"We have to get a car first, and we need to be quick." It takes thirty minutes to get to the city, so assuming no one will try to make contact with the cop before that, we have half an hour to get her. "But when we have her, we're painting the town with blood."

I climb between the two front seats and take the keys from the cop's pocket. I undo my cuffs first and then Caleb's.

"Come on," I say, grabbing the radio as I get out the driver's side door over the dead cop.

Caleb climbs out, too, and we take off down the road, running back toward town. The ditch is deep, but if you look, you can just about see the back corner of the car.

We sprint, the sun mercilessly beating down and making it hard to breathe.

"Where are we getting a car?" Caleb asks.

"The Pilkins' farm," I reply. It's the first property along this road, so we won't have to go far. They have a whole heap of beat-up cars. Easy to hot-wire. It might even take them a while to realize one is gone, so we'll have a head start before the car is reported stolen.

It'll be obvious who took it once the cops realize we've got away.

We run down the road until we come to the entrance of the Pilkins' long drive. Their house is set back away from the road, their cars parked in and near the garage, slightly hiding their line of sight.

"The Ford on the end at the back," I say. It's the farthest one away and behind two other cars, so with a bit of luck, we should be able to get it out without being seen.

I've never hot-wired a car before—my crimes are a little more upscale than that—but thankfully Caleb's criminal career began with juvenile stuff like this.

"All right," he says, rubbing his hands.

Creeping up the drive, I bend my back so I'm lower to the ground. There are a few trees lining the way, but nowhere near enough to disguise us.

Caleb reaches the car first and opens the door. Another good thing about this family is they're sweet as hell and trust the whole town. Their cars are unlocked. Unfortunately they're not so trusting that they leave the keys inside.

He leans in the car and tugs on wires.

I look around, scanning the farmhouse and outbuildings. There is no one around. Not yet anyway.

"Come on, Caleb," I whisper. Piper is waiting, and we don't have time.

"Almost there," he replies and the car roars to life.

I run around to the driver side, taking one last look at the house. No one there.

Caleb hops in the passenger seat, and we peel out of the drive. I hold onto the steering wheel with two fists as I make the sharp turn onto the main road.

Caleb thuds against the door and chuckles. "Easy, man."

"Don't be a baby. You're loving this as much as I am."

"I don't think that's possible."

No, maybe not. I was born for this. Even as a child, I didn't follow rules. There is nothing fun in doing the same as everyone else.

I speed down the empty roads. Piper lives in a quiet cul-de-sac. I know I can't drive down there, not if we've been found out. Nothing has come on the radio yet, but I'm taking no chances. The second they discover us gone, the cops will be here. We can't be trapped.

So I park on the street around the corner from her house. The only houses here are run-down bungalows, probably belonging to very old people.

"When I get out, hop in the driver's seat. I'll be back with her soon," I tell Caleb.

"Hurry up," he replies, his eyes wild as he tries to look everywhere all at once.

"Caleb, calm down."

"I am calm, and you need to get a move on."

I deadpan, "Hold it together." I slip out of the driver's seat, leaving the car running and the door open so Caleb can get in. I'll sit in the back with Piper when I get her.

The sun is setting, offering me a little camouflage.

There are two streetlights on, one near the back of her house.

I walk between a bungalow and a fence to Piper's backyard and hop over the low fence. Her yard is overgrown, but it looks recent. Her parents weren't keeping up with the lawn while she was with me.

Creeping toward her bungalow, I place my hands on the window-sill and peek through the window. The sight of her sitting on her bed with her arms wrapped around her legs steals my breath. My deadly angel. I can't wait to show her my world. She's staring blankly at something, a TV perhaps.

Her eyes, usually strong and determined, are now dull and afraid… the way they were when I very first met her.

She needs me.

There is no one else in her room. I know her parents are home; there is no way they would go out and leave her now. They probably won't ever leave her side again. Well, that is, until I take her with me.

It's hot, so her window is open, but that doesn't mean I'll be able to get through it fast enough to stop her from calling for her parents.

Right now, she doesn't know what's best for her.

I grip either side of the window frame and swing my legs up. I land on the floor inside her room before she even looks over.

When she does, her mouth opens and her eyes round.

Shoving myself forward, I slam my hand over her mouth and grip her upper arm. "Don't make a sound, Piper."

She watches me over my hand, fear swamping her eyes.

"Hey, Piper, it's me. Don't be afraid. I'm going to remove my hand. Do *not* scream." I slowly let go and run my hand from her mouth along her jaw. "Hi, babe."

"What are you doing here?" she whispers.

"Relax," I soothe. Her muscles are tense, shoulders high. "I've missed you."

"E-Evan... What are you doing? How are you here?" Her eyes flit to her door. *Don't you dare call out.*

"Leave without you? Not a chance. Caleb is waiting in the car. Grab a few things and let's go."

"What?" Her eyes dart to her bedroom door.

"I'm not letting them lock me up and leave you."

"But..."

Sighing, I say, "Caleb and I got away. We're here to take you with us. Are you caught up now? Can you start packing?"

Her mouth pops open. It takes her a minute to make a sound. "I-I can't."

"If you're not packed and in the car before your parents come back, I'll be forced to kill them."

"No," she whimpers, shaking her head. "I'll come, just please don't hurt them."

"Pack, Piper. Now."

She leaps up and runs to her closet. I stand and watch her throw clothes in a bag with trembling hands.

"I know you're scared, but there is no need. I'm about to open up your world."

Pressing her lips together, her eyes fill with tears, but she doesn't stop shoving clothes in her bag.

"You are going to love what I have planned," I tell her.

Freezing for a second, she sucks in a breath. But it only takes her a second to recover before she continues packing some things.

"Hurry up," I prompt.

She zips her bag and stands. "Don't hurt me, Evan."

What the hell does she think I am?

I close the distance between us. "I love you. That very first time I saw you, I knew there was something special about you. I felt it. We're the same, only you haven't let it out yet."

"What?" she sputters.

"You're so strong. You can take so much. Let yourself free, Piper. I'll teach you. We're going to start again. You and me, with the help of Caleb. We're moving on to bigger things. We're rebuilding. It'll be bigger and better, and it'll be you and me in the driver's seat."

With Piper at my side, there will be no stopping us. We can do whatever we want, no one to stop us and nothing to hold us back.

She looks up at me unsure, but that doesn't stop her from throwing her bag over her shoulder.

"Let's go, babe." I grin.

We're going to be one killer team.

ACKNOWLEDGMENTS

I first need to say a big thank-you to my husband and our two boys for supporting me. I love you guys.

To my Facebook reader group, who are so enthusiastic whenever I talk about a new book. Speaking to you always inspires me to write.

My editors at Sourcebooks: Annette Pollert-Morgan, Steve Geck, and Cassie Gutman, thank you for your hard work in helping me shape this manuscript. And to Nicole Hower (cover is GORGEOUS!), and everyone else who has worked on this book. I'm sorry that I don't know you all personally, but I appreciate all that you do for me.

And lastly, to the readers. Thank you so much for picking up *The Lost*. I hope you enjoyed the journey in my little house of horrors.

ABOUT THE AUTHOR

UK native Natasha Preston grew up in small villages and towns. She discovered her love of writing when she stumbled across an amateur writing site and uploaded her first story, and she hasn't looked back since. She enjoys writing NA romance, thrillers, gritty YA, and the occasional serial killer thriller.

You can visit her at natashapreston.com or find her on Facebook, Twitter @natashavpreston, or Instagram @natashapreston5.

READ ON FOR A SNEAK PEEK OF

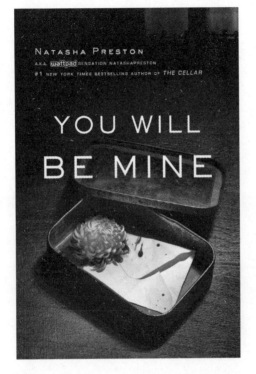

Love turns deadly in a new heart-pounding
thriller from the #1 *New York Times* bestselling
author of *The Cellar* and *The Cabin*!

ROSES ARE RED
VIOLETS ARE BLUE
WATCH YOUR BACK
I'M COMING FOR YOU

1

Thursday
February 1

Valentine's Day. *Ugh.* Of all the holidays, this one is my least favorite.

I give the paper hearts Charlotte decorated our living room with a mental eye roll. Two of my roommates, Sienna and Charlotte, are *super* into Valentine's Day.

Fourteen days until all of social media is swarmed with cutesy couple photos and declarations of love, and I'm already living in an explosion of pink and red do-it-yourself crafts.

Puke.

The theater students put on a show every year about the story of Saint Valentine. Only they use dramatic license to make it sexier and bloodier. Last year was amazing, and this year is supposed to be better.

Plus there's an after-party.

My housemates—Chace, Sonny, Isaac, Charlotte—and I are

lounging in the living room waiting for Sienna to be ready so we can head out. There is just enough space for us all in the modest room.

"Turn it up, Lylah," Sonny orders. Sonny is from London and speaks like he's a gangster. He's far too soft to be one though.

I stand and dip in a sarcastic curtsy before adjusting the volume on the speakers that are paired with Sonny's iPhone. Puff Daddy's *I'll Be Missing You* blasts through the room.

Sonny is the oldest and, like a child, thinks that gives him the right to order everyone around. He's not all bad, but I don't think he heard the word *no* his entire childhood.

He ignores me and taps on his phone, likely lining up tonight's hookup.

Chace, who is a media student like me, smirks. I stick out my tongue at him. We met on our first day at college when we got lost on campus together and then stuck together in an attempt to look like we knew where we were going. Since then, we've spent countless hours watching movies, working on projects, and hanging out. Besides Sienna, Chace is my best friend. It didn't take long after meeting him to start having feelings for him—actually, it was about three minutes. I don't think he feels the same way though, because he treats me like one of the guys. But recently he's been finding more and more reasons for us to spend time alone together. I'm definitely not imagining it. Well, I don't *think* I'm imagining it.

Sienna appears in the doorway. "Lylah, are you sure this is the one?" she asks, running her hands down the sides of her blood-red dress.

Raising an eyebrow, I reply, "No, you look awful." She doesn't and she knows it.

Sienna is stunning. Born in Korea, she and her family moved to the United Kingdom when she was two years old. Her hair is unfairly sleek and shiny, and she wouldn't be out of place on the catwalk, though she's probably a bit short for that.

"Shut up. Tonight is my night with Nathan. I'm going to make him fall in love with me if it kills me."

Two weeks until Valentine's Day, and everyone is supposed to be coupled up. Chace doesn't seem to hate the day, so maybe he'll surprise me. Maybe I wouldn't dislike Valentine's Day as much if he had feelings for me too. "Sie, don't give it away, babe," Isaac says, throwing an arm around her shoulders. "Make him work for it."

Isaac is a brave, stupid man.

Sienna's black eyes darken as she shoots Isaac a look that could kill. "Thanks for that," she replies, sarcasm dripping from each word.

Taking a step back, he drops his arm and runs his hand through his short, black hair.

"Only trying to help," he defends.

Charlotte watches our interaction with interest. She's the quiet one who came to live with us by pure chance. Over the last five months, since we've all been living together, she and I have become friends. But she's still a bit of an outsider, preferring to stay in and keep to herself, rather than joining in activities with us.

"You okay, Charlotte?" Chace asks, sensing her tension.

"Maybe I'll stay here tonight," she replies. "It doesn't exactly sound like my thing."

Charlotte is dressed in a long denim skirt and a coral T-shirt. Her pale blond hair is pulled back in a high ponytail. She doesn't look like she's going out, but I know she'll enjoy it. Every time we've managed to drag her with us, she's had a good time.

I lay back against the cushions on the sofa. "No way. You're coming."

She leans in. "I know I said I wanted more of the university experience, but I'm pretty sure a play about martyrdom isn't it."

"It's not only about the play. You know we're going for the after-party."

"Now I *know* I won't enjoy that."

"What did you do before Lylah adopted you, Charlotte? Stay home and play chess against yourself?" Sonny asks, laughing at his own comment.

I grit my teeth.

"Don't be a dick, Sonny," Chace says, backhanding Sonny's chest.

Charlotte ducks her head to avoid Sonny's gaze, and I glare at him.

Sonny sighs. "You're right. That was mean. Char, I'm sorry."

She nods, but I don't think she forgives him. I wouldn't if I were her.

"Can we move on and have a good night tonight, please?" Sonny asks. "We're all single, and since everyone"—he stops and looks pointedly at me—"well, *almost* everyone loves Valentine's Day and doesn't want to be alone, hooking up is practically a guarantee."

Sonny doesn't have a problem getting girls, but if every woman on campus could hear how he usually speaks, I don't think he would be as popular.

Charlotte looks up and nods. "It's forgotten."

Sonny's gaze meets mine. "Lylah?"

I shrug. It's really not for me to forgive him. "Sure. I just want to have a fun night." *And for Chace to realize he's in love with me.* Having fun at the party might make this time of year a little more bearable. "No more breaking hearts this year, Lylah," Isaac teases.

Here we go again...

I harrumph and point at him. "Shut up, you. I didn't break anything."

"Please. Jake left school because you rejected him."

Jake, one of our other friends, tried to kiss me last year. It was right before I went home to spend Valentine's Day, the anniversary of my parents' death, with my brother, Riley. Jake knew that I was upset and still thought it was appropriate to kiss me. *Er, no.* I pushed him away and told him he could go to hell.

Looking back, I could have been a tad more diplomatic telling him I didn't like him, but I was emotional. My anxiety was raging, and I was dreading going home. It still felt—feels—so fresh that they are gone.

He could have chosen a better time to get rejected.

"Jake did not leave because of me. He left *five months* after that happened."

"Because even after all that time he couldn't get over you," Sonny adds, winking at me.

Chace stands up. "Guys, cool it."

He's always there to tell everyone to back off when they're teasing me. I can handle myself, but they're relentless with the Jake thing, so it's nice to have Chace backing me up.

"Mate, we're only joking," Sonny says to Chace.

I'm about to jump in when the doorbell rings.

"Want to wager who's out there?" Chace asks.

"I bet it's one of Sonny's ex's who can't take no for an answer," I guess.

Sienna laughs. "I bet it's the girl who keeps following Isaac around like a lost puppy. She's a total weirdo."

"Nah," Isaac says. "I bet it's Nora trying to be Lylah's BFF."

I roll my eyes and walk to the hallway.

Nora lives in a house across the street. She's nice, and we've studied together a few times, but she's been forcefully trying to insert herself into my circle of friends. It's not that I don't like her, but we have nothing in common besides our classes.

I tug open the front door, and am greeted by an empty porch. "Guys, it's just a prank ring and run!" I call.

I'm about to shut the door when I see an envelope on the doormat. It's cream and addressed to Sonny in typed letters. There is no return address or postmark, so it must have been hand-delivered.

Bending down, I grab it and take it inside.

"Who the hell plays ding-dong-ditch after the age of twelve?" Sonny asks.

I hand him the envelope. "Must be one of your friends. This was left on the doorstep."

With a frown, Sonny rips open the envelope and pulls out a piece of paper. The next words out of his mouth are wholly unpleasant. His glare is so intense, it's like he could set the paper on fire.

"What is it, man?" Chace asks, looking over his shoulder. "Secret admirer?"

"Probably. Whoever it is, they're dead when I find them out."

I share a look with Sienna, silently asking if she's in on whatever prank has been pulled on Sonny. She shakes her head.

"Show us," Isaac orders, and Sonny turns the note so we can see.

My eyes widen as I read what's on the paper. Each letter has been cut from a magazine or newspaper. It reads:

"That's creepy. Who would send that?" I ask. Students around here hit pranking pretty hard, like any college. But it's usually stuff like replacing ketchup with hot chili sauce in the dining hall or filling communal areas on campus with pink and red balloons. People don't usually write personal notes, not that I'm aware of anyway. Usually they stick to big, public pranks with a large audience and a large laugh.

"Do you think it was one of your castoffs?" Charlotte asks, her blue eyes glistening. She's enjoying Sonny's discomfort.

"I don't think I've done anyone *that* clingy," he replies.

Lovely.

"Whatever, it's only a prank," Chace says. "Is everyone ready? Let's go."

Sienna and Isaac head out first, Sienna practically glowing with excitement. Charlotte follows Sonny out, looking like she'd rather do anything else. Chace waits for me and holds out his arm. I loop my arm around his.